"A swoon-worthy romance about following your heart, even—or especially—when it takes you to unexpected places. With sharp, vivid prose, Aashna Avachat brings the world and characters of *Love Craves Cardamom* to life. I absolutely adored this book." —**Ann Liang**, *New York Times* bestselling author of *I Hope This Doesn't Find You*

"Delightful, delicious, and deeply thoughtful. A sparkling romance that goes beyond a girl finding the boy of her dreams abroad to combine friendship, food, history, activism, and art into a beautifully immersive experience. I loved every page!" —**Amalie Howard**, *USA Today* bestselling author of *Lady Knight*

"A must-read for armchair tourists and romance lovers alike! It is a richly blended tapestry of a story about art, love, and culture told with a relatable voice and an adventurous heart." —**Timothy Janovsky**, *USA Today* bestselling author of *Never Been Kissed*

"With a swoon-worthy romance at its center, *Love Craves Cardamom* is a charming story about reclaiming art, culture, and ultimately yourself." —**Gabriella Gamez**, *USA Today* bestselling author of *The Next Best Fling*

"A thoroughly modern fairy tale that shimmers with the history and opulence of Jaipur on every page. Readers will crave even more from Archi and Shiv as they step into the world on their own terms." —**Sabrina Fedel**, author of *All Roads Lead to Rome*

"Sweet as mithai and brimming with heart, *Love Craves Cardamom* takes readers on a dazzling journey to Jaipur. Richly layered and deeply relatable, this is a warm hug of a story that will leave you swooning and craving a second helping." —**Farah Naz Rishi**, author of *If You're Not the One*

"Sweetly romantic and engaging, Archi's journey of art, love, and self-discovery is a delight." —**Emma Mills**, author of *Foolish Hearts*

Love Craves Cardamom

A LOVE IN TRANSLATION NOVEL

AASHNA AVACHAT

joy revolution

Joy Revolution
An imprint of Random House Children's Books
A division of Penguin Random House LLC
1745 Broadway, New York, NY 10019
penguinrandomhouse.com
GetUnderlined.com

In association with

ELECTRIC
POSTCARD
ENTERTAINMENT

Editor: Bria Ragin
Cover Designer: Michelle Cunningham
Interior Designer: Michelle Canoni
Production Editor: Colleen Fellingham
Managing Editor: Tamar Schwartz
Production Manager: Tracy Heydweiller

Library of Congress Cataloging-in-Publication Data is available upon request.
ISBN 978-0-593-57158-3 (trade pbk.) — ISBN 978-0-593-57160-6 (ebook)

The text of this book is set in 12-point Calluna.

Manufactured in the United States of America
1st Printing

The authorized representative in the EU for product safety and compliance is
Penguin Random House Ireland, Morrison Chambers, 32 Nassau Street,
Dublin D02 YH68, Ireland, https://eu-contact.penguin.ie.

For Arushi: I'm always on your team.
Special thank you to Mamma, for sharing Jaipur with me.

Love Craves Cardamom

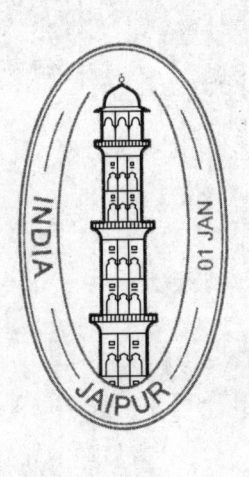

Chapter 1

Boy-Free January

Holy hell, I never knew I could be this jet-lagged.

Twenty-two hours from the airport in Washington, D.C., to Delhi, India, then two nights at a family friend's home, and now a long train ride to Jaipur, Rajasthan. If I fall asleep and miss my stop, my mother is going to kill me. And I wouldn't even blame her.

It's not that I'm not excited about heading to Jaipur. I've been texting one of my best friends, Whitney, a new photo every two seconds—a green-and-yellow sign with the name of the station painted on it, the farmland we pass, the metropolis disappearing behind me . . . I stifle a yawn. At least I'm nearing the end of the journey. Any longer and I'll show up in Jaipur looking like a zombie.

I stare out the window, focusing on the beautiful mountains in the distance to stop myself from nodding off. Thankfully, there aren't that many people on the train since the early morning commuter rush is over.

I'm on my own for the first time, and it's so different from all the family trips we took when I was a little girl. Mamma grew up here, though her family is from Punjab; Baba met her while he was here for work.

Memories wash over me of Mamma and Baba, always with a packed itinerary: countless visits to see their old friends, meetups with distant relatives who barely knew my name, poojas in temples and at neighbors' homes, shopping trips to get all the Desi things we couldn't get in D.C., and, most important, revisiting the place where my parents fell in love.

But I haven't been back in years. This time, I get to call the shots. I get to experience my parents' country, my homeland, on my own terms.

My phone vibrates, signaling a bunch of messages in the group chat with my parents:

> **Mamma:** Everything okay? Send a thank-you text to Sharmila Aunty and Rajesh Uncle for taking care of you during your first few days in India.
>
> Make sure you keep a close eye on your purse.
>
> Did you map out the way to campus from the train station? Do you need to take rickshaw?

I roll my eyes but smile at the barrage of texts from my mom. If anyone has any questions about where I get my extreme Virgo-ness, they just have to meet her. I use one hand to toy with my nose ring while I type with the other.

I tuck my phone away. I'm glad too, but this wasn't the original plan. My school, Odyssey Global High, requires students to study abroad for a semester, so I always knew I'd travel. But if you'd asked me a year ago *where* I'd be studying as an exchange student, I would have said with the confidence of a madly-in-love, delusional girl, "London, with my boyfriend." After all, in the winter semester of ninth grade, when I started dating Nick, we decided we would go to London together during the fall semester of our senior year.

Well, I mean . . . he decided.

And considering how I'm sitting on a train to Jaipur, about to spend my last semester of high school at Vidyadhar Bhattacharya International School, also known as VBIS, it's pretty obvious that plan didn't work out. The tale's as old as time: Girl likes boy. Boy likes girl. The summer before senior year, boy tells girl he has to focus on his college apps and no longer has time to put in the effort a relationship requires. Girl tells boy, "What effort are you talking about? I planned every single one of our dates!" Boy shatters girl's heart, making her question whether he ever really cared about her. Classic.

After Nick and I broke up, everything changed. No more London. No more boyfriend. I grit my teeth, reminding myself that this semester isn't about any of that.

This semester is a Nick-free zone.

In fact, it'll be a *boy*-free zone.

This semester will be strictly about Archi Dhawan.

The door to the train car opens, and the ticket collector walks in. "Ticket, ma'am?" he asks, giving me a once-over. I present it to him, my first purchase in rupees. "Chai service will begin soon," he says.

As he moves on to the next passenger, I wonder what he saw when he walked up to me. He spoke in English, not in Hindi. Did he do that because he could tell I'm American? I'm dressed in Indian clothes—a kameez blouse in pale green, matching embroidered pants, my favorite gold nose ring. And, well, I *am* Indian. Nobody at home would deny it—in fact, in the States, I feel as if some people see that I'm Indian before they see anything else about me. Here I worry it's the opposite: that people will be able to tell right away that I'm an outsider. That while my roots are Indian, I'm not *from here*. That the moment I speak, my Americanness will jump out and be the thing they fixate on.

But I tell myself that, at first glance, people won't know. I spent enough summers in Jaipur as a kid in the humid monsoon season, running up to the rooftop of my grandparents' house, feeding the cows on the street vegetable scraps from our cooking. We didn't visit for many years after my grandparents passed, but when I found myself without a study-abroad destination after the breakup and it was too late to join Whitney in Paris, I dug through the online brochures and found one with *Jaipur* on the cover page.

Suddenly, everything clicked into place.

Desi families, especially my own, love astrology, and for a moment I thought, *This is why the universe meant for Nick and me to break up: so I could go back to the place my family once called home and get a fresh start.*

Sometimes, when I make decisions, I picture an angel on one of my shoulders and a devil on the other. They argue, and it helps my brain sort through choices. The night I chose to go to Jaipur, the angel said, *In India, you could learn so much about who you are!* The devil said, *You could get revenge on Nick by having a way better study-abroad experience than he does!* At the end of the day, they were both saying yes.

I unzip my backpack and pull out the welcome packet Odyssey gave us during the study-abroad orientation, along with my journal-sketchbook, which is stuffed with papers I haven't yet glued down. If I'm going to force myself to stay awake, I may as well be productive.

I run my fingers across the cover of the eight-by-twelve book, my most prized possession. I'm on my third one now, having filled two others since I started high school. It's full of diary entries, Polaroids, receipts from cool places I've been to, and doodles in the margins. It's my memory storage, to-do list, and dream journal all in one.

I spread out my things on the table in front of me. Carefully, I paste my boarding pass onto the top of a fresh page. Below it, I write *Museum Internship Capstone Project.* Rediscovering myself post-breakup is actually the *second* priority for this trip. The first is my final, semester-long Capstone project.

Whitney did hers in the fall, and being the creative she is, she wrote, directed, and performed a one-woman play. She got an A. The thing is, I'm not a *creator*. I'm a *curator*.

Back when I was still planning on going to London, I intended on doing a curatorial internship at a museum there for class credit. I've always had an eye for art, what with Baba taking me to all the free D.C. art museums every weekend when I was growing up. We still go to the Renwick Gallery to see new exhibits, and I always find myself marveling not only at the art itself but also at the selection. Who decides what gets shown? Who decides how pieces fit together like a puzzle? Who decides which artists to feature and when to change the trajectory of an exhibit to be more risky or more political or to *make a statement*?

I want the answer to those questions to be *me*.

Curators are gatekeepers, which means they have a lot of power. I want the chance to use that power to bring more exposure to the kinds of artists I care about, the kind who often don't get to see themselves in mainstream museums. Street artists, fashion designers, digital creators. I haven't yet decided exactly what I want to do for my Capstone project, but I want it to say something about art history, the choices museums make, and my own curatorial vision. I want to do something *big*.

"Chai?" a woman asks from the aisle, and I jump at the sound.

I order a Kashmiri chai in practiced Hindi. My parents taught me Hindi before I ever learned English, and I still speak it at home, though sometimes, admittedly, it's more like Hinglish.

When she hands me the drink, I inhale the steam dancing out of my cup. It smells like home, like Mamma's mix, and it tastes even better, though I'll never tell Mamma that. Once I feel the caffeine entering my bloodstream, I get back to brainstorming. The new page in my journal fills up with notes and sketches: a bulleted list of contacts to reach out to, different artists I'm inspired by, a doodle of a train on rounded tracks so my fingers can keep moving while I think about my plans.

I'm still doing a museum internship, as I'd planned for London, only now it'll be at the Rathore Gallery, which is part of the Maharaja Sawai Man Singh II Museum in Jaipur. It was tough finding an opening at the last minute, and I had to beg my art teacher at Odyssey to write me a last-minute recommendation letter. Thankfully, the scrambling paid off. I'll be starting there next week, shadowing curators, learning about Indian artistry.

I flip a page in my journal while sipping my chai. In the corner, I glue down my offer letter from the museum, the "Congratulations!" a motivating reminder that I'm lucky I have this chance—and I need to make the most of it. I sketch an empty museum exhibit under the letter, frames yet to be filled with art. I've just started filling in the sketches with my favorite watercolor pens when four things happen:

1. The door opens from the first-class train car, where I imagine they have beds and spa treatments.

2. Someone walks in.

3. The train jolts as it rounds a curve in the tracks, sending my things flying.

4. My journal falls to the floor, landing in front of a pair of *very* expensive shoes.

I follow the shoes upward, taking in a guy about my age—tall, with wavy black hair falling in a swoop across his forehead, full lips with a perfect Cupid's bow, and a small, crescent-moon scar on his chin.

I'm suddenly wide awake. He's the first person my age I've seen since I got on the train.

This boy is dressed up, having decided against the usual bro-shorts-and-hoodie combo. He's wearing a black suit jacket, buttoned up, with—I can't believe this—a silky pocket square folded perfectly at his chest. I've never seen a boy my age wear a pocket square. This guy is put together, classy, and . . . oh . . . oh no. He's *cute.*

I blink. *Boy-free zone, Archi!*

The angel on my shoulder nudges me disapprovingly. The devil on the other side rolls her eyes. *Boy-free doesn't mean you can't acknowledge someone's objective hotness,* she says.

She has a point.

The boy looks like he should be on the cover of *Teen Vogue India.* Like the kind of guy I would have had a celebrity crush on in middle school.

He looks like a guy I would have a crush on now.

Okay, even I've gotta say this is going beyond just acknowledgment, the devil says.

"Knock it off," I mutter to myself.

"What was that?" he asks, his right eyebrow lifting in confusion.

The question snatches me back to the moment. I've been staring at the boy for far longer than is socially acceptable. My cheeks flush, and I'm ready to be called out, but the guy isn't even paying attention to me.

He's picked up my journal and is thumbing through it, a crease forming between his brows, which are thick and dark. I wonder if he gets them threaded, then—"Hey!" I say indignantly, reaching for my book. "That's mine."

Our eyes meet. His are a light brown, and a surprised smile flits across his mouth. "Sorry." He hands me back my journal. "I was admiring your work."

Oh. I take the book from his hands. "Thanks."

"The MSMS II Museum, is it? Planning to visit?"

A gentle accent softens his words, but I bristle. So he's guessed right away that I'm not a local.

"No." I clutch the book to my chest and frown. "I'm working there." I lift my nose into the air, trying to appear confident.

"Oh? As an American?"

"How'd you know?" My frown deepens into a scowl. Is there really a sign above my head, visible only to locals, that says CLUELESS AMERICAN HERE!? I know the reputation NRIs—nonresident Indians—have in India, and I don't want it to be associated with me. I've heard enough from my cousins on my dad's side. According to them, I'm an ABCD—American-born confused Desi. But I don't like how that feels. I want to be as Indian as the rest of them, even though I know our experiences are super different.

The boy smiles, seemingly amused. "You have a very strong accent."

Of course. Here I am, embarrassed again, and forgetful, as Americans often are, that we too have accents. I blush. "Right. Sorry."

"Nothing to be sorry about," the boy says. "Now, if you were British, that'd be a different story. I might expect an apology then."

A surprised laugh bubbles out of me at the quip about British colonialism, and he holds out a hand. "I'm Shiv."

"Archana," I say. "But I go by Archi."

His eyebrows go up. "You don't like your given name?"

"Excuse me?"

"You've made it more American."

I realize what he's insinuating. "I love my name. My parents gave it to me. They also gave me the nickname, which makes it feel more personal. And what about your name?" I challenge. "Shiv sounds like it's short for something too."

His mouth twitches. "It is." But he doesn't expand, and a flash of irritation surges through me. How dare he criticize my name when he won't even reveal his own? He presses on before I can address the issue. "Now it's my turn to apologize. Sorry for being presumptuous."

I do like it when boys apologize to me. Nick never did.

"I may be American," I say, keeping my composure, "but I'm Desi, too." I wonder how often I'm going to have to prove that this semester, and I fix my gaze on Shiv, waiting for him to snap back with a retort about me being an outsider.

But Shiv nods. "You are. So you're working at Rathore Gallery?"

"I got an internship at the museum."

"Are you an artist?" He cocks his head, his eyes flitting to my journal.

I shake my head. "No. I don't create art. I appreciate it. I'm going to be at VBIS this semester, studying art history." I think of my schedule. Aside from my internship, I'm taking three classes: India: Public Health, Gender & Sexuality; Jewelry as Art History; and Religion and Colonialism in India.

His smile comes back, and he leans against the wall separating my booth from the others. I probably shouldn't be divulging my daily location to a stranger, but something about this boy is . . . magnetic. We *are* strangers, but he's asking me questions beyond what's probably appropriate for polite small talk, as if we've had a million conversations before. Still, I like that I could be familiar to someone here, that this strange boy has accepted me already.

"Well," Shiv says, "there's plenty of art to appreciate in Jaipur."

I nod, wanting to show my knowledge. "I've been researching the primary schools of Rajput art, all the different styles within them."

Shiv waits, his expression a question. A test.

Luckily, I'm a straight-A student.

I grin. "Mewar, Marwar, and Dhundar." I make sure my pronunciation is perfect. "Miniature paintings, right?"

"Right," Shiv says, and I feel a flash of pride go through me until he says, "Except you forgot Hadoti. There are more subschools, too."

My jaw drops, and I realize—he's right. "I was going to say that," I lie.

A shy smile crosses Shiv's face. "I know," he lies back.

"You really know your art." I allow myself to be impressed. "Are *you* an artist?"

Shiv shakes his head. "No. But I can appreciate it, like you."

Cute *and* knowledgeable? I'm not ready to buy into it yet—Shiv seems too good to be true. And he has to be. This is a boy-free zone, remember? The universe must agree, because, right then, his phone rings. He glances at it apologetically. "Nice meeting you, Archi. Good luck with your internship." Then he brings the phone to his ear and turns to walk through the train doors leading to the concessions car.

An uncertain sensation pops up in my stomach, one I haven't felt in a long time. The conversation's ended quickly, *too* quickly. I could've talked to him for much longer—about art, the internship, Jaipur. It was so cool to meet someone new. Someone interesting.

Although I suppose it doesn't matter. Jaipur is big. I'll probably never see Mr. First Class again, but hopefully, I'll meet other interesting people in my program at VBIS. Hitting it off with a stranger on a train is clearly a sign of how well I'll do when I meet my roommate and classmates.

I check my phone and see a text from Whitney:

I watch Shiv's retreating back as he slides into the next train car.

Oops.

Chapter 2

Paneer Pizza and Graffiti Art

The walk from the station to my dorm building at VBIS is short, especially with the help of my Maps app, and I'm practically vibrating with excitement when I arrive.

It's definitely a culture shock walking through Jaipur, which doesn't seem to have many sidewalks or even marked lanes. Cars and motorcycles honk indiscriminately, somehow managing the intersections without traffic lights, and pedestrians walk on the sides of the road. There are street dogs on every block, napping in the sun, and pigeons fly in flocks around the city. I try to take everything in without getting overwhelmed, making note of shops I pass that I want to come back to.

When I get to VBIS, my fingers tingle. I did it: I got from point A to point B in a new country by myself. My dorm room door is labeled with a big, sparkly sign that has my roommate's and my name on it in both English and Hindi:

I smile as I reach for my lanyard. This is the work of a dedicated resident advisor if I've ever seen it.

Kothari Hall is the exchange student dorm building, which means my roommate will be new to Jaipur, too. As I fumble with my keys, I wonder if I should have done a social media deep dive on Mohini before coming here. I wonder if she cyberstalked me, then hope I haven't left a bad impression, what with my most recent post being from four years ago, braces and braids and all. I probably should update my profiles, but I prefer to lurk rather than post.

Before I even go to unlock the door, it swings open, revealing a wide, smiling face. "You've got to be Archana!" The girl is shorter than me but, I can already tell, much louder. She has short, curly hair and dark brown eyes framed by full lashes. I light up.

"Yes!" I try to match her energy. "And you must be Mohini."

"The one and only." She grins, then her smile falters. "I mean, it's a pretty common name. But still."

I mirror her enthusiasm. "I don't know any other Mohinis, so you're the one and only for me."

Her smile widens. "Oh, I'm going to like you." She reaches for my bags. "Need a hand? I got here yesterday, so I'm totally set up."

I follow her into the room, turning slowly to take in Mohini's eccentric decor. Her half of the room is covered in things, as though she's been living here for ages. Blankets are piled on top of her bed, lights and photos and band posters fill her walls, and her desk is stocked with chai and a definitely contraband combination of a kettle, a hot plate, and a ton of mismatched candles. A patterned, knit rug has been laid out at the foot of Mohini's bed, and along with her blankets, her bed is topped with soft pillows and crocheted stuffed animals. I see a frog and a rabbit among the masses.

Mohini follows my gaze and answers my unasked question: "I like to sleep like I'm being buried in one of those claw machines with stuffed toys inside."

I laugh. "As you should."

I turn to my side of the room, empty and waiting for me to curate a little safe haven for the semester. At home, my bedroom is covered in prints: *The Kiss* by Klimt, my favorite of Monet's Water Lilies paintings, and Munch's *The Scream*, to name a few. Beside them hang postcards from museums, and frames and textiles bought from Eastern Market in D.C. What will I fill my space with here? The wall is a blank canvas, begging me to curate a display for myself. I itch to find pieces to put together, and I envision the planning sketch I'll need to add to my journal.

In the corner is the door to our shared bathroom. It was a selling point for VBIS—I didn't know if I could handle a communal shower used by the whole hall. Now, thankfully, I don't have to find out.

"So." Mohini jumps on top of her bed. "Where are you coming from?"

"D.C.," I say. "What about you?"

"Hyderabad. My classmates went to the United States and Australia, but I really liked the idea of Jaipur. I'm studying law and politics, but I love the beautiful architecture here."

My eyes light up. "My dad's an architect! And he studied in Jaipur."

"Are you studying architecture, too?"

"Art history." I squat to unzip my leviathan-sized suitcase. I had to sit on it for the length of an entire documentary on art heists to get it to close. It pops open now like a jack-in-the-box, expanding to full size. The agent at the airport gave me a look when I weighed it, but she rolled her eyes and let me through when I gave her my best "I'm just a teenage girl!" face. "I'm interning at the MSMS II Museum this semester," I tell Mohini.

"*Oooooh.* Impressive. Your parents must be super excited. Mine don't really get why I want to go into politics."

"How come?" Law is the kind of career hypercritical aunties usually love.

"My mom's a Tollywood actress," explains Mohini. "And my dad's a producer. They don't understand why I don't want to be in the movie business. They used to put me on set when I was young, and I played really small roles as, like, the cousin-sister or something. They were sure I'd grow up and become a film star."

"But you don't want to," I guess.

"Not really." Mohini spreads herself out on top of her pillows and stuffed animals as I transfer my clothes, neatly packed, into the drawers under my bed. "In a way, my career goals are similar to theirs. My parents make things that are lasting, since people can enjoy their movies long after they come out. I want to make lasting changes in society—better laws, better programs for people who need them, better treatment of queer people, people affected by casteism, non-Hindus in India. I want *that* to be my legacy."

I nod, understanding. When it comes to my career, I want to preserve things so they'll be long-lasting, too.

Mohini and I talk for the next couple hours, getting to know each other and our class schedules, until we're called for a dorm meeting with our RA in the lounge downstairs.

Anjit, our RA, brings the room to attention as we're scarfing down Indian-style pizza with paneer and masala sauce. "Welcome, students!" Anjit waves his hands around, motioning for us all to find seats. As Mohini and I grab chairs in the back of the room, he continues: "Orientation begins tomorrow at nine, you're free on the weekend, and classes start next week. Let's begin with some ground rules for Kothari Hall and then jump into our icebreakers, okay?"

We groan. If I had to guess, Mohini's probably groaning at the ground rules, given the contraband back in our room. I, on the other hand, am not a fan of icebreakers. One of my teachers at Odyssey would make us start every class with a random prompt. If I have to come up with a "fun fact" one more time, nobody in the room will be having fun when it's my turn to talk.

Anjit hurries through the rules. "No overnight guests. No loud noises after ten p.m. No alcohol, no smoking, no drugs."

"No fun, no fun, no fun," Mohini whisper-translates beside me.

I stifle a giggle. "It's not his fault. He doesn't make the rules. He just has to enforce them."

"Whatever." Mohini rolls her eyes. "If we get caught, I'll tell my parents to make a donation to the school. Or to film their next movie here."

I snort. "Does that work?"

Mohini shrugs. "Money talks."

"Can the side conversations please come to an end?" Anjit calls out, then pointedly glances our way. I press my lips together and suppress a laugh. Scolded already.

I zone out as Anjit goes over more rules, checking my phone to see if I have any new notifications. A news icon pops up on my screen.

KAVI STRIKES AGAIN. VANDALISM OR ART? NEW INSTALLATION APPEARS OUTSIDE THE BRITISH MUSEUM.

I click on the link immediately, which leads me to a London news article about the anonymous street artist I've been following for ages. KAVI is a Banksy-like artist, popping up with graffiti-based art in public places, leaving no trace except for a temporary art installation that always includes some sort of political message. KAVI's an activist—an art activist. Nobody knows who KAVI is, but rumors have been swirling that she's a woman, a woman of color specifically.

I can't explain it, but I've always had this feeling that she's specifically Desi, like me. It's something about her art style—the colors, the recurring geometric patterns. They remind me of home. And her name—in Hindi, it means "poet." "Wise." It fits her art to a tee.

Next to me, Mohini's tapping away at her phone, and I'm afraid Anjit will have our heads if I whisper to her again, so I send Whitney a screenshot of the article instead.

Archi: LONDON!!!

It's late at night in D.C., so I probably won't get a response for a while, but I have to share the news with someone. KAVI's latest temporary installation—temporary because the authorities will probably immediately tear it down, yet somehow the pieces will end up with an art collector to be sold online for hundreds of thousands of dollars—is a collection of cloth draped across the sidewalk in front of the British Museum. It's arranged in strips, as if the walkway is being mummified. And that's probably the intent, because under the strips poke out hundreds of eyes, painted the way ancient Egyptians painted sarcophagi, the way Indians painted textiles, with thick eyeliner and stern glances. Across the sidewalk, metal letters of heavy brass are scattered like alphabet soup. When put together, they spell out STOLEN.

I shiver at the image. People are debating in the forum at the bottom of the article, some praising KAVI for her bravery, others criticizing her for vandalism and property destruction. "I understand the message," one writes. "But couldn't she have taken a more civilized approach?"

I wrinkle my nose at the words and resist the urge to write something rude back in all caps. I send Whitney another text instead.

I imagine KAVI's work showing up in the streets where I grew up and let out a happy sigh. How amazing would it be to someday hold a piece of her art in my (double-sanitized, gloved for extra protection) hands, after it was swept away from the street? Maybe if I curate my own exhibit someday, I can find a way to get KAVI's work into a museum.

Then again, KAVI is impossible to reach—I know museums have tried. Still, it feels historical, her art. As if it should be preserved instead of torn down or sent to some billionaire's mansion. I think of my Capstone. Maybe I can design an exhibit for my final project inspired by KAVI. Maybe I'll feature street artists or other nontraditional art. An exhibit on rebels, perhaps. My brain starts to buzz with possibilities.

Anjit breaks my train of thought by transitioning us to the dreaded icebreakers. "Why don't we each turn to a partner and introduce ourselves by sharing where we're from and what we're studying?"

Mohini and I make faces at each other. There are a lot of other students around, and they're probably really cool, but honestly, I'm exhausted from traveling, jetlag, and unpacking. "I'm picking you," I tell Mohini.

She grins. "Great, because while No-Fun Anjit was telling us the prison rules, I was figuring out where we should go this weekend."

I clap my hands together. "My mom told me about Hawa Mahal and Birla Mandir."

"We should go there, too, but what do you think about

touring the palace? This weekend, they're letting people tour the gardens, and apparently, they never do that. Come on. Don't you want to see how royalty live?" She does jazz hands.

"I . . . guess?" I scrunch my nose. "But don't you mean *lived*?"

Mohini laughs. "Actually, the very museum you're interning at is on the same grounds as the royal residence."

Residence? "Hold on, like, there's a king and queen of Jaipur right now? That's not just a historical thing?"

"Girl, how are you studying history and you don't know this?"

I shake my head. "*Art* history. It's a bit different. So, what, there's still a monarchy?"

"Not, like, formally," Mohini says. "There used to be a Maharaja of Jaipur, and the king ruled over what was called the Amber Kingdom. The monarchy system was legally abolished after Independence, but we still have a royal family who live at the palace."

"Whoa. No way."

Mohini nods. "The Rathores, whom the gallery you're interning at is named after, are the current royal family. The Maharaja and Maharani have two kids, the Rajkumari and Rajkumar, but their lives are kept pretty private because the prince is underage." She leans back. "They're royal in name and in wealth, but it's mostly tradition. They don't have much political power, and they keep to themselves."

A princess and a prince. And they'll be right around the corner from where I work.

I grin. "Let's go."

Chapter 3

Sensitive American Stomachs

After orientation in the morning, I walk beside Mohini toward the City Palace, smoothing down the billowy floral blouse and flowy pants I borrowed from her closet. The outfit is way cuter than anything I own. In my ears are small, dainty jhumkas.

If only my other best friend, Lilyn, could see what I'm wearing, she'd approve even though our aesthetics are completely different. She's a total goth girl. She's going to be a famous fashion designer one day and design my wardrobe when I'm running my own museum. I send her a selfie so she can admire the fit.

The walk isn't far, and it gives me a chance to practice heading to work. I take in even more than I did on my walk from the train station to VBIS. The city is beautiful and full of the warm noise and chatter of people, but it's impossible not to notice other, sadder things: the litter on the sides of the roads because public trash cans are unavailable, the kids walking barefoot, and the tiny homes covered in tarps above shops. It's tough to see extravagant architecture and obvious poverty right across the street from each other.

"We'll take auto-rickshaw on the way back," Mohini announces. "Give you a feel for that, too." She walks confidently down the main street, which is busy and noisy and colorful, filled with cabdrivers and people on scooters, kids clamoring at food stalls, and shopkeepers conversing with customers. It's a different late January than I'm used to. Back in D.C., winter's kicking into gear, with heavy windstorms and snow every now and then. I usually layer up with a puffer coat, a scarf, and gloves, but here it feels like a mild spring day, warm with a light breeze. Near the equator, the sun just feels *different.* Stronger. I can smell the delicious scent of street food as we walk, and finally, I get Mohini to agree to stop at a chaat stall.

My mouth is watering by the time our turn in line comes, and I watch the vendor pour spiced water into crispy fried-dough shells filled with spicy potatoes for the people in front of us, who ordered a tray of pani puri.

"Kya loge?" the vendor asks, nodding at me. I feel my cheeks redden in pleasant surprise. The vendor thinks I'm a local! He's talking to me in Hindi.

I glance at Mohini. "Doh pani puri?" She nods, and I gesture for two.

The vendor grabs two trays, and Mohini jumps in. "Bhaiya, bottle wala pani hein?"

"Wait, why?" I whisper to Mohini. "Why can't I use regular water in mine?"

She clucks her tongue. "You Americans. Your stomachs are too sensitive for proper Indian street food. We'll get you pani puri made with filtered water first."

The vendor grumbles a bit back and forth with Mohini until finally she pulls out extra bills from her wallet and he acquiesces.

"No, no. I want to try real pani puri." Determination blooms in my chest. "My Indian genes will pull through. I can handle it."

Mohini quirks an eyebrow at me, but I nod fiercely. How can I be just as Desi as everyone else if I have to be babied at a pani puri stall?

Mohini smirks. "Suit yourself."

When the pani puri is ready, we get our trays and resume our walk up the street. "Cheers." I knock my order against hers before shoving it into my mouth. The flavors explode on my tongue, bursting from the potato and spiced water and the crunch from the fried casing. "Oh my god." My eyes roll back into my head. "This is incredible." I wipe my mouth with the back of my hand.

Mohini closes her eyes as she appreciates her bite of pani puri. "Isn't it? Nothing beats Desi street food. Next time, we'll look for samosa chaat."

When we finally arrive at the museum, my armpits are slightly damp with sweat. I check out Mohini. She chose a plaid sweater and a satin skirt with funky, mismatched jewelry. Her hair is pinned back. Somehow, she still looks fresh.

Thankfully, our destination immediately takes my mind off this cosmic unfairness. The palace is gorgeous.

It's tall, touching the sky, with arches and intricate carvings on the exterior. It's pale yellow in some places and a soft, warm pink in others. The watercolor hues make the palace seem even grander. I lean back to take in the stunning visuals. I've seen photos, of course, but no filter beats the sight in front of us.

Mohini appears amused. "If you spend all your time out here, we'll never get inside to see the actual art."

"This *is* actual art!" I take a photo to send Baba.

"Right," Mohini says. "Architect's daughter."

We spend the next hour like that, with me taking too long at every stop, from the arched entryways to the wall plaques to every piece of art in the frames of the museum I'll be working at. A guide tells us that the palace is seven stories, only a few of which are open to tours, including a room lined with thousands of tiny mirrors that sparkle like stars in candlelight. He explains that the royal family currently lives in the Chandra Mahal, and when they're in town, the palace and all the city forts put up the royal flag. He points at a striped rainbow of pink, orange, and teal waving proudly in the breeze, confirming that the family is currently here.

We walk through a hallway that showcases portraits of the many kings who have ruled Jaipur. The guide explains that state portraits previously communicated a sovereign's right to rule their subjects. Since few people would ever see their ruler in public, the portraits became a powerful way to send a message. But now the royal family doesn't actually rule anything.

When a visitor asks whether portraits of the living

members of the royal family are shown in the museum, the guide points to the final portrait in the gallery, one that depicts the current king. He then informs us that royal policy is to keep the kids' personal information private until they become adults.

I ask Mohini so many questions, and she humors me at first, but after a while, she gets impatient. "Can we go see the residential gardens now? They're never open to the public. You'll be in the museum all the time."

On our way, we peek in at Rathore Gallery, which has its own wing of the museum, but I shy away from introducing myself to the person behind the front desk. She probably doesn't want to be dealing with interns until she has to.

The residential side of the palace is as beautiful as the museum but slightly more guarded. As we walk over, the noisiness of the Jaipur streets melts away, and we enter a secluded courtyard. Mohini spins around, eager. We follow the signs to the palatial gardens, and I snap photos of Mohini in front of various rosebushes, fig trees, and climbing vines as we roam. When we round a curve, my stomach seizes, grumbling.

"Oh," I groan, feeling a wave of discomfort, and Mohini turns to me in concern. "I think you were right."

"Obviously. But about what?"

I clutch my stomach, grimacing. "The pani puri. Maybe I should have tried the bottled water first."

Mohini covers her mouth and begins to laugh. "Let's get you to a restroom, stat."

"No, don't worry. I'll find one. You enjoy the gardens.

I'm sure I can survive finding a bathroom on my own. I'm not *that* much of a clueless American."

But maybe I am, because five minutes later, though my nausea has waned, I'm now feeling as if the pani puri wants to come out the other end, and I still haven't made my way out of the mazelike gardens, much less found a bathroom.

I stop and do a quick scan. Something about this area is different. It's less spacious, more intimate. I can't see the guards anymore or, for that matter, the signs we followed in, and that's when I realize I have somehow found myself in the *private* gardens, the ones the public isn't allowed into this weekend. The ones the royal family personally uses.

Shit. Do they still behead people?

Mohini said they were royal only in tradition, but I still don't want to piss off a king on day two in Jaipur. I have to get the hell out of here. I set down a small stone path, hoping to retrace my steps.

I hear it before I spot it: movement up ahead. I bite my lip to keep from yelping in surprise. What if the royal family is there? They'll think I'm stalking them or maybe that I'm a political assassin, and their guards will immediately take me out.

Okay, maybe not a political assassin. But a royalty-obsessed fangirl? Sure. And I can't let myself be presumed a Rathore-family enthusiast. I still have to work close by.

I take a step forward and breathe a sigh of relief. The movement has come from a gardener who's bent over a plot of soil, patting the earth with gloved hands. Whew. I can ask him for directions, right? He'll understand.

"Namaste, ji." I approach carefully, using the honorific. "Mein—" I'm about to share that I'm lost when the gardener faces me and I nearly lose my balance.

It's Shiv—the boy from the train! The one I saw all buttoned up, emerging from the first-class car. Now he's kneeling in front of me in gardening gear, covered in dirt, his face glistening with sweat. I swallow, taking in this new and strange, rugged side of him.

His face shows momentary shock, too, but he recovers faster than I do. "Very formal, ji." A smile creeps onto his face. "For someone you already know."

"Shiv!" My voice finally finds me. "What are you doing here?"

He stands, instantly so tall I have to tilt my head back to look at him, and peels off his gloves. "I'm gardening." He gives me a once-over, then furrows his brows. "What are *you* doing here?"

"I'm visiting. I got lost. You work here?"

Shiv shrugs. "I garden."

"But I saw you on the train in a suit—"

"Should I have been wearing gardening gloves even then?" Shiv is clearly amused.

"No." I frown. "It's just—" I can't imagine how a palace gardener can afford first-class tickets, especially if the royals aren't even real royalty.

Shiv pauses for a moment, then starts laughing, which makes me realize I've spoken aloud. And, as is apparently going to be usual for my interactions with Shiv, I've embarrassed myself immediately.

Luckily, he doesn't seem perturbed. "Fair enough," he says good-naturedly. "There are some perks to the job."

I blush, wanting to change the subject. He probably knows where a bathroom is, right?

But Shiv speaks first. "How's working at the museum been?"

"I haven't started yet. I've been doing orientation at VBIS. I start next week, so I'm here to, you know, scope out the scene." I wince right away. Scope out the scene? Who says that? I hurry to say something else. "I guess that means we'll be coworkers, in a sense."

A shy smile crosses Shiv's face. "Yes, in a sense. Though I rarely leave the palace grounds. Even the museum feels like a trek." He looks me up and down, and I feel my skin grow warm. "I didn't think I'd see you again."

It's amazing how cute Shiv is, even covered in dirt and sweat. Although, maybe the sweat makes him hotter. More real than the put-together, suited-up gentleman on the train. The angel on my shoulder starts to protest, *Boyfree summer!* So I cool it.

"Me neither," I respond finally.

"I hoped to," Shiv says suddenly, glancing at me with his warm brown eyes. They're the color of coffee splashed with milk. "I went back to your train car after my call. But I was too late."

Oh? He looked for me? Hoped to see me again?

A little flutter begins in my stomach, and I realize I'm feeling butterflies at the thought of Shiv searching for me on the train. I haven't felt those since—

Oh *no*. No. No butterflies. This is purely friendly. Shiv is cool, and I'm here in Jaipur to meet and learn from cool people. Anything more than that is an unnecessary distraction, one that'll take away from my ambitions for my Capstone and probably leave me hurt. Just like before. Just like with Nick.

I slap the back of my wrist, bringing myself back to reality. Shiv follows the gesture with his eyes, confused.

"Bug," I say quickly. "Mosquito, probably."

Shiv purses his lips as if he's trying to hide another smile.

"What are you planting?" I ask in an attempt to appear normal. Like there's nothing wrong. Because there isn't. We're having a regular conversation. Shiv is essentially a coworker. Really, this is a learning experience. Cultural exposure. I'm talking to someone who has an in at the MSMS II palace. And boy-free semester doesn't mean I can't talk to a boy. I simply can't catch any romantic feelings.

"Jasmine flowers. My mom's favorite, and they're great for tea."

"I bet your mom likes that she has flowers planted in her honor at the royal palace. My mom would be jealous."

Shiv blinks. "Right. Yeah. I mean, the garden is at the royal family's preference. Sometimes I get to decide what gets planted where, though, and I take the opportunity. What would you plant if you got to choose?" His voice and accent are soft, gentle.

I think for a moment. "Tulips. They're my favorite. There's a tulip garden by the Tidal Basin in D.C., where I'm from. It's called the Floral Library. We go to it every spring, and my parents always buy me tulips when they're in season at Trader Joe's."

"Ah, Trader Joe's," Shiv says. "I've always wanted to visit one."

I laugh, and his grin grows. "It's no City Palace, but the tulips there are lovely."

"Then I will plant tulips next," Shiv promises. "For when you visit the gardens again."

"Wait," I say, stunned. "No, that's— You don't—"

Shiv shrugs. "Perks of the job."

And without being able to control it, I'm remembering that Nick only ever got me flowers once, after I had *asked* for them. And they were roses, even though he knew tulips were my favorite. This is only my second time meeting this handsome, smart boy, and he's even more impressive. A tulip garden at the royal palace for *me*? What fantasy world have I entered into?

I remember when I thought Nick was perfect, too. How it felt when he took me to Le Diplomate and paid for our very expensive dinner, insisting on crème brûlée for dessert; how we'd kayak in the Potomac and watch the sunset—how Nick would take over when my arms got too tired. The way we'd whisper about our plans for the future late into the night, talking through everything we wanted to do when we got to London until our phone batteries ran out.

So many memories, once rose-tinted, now marred by the knowledge of what came after. I let a boy dictate my plans once before, and I won't let it happen again . . . no matter how cute or seemingly genuine he may be.

Shiv takes my shocked silence for discomfort. "I don't mean I'll post a sign with your name on it, saying the tulips are dedicated to you," he clarifies. "Just the next time I need to decide what to plant, I'll take your recommendation."

A recommendation. I can allow that. "Okay. But if the royal family hates it, you can't throw me under the bus."

Shiv shakes his head. "Never."

The butterflies in my stomach reappear, stronger than ever, and it strikes me—this time, they aren't butterflies. My stomach pain is back. Oh . . . I need to find a bathroom before something *very* embarrassing happens.

I try not to show my panic. "I should go. I don't want to be caught trespassing. Can you tell me where the bathroom is?"

Shiv points me in the right direction. "Are you okay? Need an escort?"

I hide a wince. "No. Thank you. I'll manage."

He gives me a hopeful glance. "Maybe we'll cross paths in the gardens again sometime?" He gestures at the impossibly lush greenery encircling us.

"I'll be around." I go for noncommittal yet honest. Technically, I'll be across the palace grounds, at the gallery. But I doubt I'll find myself in these particular gardens again. It's pure luck we ran into each other today.

Besides, why get invested in a boy I barely know in a city I'm only in for a few months? This semester is supposed to be about *me*.

I walk down the path, forcing myself not to turn around. But by the time I find my way back into the museum and head for the tourist bathrooms, I can't ignore the longing I feel, thinking back on Shiv kneeling in the garden.

Chapter 4

An Internship for Bossy Girls

A couple days later, I'm back at the palace, but this time, as an intern instead of a tourist. This is where I'll be for most of the week, with a limited course load to supplement my internship.

I check my reflection in my phone before walking through the main doors to the Maharaja Sawai Man Singh II Museum. It's two hours before opening time, and I'm dressed in a checkered blouse and a black pencil skirt, with my hair pulled back, a gold ring in my nose, and mini jhumkas from Mamma dangling from my ears. In my tote bag is my water bottle, a packed lunch, and, of course, my journal. On the outside, I'm pulled together, but my heart is pounding and my palms are clammy. Today could be the start of my dreams coming true.

I steel myself and make my way to the Rathore Gallery. "Namaste," I say to the woman at the information desk, who's sipping from a travel mug and clicking away at a computer screen. She has long hair pulled back into a braid, and she wears a simple pink salwar kameez. I clear my throat. "Mein internship ke liye aayi hoon? Archana Dhawan?"

The woman smiles. "You are expected. I'm Jassi Kaur. We'll be working together. Let me call your main supervisor, and we can get you settled in, yeah?" She grabs a phone from her desk and speaks quickly into it.

I realize now, looking at the woman, that she's likely not much older than me, maybe college aged. She has several ear piercings and a pretty stud in her nose that glints in the light. Her nails are long and painted maroon, and her eyebrows are model-thick and perfectly shaped. She's beautiful. Her style reminds me of photos I've seen of Mamma from when she was in school. Long, thick black hair, nose piercing, warm brown skin, dark brows. Classic Indian beauty.

A few moments after she hangs up the phone, Jassi waves to someone behind me. "Hey!" I turn to face an older woman with salt-and-pepper hair, wearing a long embroidered blouse with palazzo trousers, while Jassi makes introductions. "Archana, this is Kiran Bhosale. She's our managing curator, and she leads the Women in India exhibits at the museum. Kiran-ji, this is Archana, our intern for the semester!"

"It's nice to meet you, Ms. Bhosale." I press my hands together. Then I reach out to shake her hand. "I go by Archi."

"And I go by Kiran."

"Kiran-ji to us," Jassi interjects, reminding me of the honorific.

Kiran-ji laughs. "Thank you for the introduction, Jassi. Now, Archi, let's take you downstairs so we can get you all set up, shall we?"

I follow Kiran-ji to a side door, which she unlocks using a key card. "Most of our offices are in the basement." She leads me down a set of stairs. "My office is on the second floor, but our archivists and conservators work down here. I think you wrote in your cover letter that you're interested in curatorial work, correct?"

"Yes!" I pick up my pace to keep up with her. "Museums are my favorite places, and I'm fascinated by how exhibits are designed and selected. And then sometimes, I go to a museum and think . . . I totally could have done this better." I stop short. "I mean, not that the exhibits were bad—the curators were super talented, and the art was . . . I think I just like the idea of having my own say." I wince, convinced my tangled-up words have made a terrible impression on my new boss.

But when I glance up, Kiran-ji is smiling. "I know exactly what you mean. I got my start as an archivist, but I knew curating was the right place for me." She winks at me. "If you were called bossy as a kid, this is the job for you."

I beam.

"This internship, however," Kiran-ji continues, "is designed for you to get to know all the different moving parts of the museum, specifically within the Rathore Gallery. Over the next few months, you'll be on a rotational schedule, shadowing and working with each of the different departments." She opens a door. "Today, we'll get you your badge, show you around the museum, and introduce you to our staff, but after that, your first rotation will be Member Services."

"Member Services?" I try to keep the disappointment out of my voice.

Kiran-ji ushers me inside the room. "I like our interns to get to know the museum well before they work on any pieces. You'll start by working with Jassi at the information desk and graduate to giving tours once you feel you have a sense of the place. Sound good?"

Wait, so I don't get to go straight to helping select exhibits? Or even handling any of the art? The internship details in the offer were honestly a little fuzzy.

Kiran-ji sees the expression on my face and lets out a tinkling laugh. "I know you're excited to get to the big stuff, but you need to learn about our art before you take on anything else. And tours are *important.* Our main goal as an institution is to connect the community we serve to our art. What better way for you to do that than by working directly with our guests?"

She has a point. Even though I hope my Member Services role will be a quick rotation, I do want to get a feel for the museum. Now I'm determined to become an expert on the Rathore Gallery faster than any other intern Kiran-ji's ever had. When we step through a second door, I look around to see a bunch of cubicles. Some heads pop up out of the workspaces. This must be the central office, with personal cubicles for every staff member. Though I imagine much of the work involving the actual art must happen in storerooms and workshops in a different part of the basement.

"Everyone, meet our new intern, Archi!" Kiran-ji announces, and folks throughout the cubicles stand so we can see them.

The first thing I notice is that most of the staff are women. The second is that I'm way overdressed. Everyone else is wearing casual salwar kameez, or long blouses with jeans, or other everyday Desi-wear.

Kiran-ji rattles off names and introductions, and I try my best to catch everything. By the end, I'm impressed and overwhelmed. Everyone seems so *cool,* and I get to spend the rest of this semester working alongside them.

After I wave goodbye to my new coworkers, Kiran-ji tells me more about the gallery. "The palace is trying to expand the Rathore Gallery." We walk into a small filing room together. "The eldest child, the princess, has a keen interest in art. She initiated a hiring project last year to bring on more folks, particularly women. Women are still underrepresented in museum collections, so the idea is that if more of those who are working on the art selections are women, more of the art in our exhibits will be by women, too. The palace sponsors artisans to showcase their work in the museum gift shop, and the princess especially highlights women artisans."

"Are the royal family very involved with what goes on at the museum?" I ask.

"Not on a day-to-day basis, but they're involved on a broader level." Kiran-ji's mouth quirks up. "If you thought you'd get to meet them on the job, you're unfortunately out of luck."

"No worries." I laugh. "I didn't even know they existed before I arrived in Jaipur."

"They love the arts, that family. They donate works to the gallery all the time, especially historic pieces that have been around the residential palace for centuries." Kiran-ji rifles through some drawers. "The Rathore matriarch likes to redecorate, often. So pieces are always coming into the gallery. We're lucky to have a few pieces from their prized textiles collection, though, of course, that's a touchy subject."

Before I can ask her why, Kiran-ji jumps up. "Aha! Here it is. I knew we had a badge made for you." She reaches out and hands me a key card. "You'll use this to get around the employees-only sections of the museum and to get inside prior to opening for your shifts."

Back at the reception desk, Kiran-ji leads me to Jassi. "You and I will have check-in meetings every week. But for now, I'll leave you in Jassi's capable hands to get acquainted with your first rotation." She smiles, waves, and heads back to her office.

"Welcome to Member Services and Museum Tours." Jassi spins around in her chair with a huge grin on her face. "Your royal adventure starts here."

I like her already. "Tell me where to start, boss."

Jassi takes me on a tour of the different sections of the Rathore Gallery—Historic, Modern, and Women in India—to introduce me to the art I'll be telling tourists about. As we move from room to room, I take in each piece, lingering at the placards that provide context about the artists and time periods, the tiled frescoes painted with real gold and textiles dyed with colors pulled from vegetables.

Every now and then, I jot down notes in my journal. We're in the Historic section now, with medieval paintings. I examine square panels that are illustrations from Jain manuscripts dating as far back as the eleventh century. I write down some of the dates and details, thinking about my Capstone project. I wonder whether Kiran-ji will let me take on a curating assignment for my project or if she'll think that's too big a responsibility for an intern.

As I close my journal, I notice where I glued in my pass to the palace gardens from my visit. I think of running into Shiv—of his promise to plant tulips in my honor. A tribute to me, Archi Dhawan, at a royal palace. Who would've thought? I bet he's at work right now, across the courtyard from me, kneeling in the earth, making the palace grounds beautiful.

No. Stop thinking about him, Archi!

"Well, that's everything," Jassi announces when we return to reception.

"This place is gorgeous," I say. "The royal jewels were honestly amazing. And the tapestries? Oh, and the miniature paintings—"

Jassi laughs. "It's a good thing you think so, because you're going to have to talk about all those pieces about a million times on these tours. Don't lose your enthusiasm."

"Never." I flip through my journal. "Wait. We didn't see the Rathore crown or the Nihâl Chand pieces that were on the website. Did we pass by them? I think I also saw some textiles online that weren't on display. Are they in conservation?" On our tour, Jassi pointed out some things that would be back up soon but were being taken care of by the conservators, as well as rotating objects that sometimes went back to the palace residence, and she showed me a closed-off section that was temporarily on loan in Mumbai. But she didn't mention these other pieces.

Jassi makes a face. "No."

"Then?"

"Rajasthani royalty hasn't had those items in physical possession since the nineteenth century."

"Oh." I frown, processing. "Where are they?"

Jassi scowls deeper. "In London."

"On loan?"

She snorts, but she's not smiling. "As if. The British colonized our country and looted our art. They sold prized pieces to private collectors, who eventually gave them to museums in London. Some of them, anyway. One imagines there's a lot of historic Indian art in somebody's attic in the UK, likely because their grandfather was a thief during the British Raj." Jassi's tone is bitter.

I feel sick to my stomach. Of course, I know about how much looted art the UK has. Every Indian person knows of the Kohinoor diamond, one of the largest cut diamonds in the world. The gem is now part of the English crown jewels. And who isn't aware of the hundreds of stolen artifacts from colonized countries in the British Museum? I'm reminded of KAVI's installation outside the museum, and I think of how I almost went to London for my semester abroad: Could I have been working in one of those museums, selling out my ancestors? I realize now why Kiran-ji said the prized textile collection was a sore subject.

"The information stays on our website," Jassi says, "because the art is ours. It's Rajasthani art. But the museums refuse to repatriate the pieces."

"If they repatriate some pieces, they'll have to give back all their stolen artifacts," I whisper.

"And then their museums will be empty. So they refuse, no matter what."

"Despite its being Rajasthani property."

"What is it you say in America?" Jassi sits down in her swivel chair. "Finders keepers."

For the rest of the day, Jassi guides me through my primary responsibilities for my first rotation. I try to focus, but I can't stop thinking about the missing art. The crown, the miniatures, the textiles. Art that should be here. Later, I shadow a couple tour groups. One guide mentions the stolen art on his tour. The other doesn't. I guess it's hard to talk about loss.

People should be talking about this way more, though. We *should* be forcing people to think about the long-lasting effects of colonialism. I think again of KAVI, drawing attention to important social causes. If only KAVI could help call attention to the Rathore Gallery specifically. In the meantime, maybe I can do something about it myself.

I flip forward to get to the page in my journal titled *Museum Internship Capstone Project*. It's the page I was filling in on the train when I first met Shiv. Shiv, who's probably only some yards—meters, perhaps—from me right now.

I could try to get lost in the gardens again. . . .

I almost want to go, take my mind off what's missing from the museum. But I don't. It was nice seeing Shiv a second time, but I can't let him take me away from my purpose here. I have more than enough to do. For one: figure out how to incorporate the stolen art into my Capstone.

In the middle of the page of discarded ideas, I take out my pen and write in block letters so it jumps out from the rest of my scribbles.

PROJECT: BRING OUR HISTORY HOME.

Chapter 5

Sisterhood of the Traveling Polaroid

The following week, I've just gotten off the phone with my parents when Mohini walks into our room, her arms full of boxes.

"What's all this?" I jump up to help her.

"My mom sent me a million care packages." Mohini sets everything down on the floor between our beds and places her hands on her knees, letting out a long breath, as if she's winded. "Oh, and"—she looks up, her eyes sparkling—"I did some online shopping."

I laugh. "Where do you have the space for more things?" Mohini's side of the room is already overflowing.

"Fear not." She rummages through the boxes. "Some of these packages are for you."

"For me?"

"Yup. You have one from Whitney, a letter with no return address, and"—she gestures at a box in front of her—"I got you some more casual Desi fits for your days on the job."

"Mohini!" I hug her. "You did not have to do that."

"Don't worry," she says. "I barely did. They're PR packages. I have a ton of followers online because of my parents, so brands send me stuff to unbox on camera. Literally spent nothing on them. I usually donate the things I get anyway, after posting a photo online, of course."

I tear open the box and run my fingers over the sequined fabric inside. The dress is butter yellow, with a square neckline. Who would've thought I'd get so lucky to have not one but two friends to help me with fashion? And they're both influencers?! I take a photo and send it to my group chat with Lilyn and Whitney. Lilyn would *love* Mohini.

Speaking of . . . I reach for Whitney's box and use a pair of nail scissors to slice it open. When I open the flaps, I let out an excited squeal.

That catches Mohini's attention. "What is it?"

"Our traveling Polaroid!" I pull a lavender Polaroid camera out of the box and turn it on, pointing the lens at Mohini. She makes a funny face, and I snap a pic, laughing in excitement. "We're passing around a camera on our semesters abroad. Whitney took it with her to Paris last semester, and she took a bunch of photos documenting her adventures. She had the idea to pass it to me when she got back from France."

It's our way of staying connected to each other despite being separated by continents. Our very own Sisterhood of the Traveling Polaroid. We're sending around a photo album, too. Whitney's photos are already in there, and there are empty slots ready for mine and Lilyn's. Whitney's shots include a picture of the Eiffel Tower, her dorm room, and her and her boyfriend, Thierry, at the Pont des Arts. They are adorable.

Lilyn's a junior, so she's going to fill up the album after me, when she does her Capstone in Tokyo this summer. I hold the camera in my lap and smile, feeling the bittersweet taste of homesickness. I follow up my text in the group chat with an update that I've received the Polaroid.

Archi: It's here!!! 📷

Whitney: ♥♥♥

Lilyn: Yesssss

"Hold on." I peer back up at Mohini. She's cutting through cardboard, organizing her PR packages by brand. "Did you say I had a letter?"

"Yup." Mohini fishes for something in our pile of discarded packaging. She waves a creamy, pale-gold envelope.

I grab it out of her hands. The envelope is weighty, like it holds something important. On the back is my name in carefully printed calligraphy. And on the front— I gasp. "A wax seal?"

"I know. Fancy." Mohini leans over and runs her finger over the red wax, which is stamped with the outline of a tulip. "Is this an invitation to one of those secret societies people say are at VBIS?" She frowns. "How come I didn't get one?"

Something about the tulip seal sends a little buzz to my chest. Then I furrow my brow. "I don't have the time to be in a secret society, what with my internship and my classes—"

"Oh, hush," says Mohini. "It could also be from a secret admirer. Open it, open it!"

I almost feel bad tearing through the envelope, but curiosity gets the better of me. Mamma used to hate it when I opened presents on birthdays. I'd rip up the wrapping paper, aiming greedily for the gift inside. After a few parties during elementary school, she insisted on opening my presents for me so she could save the paper, still perfectly creased, and reuse it in the future. But old habits die hard, and this fancy envelope is no exception. Even Mohini winces as I throw half the envelope aside and pull out the card.

"'Archi,'" I read aloud, but before I can start reading the rest, my eyes automatically skip down to find the name at the bottom:

—Shiv

"It's from Shiv!" I drop the card like it's red-hot.

"Shiv? The guy from the garden? The same one from the train?"

The tulip on the seal makes a lot more sense now. Something squirms in my stomach.

"Oh my god." Mohini swats me. "You're blushing."

"Am not."

She grabs my Polaroid and takes a pic of me, then shows me the photo that develops. "Try denying it now."

I *am* blushing. "Well, I shouldn't be blushing, because I haven't even read the letter. Who knows what it says? And how did he know where to find me?" I pause, frowning.

"Actually, isn't this creepy? A letter from a boy I've run into twice, without a return address?"

Mohini clucks her tongue. "Read it first. Decide how you feel after you've seen what he's said."

I reach for the card again, my fingers buzzing.

"'Archi,'" I read, starting over. "'Sorry for the unsolicited note. I didn't know how to get in touch with you, but I remembered you said you were going to VBIS, so I'm putting this together at the VBIS mail room. I guess you're the only Archana in the study-abroad program. If you're totally creeped out, please ignore this, and I promise, it'll be the last you'll hear from me.'"

"Thoughtful boy," Mohini says.

Okay, if he's preempting my concerns, he can't be creepy, right? Now I feel less nervous and more . . . flattered. This guy saw me twice and went on a *quest* to find out how to reach me?

I keep going:

"'If not, I only wanted to say that it was really great running into you at the garden. I'm sorry you didn't get to see much of it, because it's a really special part of Jaipur, at least to me. I know you're here to learn more about the city and explore. So I was thinking, if you're available and willing, would you like to meet me tonight? I'll be at the west entrance to the royal gardens an hour before sunset. I hope to see you there. Shiv.'"

When I glance up at Mohini, her jaw has dropped.

"Is he . . . asking me out?"

Mohini is flabbergasted. "Romantic or not, he's definitely asking to see you again." She pauses. "Do you *want* it to be romantic?"

I shake my head adamantly and ignore the devil that has popped up on my shoulder. "I'm not dating anyone this semester. I promised myself!" I press my hands to my cheeks. "What do I do?"

"You have to go. Obviously."

"But what if it *is* a date?"

"Well, you won't know until you show up. And don't you want to see him again, too?"

I think for a moment about how easy it felt to talk to Shiv, to even argue with him briefly. It was fun. As easy as talking to Mohini. And I could use a friend at the palace. "I guess so."

"Then go. Suss out the vibe, and if you're not feeling it, tell him that you're only open to being friends."

"You're very wise, Mohini."

"That I am. I'm also curious about how this guy is arranging a meetup at the royal gardens." She leans over and looks at the note. "He has good handwriting. And where did he get his stationery? Actually, can you ask him that? I want some, too. Maybe monogrammed."

"He's a palace gardener," I remind her. "This is probably palace stationery."

"Still. It's very cool. And mysterious. You have to go to find out what his deal is."

"But—"

"No buts!" Mohini crosses her arms. "You can't turn down an invite to the palace gardens. Do you understand how unique this opportunity is? Besides, it's not like you're agreeing to marry him."

"True." Her logic is impeccable. "And we could be reading way too much into this. Nowhere did he specify it was a date. He asked me to hang out. I can do that."

"Exactly." Mohini blows out a long breath. "Thank god. Because if you'd said you weren't going, I would have dressed up in your clothes and pretended to be you tonight. One of us should get to explore more of the royal palace. I mean, we saw only a fraction of the gardens when we visited. Imagine how much more a royal gardener could show you! He probably knows about all kinds of secret pathways and hidden alcoves. And you'll get to see all of that after hours, without tourists nearby." She sighs dreamily, clearly caught up in her fantasy.

I snort. "What about Anjit? Doesn't he have a dorm social planned for us tonight? Won't he realize I'm missing?"

"It'll probably be a lame movie. I'll cover for you. I'll say you studied so hard you got a migraine. If anything, he'll be proud of you."

"Okay," I say.

"Okay?"

"I'll go. I don't want to stand Shiv up, and you're right. It *is* super cool to get invited to the royal gardens. But if this ends up being anything weird, I'm texting you to come get me right away."

Mohini grins. "Perfect. Now let's figure out what you'll wear." She gestures in front of her. "Lucky for you, we have about a thousand PR packages to choose from."

Two hours later, I'm standing around the corner from the private west entrance to the palace gardens.

From here, I can see the roof of the museum and the top of the courtyard meeting room that the guide talked about during my first visit to the City Palace. It's made of pillars, without any walls, and the royals used to host important meetings there. Walls have ears, they used to say, so it was better to have no walls at all.

It's strange, being at the palace after hours. There's way less noise than usual—no guides clamoring to get tourists to use their services for only a rupee an hour (which to me feels criminally underpaid), no street sellers advertising their Jaipur souvenirs in the languages of passing tourists (I remember the shock of hearing "¿Mira, mira, te gusta?" out of the mouths of Rajasthani locals when they spotted Spanish tourists), no farmers herding their cows past the front street and blocking traffic.

The sky is still bright. Mohini and I checked to see when the sun was supposed to set, and I'm here exactly an hour before that, so I hope I'm punctual. Seriously, what kind of meeting time is *an hour before sunset*? Just give me a number!

Before I left campus, Mohini outfitted me in a flowy pink blouse with a triangle pattern embroidered in cobalt blue and sunny yellows. I braided the hair at my crown and put in a pair of dangly gold earrings. I swapped my simple nose ring for one with a twisty gold detail. With my blouse, I chose blue jeans and comfy sandals. A little dressed up, a little dressed down. It seemed the vibe for an evening I have no idea what to expect from. For all I know, Shiv could show up in his suit, his gardening gear, or anything in between.

My heartbeat quickens. I've brought my purse, too, and in it is the Polaroid Whitney sent. I remember how her photos from Paris told a story, from sightseeing to unexpectedly falling in love. I wonder what story my photos will tell.

On the street corner, there's no sign of anyone, not even any guards. I remember passing the last guard about a block away, but shouldn't there be more, this close to the garden entrance? Trepidation builds inside me. What if this is a con? What if this is how I get kidnapped? I fire off a text to Whitney. It's earlier in the day for her, back in D.C.

> **Whitney:** You're at a palace. That's literally one of the safest places you could be.

> **Archi:** Yeah, when security guards are present!

> **Whitney:** Maybe they have high-tech lasers now, and they don't even need guards.
> Stop texting me and find the boy!!!

Hesitantly, I round the corner. There, on the other side of the street, are the gates to the palace garden. They're not as grand as the ones by the visitor entrance that Mohini and I used when we were touring. They look older—bronze and tall. There are no guards there, either. Instead, by the gate stands Shiv, his hands clasped, his weight shifting from foot to foot.

Oh.

He's dressed up, too—not suit-and-tie dressed up but

put together, with his hair pushed back like a movie star's, and wearing crisp trousers and a white button-up shirt. A sweater is tied over his shoulders and around his neck, prep school (or Shah Rukh Khan) style. His shirt sleeves are folded up, so I can see his biceps as I walk closer. I swallow.

He looks *good.*

When he sees me, his face breaks into a smile. The nervousness washes away from me.

"Archi," he says, knocking the wind from me. "You're here."

I duck my head. "The invitation was too good to pass up."

"Sorry it was so out of the blue. It was either that or show up where you work, and that seemed a bit much."

I can't help but smile. "I mean, I showed up where *you* work last time."

Shiv laughs, and the sound cuts into my stomach, firing up those butterflies that really shouldn't be fluttering. "Good point." He swallows, gesturing toward the garden. "Ready?"

"I think so." I follow him in toward the sweet smells of rose and honeysuckle. "So we're really going to explore the garden?" I tuck a strand of hair behind my ear. I don't know how to ask whether this is a date, how to preempt any romance, so I dive into other questions instead. "Why aren't there any guards here? And how did you even arrange this? Did you send me the letter on official royal stationery?"

Shiv's mouth twitches. "I, uh. Let's just say I helped out the royal family with a floral crisis. You know royals—"

I don't.

"They like to be grand with their words. So when they said I could ask for anything in return, I asked for an evening in the gardens to myself. And a guest to invite."

Huh. The royal family seems a lot more generous than I would have expected, especially toward an employee. "I would've asked for more money."

Shiv laughs again, and I feel something like pride at having been the cause of the sound. It makes me want to do it again—make him laugh. "The stationery did come from the palace. But don't worry, I didn't use the king's official seal. The courier had a whole collection of wax stamps. I got lucky with the tulip."

"You remembered."

"You're memorable."

There must be a garden in my gut, the way the butterflies are flapping around in there. I glance down at my shoes, then back up to find Shiv smiling at me, his eyes soft and kind.

"Shall we?" he asks.

Shiv leads me inside, and I follow.

Chapter 6

Whatever Happened to Feminism?

"Here, look at this," Shiv says when we find ourselves under a flowering tree deep within the palace garden.

We've been walking on a narrow stone path through a labyrinth of watercolor flowers and lush green leaves, the scents of honeysuckle and lavender and mint around us. Shiv was right when he said there was so much more of the garden to see.

It's been mostly small talk so far, learning little things about each other we didn't get a chance to ask on the train or in our run-in last week. I tell Shiv about home, about Mamma and Baba. I tell him about Whitney and Lilyn and school. He tells me about his family—he has an older sister who loves to paint, which is how he knew so much about the Rajasthani styles when we spoke on the train. He has a puppy, a stray he begged his parents to let him adopt, and even though they had their qualms, they eventually gave in. He graduated a semester early, but he's my age.

He's smart and funny, and his smile makes me smile.

I can see it already: we could be good friends.

I follow Shiv's movement to see him pull a low-hanging branch toward him and clip a few flowers to put in a small wicker basket that hangs on the crook of his elbow. Around us are trees laden with ripe fruit, banana plants with wide leaves, and vines of vegetables crawling over raised planters. He's been clipping flowers and ferns the whole walk, pointing out species and native plants. He saves one of the flowers from the tree above us and holds it out to me. "Papaya flower." The flower is light green and white with a golden-yellow stamen. "It's edible."

I pluck the flower bud from his fingers and put it on my tongue. It tastes fresh and bitter and like . . . well . . . *plant.*

Shiv laughs at the expression on my face. "Uh, just because they're edible doesn't mean you should immediately put them in your mouth."

I frown. "I'm not sure I'd call these *edible.*"

"Have a little patience, please."

"What, you're gonna whip me up a five-star meal made of papaya flowers?"

Another laugh, and despite myself, I feel proud again, as if I'm getting gold stars for each chuckle.

"Maybe," he teases as he touches the back of my elbow gently. "Patience. Come on." Shiv reaches into his basket and pulls out a few more plants. "Try these instead."

"No, no," I protest, "not after the papaya flower."

"Well, I didn't *tell* you to eat that," Shiv points out. "So this is already different."

I peer at him suspiciously.

Shiv stares deep into my eyes. "Do you trust me?"

"No!" I say immediately. "I barely know you."

He pauses, taken aback, and I wonder if I've offended him. Then he starts laughing. "Okay, fair enough. But I *do* know this garden. Do you trust that?"

"I'll allow it."

"Give this a go." Shiv hands me the blossom. "Honeysuckle."

Keeping my eyes on Shiv, I put the flower in my mouth and crush it between my teeth. He holds my gaze, not even dropping his eyes to my lips. Not taking the bait, I realize. Then it occurs to me that I've put out vibes without even meaning to.

Barely know Shiv or not, boy-free semester or not, I'm instinctively flirting with this guy. I shouldn't be. I'm here to be friends. I force myself to focus on the taste in my mouth, which is sugary and light, a pleasant surprise. "Oh," I say. "This is nice."

"Something sweet." Shiv smiles knowingly at my reaction. He reaches into his basket and pulls out a seedpod. "Smell this. You probably don't want to eat it raw."

I sniff. The scent is warm, intoxicating.

"Cardamom," he explains. "It's best in hot dishes and drinks. I think it's one of my favorite spices to cook with. Plus, it's easy to grow." Once more, he pulls something from his basket. It's a green stem with leaves.

"I know this one. Mint!"

"All right, smarty-pants." But he's still smiling.

I take it and inhale deeply. "Mmm. So do you go around eating royal property when you're on the clock?"

"Technically, I'm not on the clock right now."

"You really have to correct me on every little detail, don't you?" I roll my eyes.

"It's a little too fun not to." He traces my face with his eyes. "You get all pouty."

"I do not!" I pout.

Shiv smiles again.

We walk farther down the winding path, deeper into the scent of flowers and fruit trees. "Whatever happened to feminism?" I grumble. "And the girl always being right."

Shiv's lips twitch. "How could I be so thoughtless?" He reaches to the side of the path to clip some daffodils and adds them to his basket.

"That's the spirit," I say, bumping his shoulder with mine. He stumbles briefly, and his fingers land on my lower back as he rights himself. I suck in a breath. His hand is gone in a second, but I can still feel where he touched me, at the bottom of my spine. My skin buzzes, electrified.

A faint voice in the back of my mind reminds me, *Boy-free semester*. I know I have that rule for a reason. For a *Nick* reason. Because as nice as this is—being giddy in a literal palace, wandering secret paths, learning about flowering plants—dating Nick was nice at one point, too. Until it wasn't.

Shiv continues, oblivious. "I sometimes help set the table for palace dinners. Since I know so much about the garden, and we harvest a lot of the vegetables and herbs for meals, I can give my input on what might be good for the menu."

"You're really involved in palace life," I observe.

"You could say that."

"Is it weird? Working for the royals?"

"What do you mean?"

"Like, being in service to people who did nothing to deserve their titles and privilege except having the luck to be born into the right family?"

Shiv pauses, mulling over my words. "It is weird in that way, I guess." He moves his basket from one arm to the other. "It's not fair, obviously. People always like to think, now in a postcolonial world, that we should go back to how it was before British imperialism in India. But I wonder sometimes about the idea of preserving monarchy. If it's merely getting rid of one unjust regime for another."

I'm stunned by Shiv's words. He's right, of course. As an Indian American, I romanticize India before British colonization. And there definitely is so much to romanticize—the art, the agriculture, how gender-fluid ancient India was, the diversity of languages and religions, the rich history and blending of cultures. But no place is perfect, and there's a lot in India's own history that's bitter and wrong. The structure of monarchy is one of those things.

I nod. "It has historical value, I guess?"

"Sure," says Shiv. "The palace. The grounds. The museum. But do we really need a king and queen in this day and age? A prince and a princess? I suppose it depends on what they do, though. If you're born into power, you have a responsibility to your community, you know? I don't know that our royalty balances that power with enough responsibility."

I jerk my head around, checking to see if any guards have followed us. "Are you allowed to be saying these things on royal property? Isn't this blasphemous?"

Shiv laughs. "You worried about hidden cameras, *Bigg Boss* style?"

"I hadn't even thought of that!" I remember the Indian version of *Big Brother* my parents watch sometimes. "Now I'm even more nervous. You know, if I get into trouble in India, it's a big deal. I'm a foreigner."

"Don't worry. There are no cameras. It's just us. And I'll make sure you're safe."

I smile. "With your extensive royal gardener privileges?"

"Exactly."

The sun has set now, officially. It's dusk, and the evening settles around us. A breeze travels past us, and I shiver as it grazes my skin. Shiv notices immediately. "Cold?" he asks, moving to undo his sweater.

The utter sweetness of the gesture strikes me, and the voice in my head comes back with a boom. Nick seemed sweet, too. Didn't he?

Oh, no. I can't do this.

So I jump forward in the path. "No," I insist. "I'm good."

Shiv eyes me with an amused expression. "Are you?"

"Yup!" I jog in place a little, aware I look ridiculous. "Just need to get my blood flowing." At this point, I'm so embarrassed, I want to run away. So I grab the basket out of Shiv's hands and turn on my heel. "Race ya!"

I take off on the path, hearing Shiv call after me, "To where?!"

But I'm flying down the path, my hair floating around my face, trying to get rid of my blush, or at least make it appear as though it's a product of the run and not Shiv. I run around a corner, hearing Shiv following behind me, and come to a screeching halt.

The path ends at a beautiful gazebo, strung with flickering fairy lights. The structure is the same terra-cotta pink as the palace, a bright contrast against the darkening sky. Heat lamps dot the space, and in the middle of the gazebo is a table with cookware and dishes. Behind it, on the other side of the gazebo, is a shimmering pond filled with pink lotus flowers, reflecting the evening. At the bank of the pond is a knit picnic blanket, cozy and inviting.

"Oh," I breathe, my eyes filling with wonder at the sight.

There's a rustle behind me, and Shiv catches up, letting out a long breath. He doesn't seem winded, but his cheeks are pink, his hair a little mussed. I resist the urge to fix it for him.

He meets my eyes. His irises are dark—deep—in the evening light. "It was supposed to be a surprise." His voice is quiet.

I hold his gaze, and something in my belly stirs. "I'm . . . surprised."

Shiv's shy smile makes me want to melt into the earth.

I look around at the gazebo and pond in bewilderment. "What . . . what is all this?"

"It's dinner." Shiv takes his basket back from me and

adds another fistful of flowers to it. "If you're hungry?" He says it like a question.

My stomach rumbles at the mention of food, and I realize that in my rush to get ready with Mohini, I only picked at lunch and had crunchy Kurkure chips in our dorm.

Shiv grins at the sound of my stomach growling. "I'll take that as a yes."

"We're eating here? In the palace garden?"

Shiv points to his basket. "With palace ingredients."

"Oh my god." I'm amazed. "The royal family *really* meant it when they said you could ask for anything."

I follow Shiv into the gazebo, where he sets the basket on the tabletop and pulls out a cutting board from a shelf underneath. "I told you to be patient with all the edible plants," he reminds me. "Now you'll see how you're actually supposed to eat them."

"Can I help?"

"Nope." Shiv pats the end of the table, which is empty. "You can sit and talk to me while I take care of the food."

I don't think I've ever heard hotter words come out of a guy's mouth. Even though, of course, that is not the point. I'm a guest, and he's cooking for me. That's all this is. I lean back, watching as Shiv deftly cleans some of the garden veggies and starts chopping away. "What are you making?"

"Raw papaya curry and chaat." He lifts a pair of papayas out of the basket. "Does that sound okay to you?"

I gasp. "I'm allergic to papaya."

Shiv pales, then glares at me. "Yeah, yeah, says the girl who immediately put a papaya flower in her mouth."

I laugh.

"I bet you're also allergic to chaat, huh?"

"Anything to make things more difficult for you."

"Lucky for you I like a challenge." The corners of Shiv's lips turn up.

We're silent a moment as I watch Shiv cut vegetables and pluck edible flowers from their stems. Crickets chirp in the garden, and the rhythmic chopping of the knife, combined with the heat lamps brightening the dusk, lulls me into warm relaxation.

"Have you had dal baati yet? I didn't want to make it in case you've already had it from somewhere that makes it better than I do."

"Good thinking." I picture the popular Rajasthani food. "A group of us on my floor went out for dal baati during our lunch break at orientation. It was delicious. I'd have it again." Even at a mention of the dish, I can taste the crispy baked dough dipped in piping-hot dal. I sigh happily.

"I'll keep that in mind," Shiv says.

The tendons in his arms flex as he chops herbs. To my amazement, he brings out a mortar and pestle and starts manually grinding mint and cilantro into a spicy, tangy blend. It's an advanced move.

"You're making chutney," I whisper. "From scratch."

Shiv raises an eyebrow. "Mm-hmm?"

I shake my head. "Wow."

A blush glows on Shiv's cheeks, and I realize I've flattered him. "So," he says, glancing back up at me, "tell me something."

"About?"

"You. Your work. Your home. What you want out of your time here. Anything. I want to hear you."

Now it's my turn to be flattered. This boy—who collects favors from royalty, who knows flowers and herbs like he's a botanist, who has asked me to sit while he cooks me a meal—wants to hear about me.

"My internship's off to a good start," I begin, watching Shiv's reaction. His eyes are ahead of him, dropping cubed raw papaya into a bowl, but he nods, actively listening. "I like working here—learning about Rajasthani art. But I learned more about the pieces that are missing from the museum. Did you know about that?"

Shiv nods again, gravely. "Yeah. They're in England."

"Yeah!" I ramp up. "The pieces were taken by, like, lords and ladies, who sent them back to their families as gifts. Some are in London museums now, but others are probably in somebody's attic, passed down as 'family heirlooms' even though they were stolen."

"I remember reading about a woman who had an auction for the things she found in her father's home after he died. She donated a bunch of things to the British Museum, and everyone thought it was so generous of her, but"—Shiv adds spices to the papaya chunks he's sautéing in the pan—"those items were never hers to give away."

"She should have 'donated' them back to the original owners!" I grit my teeth. "Doesn't that kind of thing piss you off?"

"For sure. But it's hard to do anything about."

I nod. "I have to come up with a Capstone project by the end of the semester—something from my internship. I was thinking of doing something about the stolen art. And I want my project to be related to my curating goals—like, maybe I could help curate a gallery. But how can I curate a gallery without having access to the art?" I tuck a loose piece of hair behind my ear and watch as Shiv plates the curry and, in two bowls, adds a bunch of raw veggies with what looks like precooked, spiced chickpeas, spooning the chutney on top. He garnishes the dish with papaya flowers. "I don't know," I finish. "I have a lot to think about."

Shiv grabs another set of flowers he clipped earlier and placed into his basket and arranges them quickly into a little bouquet. "You'll figure it out." He ties a piece of twine around the bouquet and holds it out to me. "I'm sure of it. And I'll bring you a bigger bouquet when your gallery opens."

My chest warms, and I take the bouquet, marveling at the purple and pink and yellow petals between my fingers. *When.* Shiv said *when,* not *if.* His belief in me is stunning—literally. I feel glued in place, and I try to remember whether Nick ever told me he believed in my goals. He prided himself on being "realistic." And he always spoke in ifs.

I help Shiv bring the tray of food to the picnic blanket by the pond, and we sit together, our legs dangerously close. I dip a spoon into the curry and take a bite, instantly melting into the flavors. "Oh," I groan, closing my eyes. "This is *so* good. You should be doing this professionally."

When I open my eyes, Shiv is staring at me with an expression I can't read. His eyes are molten, dark and endless. "Thank you. Try the chaat?"

I do, and it too, crispy and spicy, is fantastic. We eat for a while, me diving quickly into my food, both because I'm so hungry and because it's delightful. The pond glitters in front of us while we eat.

"Shiv," I say quietly. Because it's been enough time not addressing it. Ignoring it. Although, I wonder, what if *it* is just in my head? "Why did you ask me to meet you here?"

He frowns. "You mean, as opposed to somewhere else?"

"No." But my lips twitch. "Why me? We only met by accident." I hope it's clear what I'm asking, even if I'm not being direct. What does he *want* from me?

Shiv thinks about this for a moment. "You surprised me," he says simply.

I raise my brows in question.

"When we talked on the train, you were so sure of yourself. And you were ready to call me out. It's been a long time since someone's done that—since I've . . ." He pauses. "Made a new friend, I guess. There aren't a lot of people my age at the palace. And in some ways, it's isolating. I thought, when I saw you again by accident, that it was a sign I should try to get to know you on purpose."

"A friend." I repeat his words. "You want to be friends?"

Shiv looks at me strangely. "Well, I hope you didn't think I asked you here to be enemies."

I giggle, and Shiv seems pleased by my reaction. He leans back on the picnic blanket and peers up at me. "Well, you called me out, too." I replay the moment he tested my knowledge on the train. "That's frenemy behavior."

"You yelled at me," Shiv points out, grinning.

"And yet, here we sit." I smirk. "So I guess that's what you're into."

Shiv laughs—a full belly laugh. "See?" he says. "Surprising."

I want to sigh happily, studying his face, his messy hair, his dark, thick eyebrows. His high cheekbones. My belly is filled with amazing food and an oozing, gooey feeling that could be dangerous but simply feels . . . nice.

"Okay," I say.

"Okay what?"

"I'd like to be friends. Not frenemies. Just friends."

"Not just strangers who run into each other on a train?"

I smile. "Or in a garden."

"Unless it's on purpose."

A laugh escapes me. "Exactly."

This is good. I'm focusing on my goals. I'm staying on track. And I'm meeting new people. Mohini will be proud, I think. And my parents! They'll be ecstatic when I tell them I got to tour the private palace gardens, *twice*.

Shiv interrupts my thoughts, turning the question on me. "Why did you say yes? To meeting me here?"

I study Shiv's face. His expression is completely unguarded. I swallow, and the words come out rough. "You surprised me, too."

A smile builds on Shiv's face, and it feels, again, like getting a gold star.

"And it would have been pretty rude to leave you hanging."

He bursts out laughing. "I would have survived. Probably."

"Thank you for this," I say. "For tonight. I'm glad we got to see each other a third time."

"Anytime." He cocks his head. "Can we—can we do this again?"

"You going to send me another engraved invitation?"

His eyes crinkle. "If you want. Or I could get your phone number to text you? Since that's what friends do?"

Chapter 7

Hands-On Learning

The first thing I see later in the week when I open my eyes is the little bouquet Shiv made me. It sits on my nightstand in a mug of water.

The second thing I see is Mohini at the foot of my bed, fully dressed. "Get your ass up! We're going to Johari Bazaar."

Crust covers my eyes. I'm pretty sure I was having a particularly pleasant dream, set in a lush garden of wildflowers and lotus petals, and I'm irked to be awakened from it. I grumble as I sit up and reach for my phone. "It's a school day. I have class in two hours."

"We're going to bunk today."

"Bunk?"

"Skip. Ditch. Blow off." Mohini tosses a pillow from her bed at me, and I catch it square in the chest. "What do you guys have in America? Senior Ditch Day? Consider that today."

"We already did Senior Ditch Day in the fall," I say,

stretching out. I crack my neck and twist my lower back until it makes a satisfying popping noise.

"Ew." Mohini scrunches up her nose. "Don't do that again, please. And you haven't done a ditch day at VBIS. Consider it a clean slate."

I run a brush through my hair and squint in my desk mirror at the new eyebrow hairs growing in on my face, far beyond the clean lines the eyebrow Aunty back home threads them into. I twist my nose ring. "Okay, I'll bite. What's Johari Bazaar?"

"Only the coolest open market in Jaipur. We're going shopping!"

"Don't you have enough things? You just did some online shopping." I eye Mohini's overflowing side of the room.

"This is different. Let me support local businesses in peace," she replies. "What class do you have today, anyway?"

"Jewelry as Art History." I do seriously like the class—but three hours of any lecture is way too long, especially first thing in the morning. I have to down a tumbler of strong chai to stay awake.

"Well, today will count as hands-on learning instead of class. Johari Bazaar has an incredible selection of jewelry." She slaps my Polaroid camera into my hands. "Make sure to get some photos. You're definitely going to want some for your journal."

"Ah, yes," I say. "Let me document proof of us skipping classes for a personal adventure. Then, if we get caught, we won't even be able to deny it!"

"We'll be fine. And besides, the real world is the best educator," Mohini retorts sagely.

We take a rickshaw to the bazaar. I try to pay Mohini back for the bills she gives the driver, but she waves me off. "When I come visit the United States, you can pay for me."

I twirl around in amazement as we land on the street. We're in the old part of Jaipur, in the middle of a long, busy stretch of road. A ton of drivers move quickly through the street, honking their horns and yelling exasperatedly through their windows at other cars. And on either side of us, filling our sights with bright colors, are open-front shops selling jewelry, clothing, incense, spices, shoes, and handbags. It's a feast for our eyes, and both Mohini and I take everything in slowly.

"The photos don't do it justice." Mohini sighs happily. "Where should we start?"

"Jewelry and clothing?" I suggest. "I promised Lilyn I'd report back on Rajasthani fashion. Then we can do food."

Mohini grins. "Today is going to be incredible."

We stop at a jewelry stand first, where I run my fingers over wide, intricate rings with sparkling stones and necklaces with gems dripping like teardrops. "Wow," I whisper. "These are stunning."

"Aren't they?" Mohini holds a red-and-green choker up to her throat. "I want to be buried in all this. Isn't this a million times better than going to class?"

I nod begrudgingly. "I care more about my internship than class anyway."

"How's work going?"

"Good, I think?" I spin a pair of dangly green earrings between my fingers. "I'm still doing tours, which is a little frustrating, but I'm learning more about the museum because of it." I don't mention I got so turned around giving one of my first tours that a *kid* in the group had to point out that the art I was talking about wasn't even in the room we were in. "There's a space in one of the wings that's kind of quiet. I want to pitch an idea to Kiran-ji to turn it into a mini gallery that hopefully I can curate for my Capstone."

Mohini screeches so loud the storekeeper glares at us. I make a face in apology. "Oh my god!" Mohini yells. "That's the best idea."

"Only if she says yes," I agree. "And only if I can secure art to showcase. I'd want to include something about the stolen art if they let me. But I don't know how yet."

"Well, when you get approval—"

"If," I correct.

"*When* you get approval, because you will, you could write a letter to UK museums," Mohini suggests. "They're not going to give the art back, but the letter could bring attention to it. I could post it to my socials, too, where I'm sure it'd get a lot of traction."

I hold the emerald-colored earrings next to my face in the shop mirror. "I like that. Something to communicate our demands."

Mohini comes to my side and gives me a squeeze. "You're going to kill it, no matter what. In the meantime, let's get you some retail therapy." She cups my chin. "Those earrings look great on you. Green is definitely your color. You must get them."

After I buy the earrings, we walk into a clothing dukaan. Mohini points to a purple anarkali. The gorgeous Desi gown is heavy with glittery designs. *"Ooooh,"* she breathes, admiring its gold-embroidered pleated skirt. "That's beautiful. Try it on."

"Mohini, that's a wedding dress! And why don't you?"

She leans in close to me. "They don't know you're not getting married." She gestures at a baby pink anarkali beside the purple one. "I'm going to try *that* one."

Before I can protest or agree, Mohini barrels straight through the other customers perusing anarkalis and lehengas to the counter where the owner stands. "Yeh doh, bhaisab."

They speak for a bit as I run my fingers over the long, elegant skirts and then a casual, traditional Rajasthani blouse in jewel tones, decorated with mirrorwork. On another rack is a collection of bandhej saris, tie-dyed in an Indian style in printed and beaded floral patterns. When Mohini comes back, she's grinning widely. "We can go to the back to try them on," she practically squeals.

As I emerge from behind the curtain, Mohini is already outside, her beaded pink anarkali glittering in the daylight. She looks incredible: her deep brown skin shimmers from the light the sequins cast around her, and her eyes, rimmed with dark liner, shine brightly at me in the reflection of the mirror she's facing.

I come up from behind her and stand to her side,

checking out the two of us in the mirror. Her pink complements my violet nicely, the bright hues reminding me of a set of rose quartz and amethyst crystals on display at a booth we passed on the way here. I remember visiting Desi clothing shops as a kid with my mom when we'd visit my grandparents, and trying on clothes as Mohini and I are now. But today feels grown up.

"Whoa. You look amazing," I tell Mohini.

"I know, right?" Her reflection grins at me. "I don't think I'd wear this to my own wedding, but to a movie premiere for sure." Mohini spins around to take me in. "But you! How do you feel?"

I stare at myself and smile. "I feel like royalty."

"Princess Archi," Mohini says. "I'd be your knight in shining armor." She holds up her phone, zooms out to point-five, and takes a bunch of photos of us. "Although I might have some competition. . . . When are you going to see the royal gardener boy again?"

I smile. "Speak of the devil. I just got a text from him."

"*Ooooh*. That's exciting." Mohini holds her hand out to me, and I give her my phone, open to the notification.

> **Shiv:** Free Wednesday afternoon?
> I'll pick you up.

Simple, straight to the point. I like the directness.

"Wow, we love a planner," says Mohini. "Is he a Virgo, too? I love Virgo women." She then scrunches her nose. "But Virgo guys scare me. They can be intense."

"Um."

"You have to ask him for his birth chart. Chandana in the room next to us does readings. She's great at them."

"Okay," I agree. "What if he ends up being a Virgo guy?"

Mohini grins. "Run for the hills." She taps at the screen. "What's his name again? We need to internet-stalk him."

"Shiv." I frown. "It's short for something, but I don't know what. I . . ." I pause. "I don't actually know his full name."

Mohini *tsks*, handing me my phone back. "Well, there's your mission for the next time you hang out."

After we change back into our clothes and tell the disappointed shopkeeper we won't, in fact, be purchasing wedding dresses, we wander through a few more stalls. At one, I end up buying a dupatta with intricate gota patti work, a lovely style of layered embroidery. The shawl is a bit dressy, but I imagine I can wear it with a basic top and flowy pants and let the drapery do the talking. I send a photo to Mamma. I want to get her something from the bazaar, too, something to remind her of what was once her home.

The rest of the day, I barely remember that I'm supposed to be in class. Mohini was right. I learn so much while at the market. We pass a little shop of traditional Rajasthani puppets, and I spend probably too much time marveling at the craftsmanship, the bright colors and painted patterns of their clothes, their expressive faces, and even the fact that they have their own jewelry. Storytelling is such a big part of Indian history, and these puppets are art and history combined: the owner of the stall, who makes the puppets herself, explains that performers use the puppets to tell stories of great wars and heroes from long past, and it's a community activity to get together and watch the little plays.

Another shopkeeper tells us about his daughter, who's our age, and how she's planning on studying abroad, too, in Australia. Yet another lets me successfully haggle with him, likely out of sympathy for my amateurish efforts and not my actual persuasiveness, but Mohini cheers me on anyway. Talking to people in the market makes me think of why I was so drawn to Shiv. In some ways, he feels like my connection to Jaipur, my connection to a place that could have been my home if my parents had stayed.

When Mohini buys herself a pair of mojari, colorful leather slip-on shoes, I tell her about their history, based on my knowledge from artifacts at the museum. We spend a good amount of time at a quilt shop, studying block prints, and I take notes on my phone for ways I can incorporate these local traditions into my Capstone.

At the end of the day, spent, we find ourselves in a sweets shop drinking cardamom chai and eating pistachio-topped mithai. "So," Mohini says, her eyes a challenge. "Do you think your next hangout with the gardener will top today?"

I snort. "As if." I smile at Mohini. "Today was perfect. Nothing beats that."

Chapter 8

If I Die, I'm Suing You for All You Have

Wednesday rolls around, and I'm almost done getting ready when my phone buzzes.

Shiv: I'm here.

I turn to face Mohini, who has just changed into her robe to take a shower. "Do I look okay?"

She gives me a once-over. "You're gorgeous. Stunning. A wonder of the world." She waggles her eyebrows at me. "But why does it matter? You're just friends."

"Hey," I say. "I dress to impress everyone. Even you."

"And you always succeed, my dear." She pops into the bathroom and closes the door behind her. Within a minute, I hear the water running.

Archi: Coming! Meet you at the corner?

His typing bubbles come up, and then:

Shiv: Um.

Three bubbles again. Then a photo comes in, of my and Mohini's names in Hindi and English on our door. I gasp. "Mohini!" I whisper-yell. "He's *here*!" I try to knock on the bathroom door without alerting Shiv.

The water stops and the door cracks, steam escaping. Mohini sticks her head out. Her hair is dripping wet. "What?"

"He's *here* here."

Her jaw drops. "Well, let him in! I'll eavesdrop from the bathroom."

So I head to the door and swing it open. Standing there, in the VBIS dorm hallway, is Shiv, soft hair and kind eyes, lips turned up in a hesitant smile. The skin by the crescent scar on his chin dimples. He's wearing a hat that shields his face, but since I'm shorter than he is, I can still see him fine.

In his hands is a small bouquet of wildflowers.

"Hi," I breathe, drinking him in.

"Hi."

He looks me over, too, and the moment lingers until Mohini pipes up from the crack in the bathroom door, "How'd you find our room?" You can barely see her, but her voice carries. "Are they letting random people inside? You know I'm really rich, right? I can hire someone to take you out, no problem. I'd do it myself, but I'm a little occupied right now."

Eyes wide, I turn toward Mohini, hoping my expression screams *Do not embarrass me in front of Jaipur's royal gardener!*

But Shiv just laughs. "I tailgated in. Maybe they should hire someone for better security here. And I know VBIS pretty well. My friend Tushar went here last year. He grew up in London—our parents know each other." Shiv scratches the back of his neck as he shifts his attention back to me. "I wanted to bring you these"—he gestures at the flowers— "but I didn't want to make you have to go back upstairs to drop them off." I frown. Do *friends* bring each other bouquets every other day?

"My family would kill me if I showed up to meet anyone empty-handed," Shiv adds.

Oh. Yeah. I smile down at the flowers. That's low-key true of all Desi parents. Mamma and Baba bring a dish or a gift to every dinner they're invited to, even if it's explicitly *not* a potluck. Even if they're simply returning something that someone let them borrow, like a Tupperware container, they'll always put something new inside before they give it back.

Which makes me think—I didn't get anything for Shiv. Not this time or last time. I pat my pockets as if I might find something in them. "Thank you," I tell him. "I'll get us chais. My family would kill me if I didn't repay you."

He grins. "Deal."

Mohini interrupts, seeming far less impressed. "And what about me? No flowers for the roommate?" Her head pokes out from behind the bathroom door. "You come to my place of living, and you don't even bring me a gift?"

Shiv presses his lips together, amused. "The flowers are really for both of you, but . . ." He pulls a long white-petaled flower out of the bouquet without disrupting the rest and waves it toward Mohini. "Will this suffice as an individual gift?"

I can tell Mohini is surprised that he played along with her giving him a hard time. She pauses. "Thanks," she says, like she can't even think of something snarky to say in response. "You can leave it on my side of the room." She shuts the door.

"I'll remember to bring something more special next time," Shiv promises. *Next time.* My chest warms in me at the thought. He turns to face me, hand out with the bouquet, which looks as full as ever. "Ready?"

I take the flowers and put them on my desk. "I'm going to have to start buying vases."

"I like the mug on your nightstand," he comments, and I blush. He's noticed I kept the flowers from last time.

"Don't let it go to your head. Those were royal."

Shiv laughs.

"Be good!" Mohini calls from the bathroom as we leave. "Bring her home at an appropriate time, or else—" We don't hear the rest of what she shouts.

Outside, it's a beautiful day—warm, but there's a breeze. My kind of weather. We rarely get days like this in D.C., which seems to operate as though winter and summer are the only seasons that exist, except for the two weeks of spring in between. "So," I say as we make our way down the block, "where are we going?"

Shiv points to some hills in the distance, then gives me a wicked smile. "We're going up there."

"Shiv," I groan. "You better not be taking me on a hike. I am *not* dressed appropriately!" I check out the sandals on my feet.

"Don't worry. We're going to Jaigarh Fort, and this"— Shiv comes to a stop—"is how we're getting there."

In front of Shiv, parked by the curb and leaning a bit to the side, is a black-and-silver motor scooter, which looks like a cross between a moped and a motorcycle. "No way." My voice is a whisper.

"Have you ever been on a scooter?"

"Never." I've always wanted to, though. It's amazing how the drivers in India get around on these things. I'm already used to scooter and motorcycle drivers caring little for the laws of the road, zipping through traffic like they own the streets, maneuvering narrowly through crowds of cars and taxis. It's the best way to travel around here, it seems: efficient, fun, and also extremely terrifying. I eye Shiv suspiciously. "How do I know you're a good driver?"

"How do you know I'm not?"

"I'm not sure that's a bet I'd like to take with my life."

"You can wear the helmet."

"The helmet, singular? You're not going to wear a helmet?!"

"Come on, Archi. It's common to go without a helmet here. I'm used to it."

He's right, but that only adds to the danger. "If I die," I tell him, "I'm going to sue you for everything you have."

I get another laugh from him at that, and I smile despite myself. Gold star for Archi.

"If you die, I will have the Indian government create a new Taj Mahal in your honor," Shiv promises, and I recall that the palace in Agra was created as a mausoleum for Shah Jahan's favorite wife.

"And how would you be able to do that?" I play along.

"I wouldn't." Shiv grins. "That's how confident I am that you're going to be fine."

With that, he hops onto the seat and gestures at me to join him. Oh, what the hell. I put the helmet on and clip it under my chin. I swing a leg over the seat to sit behind Shiv. Hesitantly, I place my hands on his shoulders. They're broad and warm under my palms. I take a deep breath, and as Shiv's shoulders rise and fall, I realize he's taking a deep breath, too. "Is this okay?"

"Yeah," Shiv says. His voice comes out gruff. "Ready?"

"As much as I can be," I tell him. Shiv kick-starts the scooter and we're off, soaring through Jaipur's streets, barreling down the intersection, headed for the hills.

I let out an involuntary screech, and before I can help it, my hands slide down to Shiv's chest. I wrap my arms around him and lean in so I'm holding on tight. I squeeze my eyes shut. The noise and movement fade into the background as my vision goes dark, and all I can feel is the wind in my hair and the warmth of Shiv's back against me. I can feel his heartbeat with my fingers. I begin orienting myself to his breathing, trying to slow down my heart.

When my heart rate is calm again, Shiv's voice rings in my ears, low and gentle: "You can open your eyes now."

I flick them open—my forehead is resting on Shiv's back. "How did you know I had my eyes closed?"

There's a lilt in his voice when he answers, "Lucky guess." He lifts one hand from the handlebars and places it over my hand at his heart. "Look around. I promise it's worth it."

So I do, lifting my head, and I realize we're climbing into the hills. The scooter isn't going as terrifyingly fast as I feared, and as we round a turn, I nearly gasp.

Shiv seems to know exactly what I'm feeling. His hand is back on the handlebars. "Isn't it beautiful?"

From this vantage point, we have a perfect view of the Pink City. The sun shines on all the terraces and family homes and shops crowding Jaipur. At this height, the people and cars in the streets are the size of Lego figures. I wonder how many of the people are locals like Shiv, how many are tourists like me.

These hills weren't on Mohini's bucket list or mine. We've been sticking to things mostly accessible by transit or quick rickshaws. Jaigarh Fort wasn't part of the plan, but . . . this deviation is perfect. As we round another curve, a new view comes upon us. A shimmering lake appears in the distance, with a palace-like structure in the middle of it, emerging from the water. "What is that?" I say into Shiv's ear so he can hear me above the rushing wind.

"It's the Jal Mahal. When we get to the fort, I'll give you the whole history lesson."

"Hurry up, then," I say, finally comfortable on the back of the scooter. It's thrilling, honestly, being here, and I do feel safe with Shiv. "Please."

Shiv laughs, the sound soaring through the air. "As you wish." And he hits the gas, throttling us up the hills, leaving me laughing and holding on to him for dear life.

Jaigarh Fort is a gold-pink structure jutting out of the Aravalli Range on the edge of Jaipur.

Stone paths lead us to and through the fort. A thick forest covers the mountain range, and a defensive wall of pink extends down the fort, connecting it to other structures along the hills. At the admissions booth, the ticket prices are different for Indian citizens and foreigners. But the guard doesn't even bat an eye when I pay the price for locals, and his assumption that I count as Indian enough fills me with genuine pride.

After getting our tickets, we explore the temples, the armory, and the winding pathways to a stunning estate with bright-pink flowering trees. A guide tells us about the Jaivana Cannon at the fort, which was, at the time of its creation, the world's largest cannon on wheels, and about the three different water supply systems that, legend has it, once held a great treasure. There are remnants of frescoes on the walls, and I feel like I'm literally walking through history.

It's so *cool* being here. When I visited Jaipur with my parents, we rarely did touristy things, since we always had so much family to see. This feels like exploring uncharted territory. I smile to myself. Mamma and Baba are going to love my updates on our next phone call. They got to see all this when they lived here. Now it's my turn.

Shiv takes me to the wall that guards the fort, where other tourists are snapping photos of the view. Some are climbing onto the wall to stand or sit on the ledge and see the city better. There's some graffiti on the walls, with people writing their names and drawing hearts. I wonder if they felt like the fort was protecting their love stories. We walk alongside the wall toward the top of the structure, overlooking the eastern part of the city; and after some protests, I let Shiv help me up onto the top of the wall. It's a more private spot, away from the groups of tourists. Shiv seems to prefer that, being away from crowds.

We sit with our legs dangling and gaze out over the lake and palace. "This fort was built in the seventeen hundreds," Shiv says. "For defense, even though it has never actually come under attack. Now it's a historical spot. On the other side is Nahargahr Fort, which has centuries-old residences. It's a little smaller."

I think of the names: Jaigahr, Nahargahr. "Ghar means 'house,' right?"

Shiv seems pleased. "Yes. Nahar means 'tiger' in Sanskrit, so literally, Nahargahr is the home of tigers. Some people think it's named that because tigers roamed the forests here, but there's a more popular legend that a prince once lived here, and when the fort was constructed, his spirit haunted the area and wouldn't let anyone build until the king created a temple in his name."

"I would do that," I say, and Shiv snorts.

"What do you mean?"

"I'd totally haunt my home if someone tried to come and build something new there. I'd demand a temple, too."

Shiv shakes his head, clearly amused. "You really are something."

There's a Bollywood line that would be a perfect response, but I'm not ready for that level of vulnerability yet. "Something amazing," I counter. "Tell me about the lake palace."

"Right. So the palace was built in the late sixteenth

century, and the lake was created in the early seventeenth century." Shiv catches my eye and smiles. "It's man-made, from a dam. The first Raja Man Singh had it constructed."

"Damn," I say, and Shiv rolls his eyes. "The palace looks like it's in the water." I try to examine it closely—it doesn't appear to be on an island or anything. It just comes up out of the lake.

"It is." Shiv shifts the brim of his hat to shade himself from the sun. "When the lake is full, the lower levels of the palace are actually underwater. There's a garden on the terrace, because there's no real ground level. It lights up at night, and it's beautiful."

"I can't even imagine," I whisper. "I've got to take some photos for my friends." I reach into my bag and pull out our traveling camera.

"Polaroid," Shiv observes. "Old school."

"It feels more serious, you know? Like, something has to be important enough that I want to take a photo of it with this instead of my phone." I point the lens at the Jal Mahal and snap the shutter. "My friends and I are passing this around on our study-abroad trips. I told you about Whitney, my theater nerd who went to Paris. She took amazing photos. Now I get to do the same."

I capture more photos of the water palace, collecting the photos in my pocket, then turn the focus on Shiv. "Say 'cheese,'" I instruct, and he immediately gasps and covers his face. I get a delightful—and adorable—shot of him blushing from behind his hands. "Camera shy?"

"I like to live a more behind-the-scenes kind of life. Trust me, I'm not photogenic."

I scoff. "That's something you're definitely lying about."

Shiv shakes his head and gestures for the camera. "Let's get some photos of you. Your friends will want those, not shots of some random guy you met on your trip."

I roll my eyes at that before patting down my hair and smiling for the camera. Shiv takes a regular photo of me, then makes me do a "silly one." He tells me more about the palace and the forest, about a time he visited the fort with his sister and parents when he was younger, his first memory of being this high up in the hills. He tells me that when he was little, he was scared of the buildings that sat atop the hills, worried that they'd succumb to gravity and one day topple over.

"But my father told me that this architecture has been here for hundreds of years," Shiv continues, "and the hills have been standing since near the beginning of time. He promised they wouldn't fall, but it's something I think about a lot. How so much withstands the test of time. How generations before us built beautiful things to last, and we can, too."

I nod, listening carefully. It feels so special to hear about Jaipur from him, this boy who grew up here. Jaipur is *his*, and he's sharing it with me.

We wander over to a café, and I get us those chais I promised him. At the outdoor seating, we sip our drinks and take in the city. Shiv's eyes go wide. "Oh! I almost forgot." He grabs his knapsack and pulls out a small box. "Here."

"Shiv," I say in protest. "You're making me look so bad. You showed up with flowers, and now that I've made it even with our drinks, you're putting me in your debt again with a gift?"

This is very Desi of us, battling back and forth for who can do something nicer for the other. The same way Mohini and I argue over who's paying for the rickshaw or who's letting the other borrow something from their closet. (Well, usually Mohini ends up lending me things, but that's because she gets way cooler designer stuff for her social media.)

"Don't worry. This is just food, and the flowers were free, literally picked from the wild. You can bring something for me next time. And really, getting to come here because of you is a gift in itself. I haven't been back in ages. My family isn't that excited anymore about the touristy stuff."

There it is again—*next time,* the words falling so naturally out of his mouth. A sign he likes hanging out with me as much as I do him. I think of how I fall in love with D.C. a little more every time I get to take someone new on a tour. Maybe that's how Shiv's feeling, too.

I reach for the box and pull off the lid to reveal a collection of mithai—milky sweets decorated with flowers and edible gold. They smell amazing, and my mouth immediately waters. "Whoa."

Shiv grins, picking up one sweet and handing me another. "This one's a traditional Rajasthani ghevar. A mini version, at least." The mithai is a golden disc that has a honeycomb pattern. I remember seeing the normal-sized options, stacked on top of one another, at a shop near Johari Bazaar. They were too big for Mohini and me to share, but these are bite-sized. Perfect.

He knocks his against mine. "Cheers."

I pop the mithai into my mouth and close my eyes. "Oh my god." Mamma makes mithai back home, and there's no type of dessert I love more. "Where did you get these?" I ask, transported to food heaven. "I've been meaning to send my mom a box of her favorites but don't even know where to begin."

When I open my eyes, there's a pink tint to Shiv's cheeks. "Uh . . . ," he begins.

"No way," I interrupt. "Don't tell me you *made* these."

He holds up his hands. "Guilty."

"They're incredible. How can you—how can you do *everything*?"

"What do you mean?"

"You cook, you garden, you know everything about Jaipur's history, you drive, you make mithai. Is there anything you're bad at?"

There's that amused smile on Shiv's face again. "Polo. My parents tried to get me into it as a kid."

I frown. "Polo? Like the game played on horseback? Where do you even do that here?"

Shiv's face flushes, and he stammers uncharacteristically. "That might be why I'm bad at it. Not a lot of places to practice. But anyway. I'm not good at everything. You're acting like I won a Nobel Prize."

His comment succeeds in distracting me. "Well, maybe you should! For exceptional sweets recipes. I bet these could bring world peace."

A gold-star laugh escapes him. "Archi," he says.

I raise my eyebrows. "Mm-hmm?"

"Nothing." Shiv shakes his head. "I just wanted to say your name."

My face heats up. "When did you start cooking?"

"When I was little. I was a picky eater as a kid, and I found that I liked food more when I made it myself." He hands me another sweet, a Rajasthani mawa kachori, which is almost like a cookie, except deep-fried and coated with sugar syrup, rose petals, and shaved pistachios. It's—as expected—divine.

"I might like food more when you make it, too," I say. "My mom does most of the cooking in our family, but she didn't do it much growing up. It didn't come natural to her, so I never learned when I was younger, either. She only got into cooking when she joined a group of Aunties at the temple we go to. They host so many potlucks that my mom was forced to learn from another Aunty."

Shiv laughs. "My parents don't really cook, either."

"And yet, look at you."

"They do appreciate my recipes," he admits. "I'm in charge of the menu for all our family functions."

"What's next on your list to make?"

"I'm not sure." Shiv raises an eyebrow at me. "What's something you've been craving?"

"Chole bhature's my favorite. I like the VBIS cafeteria, but I miss home-cooked food."

He pretends to jot down a note. "I'll keep that in mind."

As the sun sets, Shiv and I go back and forth sharing stories and teasing each other. He's incredibly attentive, nodding thoughtfully when I tell him about myself and home and asking questions to follow up on little things

I say. I ask him questions, too—because I'm so curious about him.

"Do you like your job?" I ask as we cruise back to VBIS. "Do you know what you want to do years from now?"

"Honestly, I've been thinking about it a lot. I want to do something I care about. I love making food for people and taking care of plants and the earth. I want to do something that lets me share good things with people in my life and community. I haven't figured out exactly what that is yet."

We pull to a stop outside VBIS, and I nod. "That's a big reason I want to do curation, you know. To share good things with people. For me, art is that good thing. You'll know what it is for you eventually, too."

We hop off the bike, and he takes a step toward me. Carefully, gently, he undoes the helmet buckle under my chin, keeping his eyes on mine the whole time. I hold my breath as Shiv removes the helmet from my head and hangs it on the scooter's handlebars. We stare at each other for a long moment, like we don't know the protocol for saying goodbye. And then Shiv—as if he's been debating what to do—leans in and wraps me in a tight hug. My brain goes numb, and I put my arms around his neck. He's soft but sturdy and smells like mint. And it feels . . . nice.

When we separate, I remember something Mohini said to me.

"Hey," he says, just as I blurt, "What's your last name?"

"What?" he says.

"Sorry, you go ahead."

"I was going to ask if you wanted to do this again. Did you ask me what my last name is?"

"Yeah." I pause. "I mean. Yes . . . to both." It's too easy to say yes now. I know I should be more careful, but I can barely see the angel and devil on my shoulders anymore. "I'd like to do this again. And I did ask you what your last name is."

Shiv grins, his face lighting up. "It's Kandari. Why?"

I don't tell him I'm going to Google him the moment I get back to my dorm. Mohini will be able to help me do a deep-dive social media check. "Just wondering." I bite my lip. "Can I pick the next location?"

Shiv nods. "Tell me when and where."

Chapter 9

I'll Be the One with the Flowers

After another week at my internship, Kiran-ji finally gives me the go-ahead for my Capstone idea.

"A gallery, no matter how small it is, is a big responsibility," she tells me. "You'll have to work with the team and plenty of moving pieces. I'm impressed with your plan for highlighting our stolen artifacts, but you'll have to prove to me you can turn the idea into action. I want a full proposal on my desk by the end of the day."

Going from giving tours and shadowing conservators while they show me how they restore art to designing a proposal for a new exhibit is a jump, but I want to show Kiran-ji that I can do it. That I'm not going to waste this huge chance she's given me.

I sit in an empty office in the basement and flip through my journal, alternating between making crowded notes on my brainstorming pages and doing Google searches to track down pieces of history. After a few hours, I take a lunch break, unwrapping a foil-covered aloo paratha I snagged from the Kothari dining hall to sate my appetite.

Then I reach for my phone. I need some human contact in this quiet basement office. I should text Whitney or Lilyn. It's nighttime back in the States. Or I could text Mohini. She's in class, but she's probably on her phone anyway. Still, when I click through my texts, my thumbs go to Shiv's contact.

Shiv Kandari. Last name and everything.

> **Archi:** Hey

I stare at the screen, wondering if I should put my phone away and check for a reply in half an hour, like an appropriately chill person would do, but then Shiv's typing bubbles appear. And then a text.

> **Shiv:** Hey 😊
> How's it going?

I smile, appreciating that he doesn't leave me on Read in some misguided attempt to seem cool. The way Nick used to.

> **Archi:** I'm at the museum. I have the day to work on my Capstone proposal, and I'm struggling already. I only need to write out a plan, but it's such a short turnaround.
> Are you at work?

> **Shiv:** I'm in the garden

I look to my right, even though I'm in the basement and there's no view of the gardens. Shiv is out there, a short distance from me. I marvel at the fact that we're so close.

> **Archi:** You can't see me, but if you wave from the garden toward the museum, I'm waving back

His reply comes back quickly, cheesy as ever.

> **Shiv:** You can't see me, but I'm drawing your name in the soil by the flowerbeds

I bite my lip, immediately shutting down the excitement bubbling in my chest as I remind myself that there's no indication that's a romantic gesture. After all, this is something I'd easily do for Whitney or Lilyn—how many times have we written each other's names in the sand on a Delaware beach? And I don't want this to be romantic. It can't be if I'm to stick to my boy-free-semester plan. A plan that is in place for a reason.

Another text pops up from Shiv, back to normal conversation, no hints or worries about potential flirting.

> **Shiv:** Why are you struggling?

I sigh.

So far, I've been trying to track down where different stolen pieces are. We have some records of where items have gone, especially if they've resurfaced at British museums, but others seem to be lost to trade and inheritances. The notes in my journal are a series of dead ends. Beyond that, I can't fill a gallery with emptiness, stolen art or not.

Despite my hyperfixation on the missing pieces, I actually need to curate artwork that's *here* for my exhibit. And though I know I also want to focus on the resilience of Rajasthani postcolonial art, the resistance of continuing to create despite losing precious history and artifacts, I don't know exactly how I want to source this art. Where I hope to get it from, how I'll choose which pieces matter more. I want to honor the pieces that were taken but also the art still growing and flourishing in Rajasthan and specifically Jaipur. I need to figure out a way to pull together a cohesive plan for all that to be put into a single exhibit . . . by the end of the day.

As I text, Shiv reacts to each thing I tell him.

> **Shiv:** How can I help?

> **Archi:** Honestly, just you talking to me is nice. It's a great mental break.

> **Shiv:** Happy to be a distraction 😊

With a lull in conversation, I take the opportunity to ask him about something that's been nagging at me. As soon as I mentioned to Mohini last night that I had learned Shiv's last name, we dove straight into cyberstalking . . . and found nothing. No social media. No photos. Only one random article about the royal palace, but it didn't even mention Shiv. How can anyone *not* have an internet presence nowadays?

> **Archi:** I looked you up
>
> How do you have ZERO online presence? All I found was a link to something about the royal palace, but it didn't even mention you

His reply is quick.

> **Shiv:** Hahaha
>
> I'm . . . not that into it? My sister's online more, but she uses aliases for all her profiles
>
> If I was trying to keep up with social media on top of everything else, I'd never get any gardening done 😊

> **Archi:** Or any cooking

> **Shiv:** Exactly

I can't imagine what it must be like—not being on five million feeds at once at all times. It sounds both terrifying and relaxing. I may not update my profiles as often as I should, but I know I'd get FOMO if I deleted my apps and didn't even have the option to lurk.

I try to imagine what Shiv's social media feed would look like: definitely something like a lifestyle influencer, I bet. Aesthetic food pics, close-ups of greenery and morning dew on flower petals, interspersed with sunset shots of the Jaipur skyline.

> **Archi:** So when are you going to make me chole bhature?

Shiv: Right, your favorite

I think you'll have to come help me make it, though

> **Archi:** Whoa whoa whoa
>
> I didn't sign up for that
>
> You're the chef, not me

Shiv: You're right you're right

A man's place is in the kitchen

This remark makes me laugh out loud, echoing in my little workspace. I can't help it: I take a screenshot to save it for posterity.

> **Archi:** ☺

Shiv: How about I cook, you taste-test?

> **Archi:** I thought I was planning our next thing, though

Shiv: You are

This can be the next-next one ☺

After working for a couple more hours, I get a call from Lilyn. Her face appears on the screen as I accept.

"Isn't it late for you?" I ask, by way of greeting.

She sighs, holding her favorite stuffed animal. "Yeah.

But I can't sleep. I've been scrolling for ages for fashion inspo, and now there are no new posts. Thought I'd call you so you could entertain me."

I roll my eyes jokingly. "If you really want to fall asleep, you should put your phone away."

"Boooooo. Be more fun. Any updates with you and hot gardener-chef-historian-dreamboat boy?"

I groan. "Don't call him that! I'm not trying to objectify him."

"Well, I am," she retorts. "You have a cute guy who's bringing you flowers, and you're still insisting on being friends?"

"It's the right thing to do. No distractions."

"And how'd that work for Whitney?"

I make a face.

She grins, victorious. "Tell me the updates."

"We've been texting," I admit.

"At work? Okay, Miss No Distractions."

"Excuse you. I was telling him about my Capstone. He was helping. I'm stressed. There's so much stolen art, and in an ideal world, I could do an exhibit focusing on the pieces that were stolen and actually get them *back,* you know? I don't know how I'm supposed to feature the missing pieces if I can't show them off. And that's not even getting into the difficulties of finding new art to showcase, too."

Lilyn nods. "Yeah. A heist exhibit would be really cool."

It's the word she uses—*heist*—that gets me.

I gasp. "Oh my god. Lilyn. You're a *genius*."

She laughs. "Yeah, I am." Then she pauses. "But for extra clarification . . . what did I do?"

"A *heist* exhibit!" I repeat, excited now. "This obviously isn't the first time art's been stolen. It's a unique situation, because we actually know where most of the art is now but we can't get it back. But the biggest *unsolved* art heist in recent history has its own place in a museum." I'm talking fast now, the ideas spilling out quickly. "Something like this has been done before. I can just modify it for *here*."

Lilyn holds up a hand. "Sloooow down. Context, please?"

"The Isabella Stewart Gardner Museum in Boston. In the nineties, there was this ridiculous heist. A couple guys dressed as cops walked in and overpowered the guards after hours and then literally walked around and stole a bunch of art. Famous stuff, too, like two Rembrandt paintings, a Vermeer, and five Degas sketches. They never found the stolen pieces. Gardner, the woman who founded the museum, had wanted everything in the collection to be permanent, so under her will or whatever, nobody could legally remove anything from her museum. The thieves cut the paintings right out of their frames, but because of Isabella's rule, the museum couldn't remove the empty frames." I grin. "So now, if you go to the museum, you can see them, still on the walls. Some people go there just to see empty frames. It's infamous. It's more about the missing art than the art that's still there!"

Lilyn gasps. "You're right. That *is* genius."

I'm on a roll now. "Art stolen during British imperialism and colonization is worthy of at least as much lore and drama as thirteen stolen pieces from the ISG get. Thousands of works were looted from former British colonies.

What if . . ." I run a hand through my hair. "What if the MSMS II Museum did something similar to what ISG did? What if I combined contemporary art with empty frames to symbolize the stolen pieces? For a sculpture or artifact, an empty outline could be symbolic." My mind is going a million miles an hour, and I start writing the ideas down in my journal.

Lilyn nods vigorously. "YES. I'm obsessed. Now I can sleep in peace—maybe this is what was keeping me up. The universe wanted me to help you figure this out."

I snort. "That's definitely it. You are the best."

Two hours later, I hand Kiran-ji my proposal and give her an elevator pitch in her office. As I speak, she nods thoughtfully. I take a deep breath when I'm finished, waiting for her to respond, to react, to do something.

She pauses for a long moment, spinning a pen between her fingers. I can sense she's calculating something. Is the project too big for an intern? Is the idea silly? After all, the ISG kept the frames up because they legally had to, not because they wanted to make a point.

And then Kiran-ji speaks. "I've heard about the ISG. And not too long ago, the Acropolis Museum in Greece did something similar for pieces of the Parthenon that the British still have and refuse to return. They used plaster replacements." She marks something on my proposal. "I like this plan, Archi. Let me share it with the rest of the team, but I think this could be something great."

My mouth falls open. "Wait. You like it? My idea?"

She raises her eyebrows. "Should I not? You put together a solid proposal. I think it's viable."

A wave of excitement comes over me. "I can't thank you enough. I'm going to make this work. It'll be a really good exhibit, I promise. I'm going to work so hard—"

"I still have to run it by the team," Kiran-ji reminds me. "But I have a feeling they're going to be on board. So, as a reward for your work, I'm assigning you more work. Tomorrow, after our staff meeting, you'll need to start contacting folks and building a plan with the team to advertise the exhibit. The other thing is, people might not be interested in coming to visit a bunch of empty frames. You'll need to add a noteworthy attraction they can actually see."

I nod vigorously. "I'll find something for balance, showcasing contemporary art and sending a message."

Kiran-ji appraises me. "Good. You're about to join a line of pretty amazing postcolonial curators, you know?" She smirks. "Now get back to work."

Later, I call Mohini to tell her the news. Then I ask her for ideas for my next hangout with Shiv. Immediately, she tells me about Galtaji Temple, and I look it up on my phone before oohing.

"Chandana from next door asked me if I want to go with her," Mohini tells me. "So I could do that, and you could go with the boyfriend."

"Not my boyfriend," I insist.

"Tomato, tomahto."

And then I text Shiv again. The conversation is quick, the two of us firing back messages. I wonder what he's doing—if he paused his work to check his phone, the way I have.

> **Archi:** My Capstone is a GO!!!
>
> And I know where we should go next

> **Shiv:** !!!!!!! I knew you could do it.
> Can't wait to hear about the project.
> Where are we going?

> **Archi:** Mohini suggested Galtaji
>
> Another architectural delight
>
> And I want to see the monkeys at the temple 😊
>
> You in?

> **Shiv:** Let's do it

Then he sends me a text that has me melting, against all my best efforts as always.

> **Shiv:** I'll be the one with the flowers

Chapter 10

The Monkeys Will Straight-Up Rob You

Galtaji Mandir is in the Aravalli Range, on the outskirts of Jaipur. It's an ancient Hindu pilgrimage site, with temples jutting out of the mountains and lush greenery all around.

After class yesterday, I asked my Religion and Colonialism professor about the temple to get context. He told me the mandirs are built into the crevices of the hills, and they've been around since the fifteenth century. Even before the temples were built, the spot was a holy ground for yogis, and it's believed that Tulsidas, a revered Indian poet, wrote some of his most important and religious works while he was here, including a retelling of the *Ramayan*, a Hindu text about a prince in exile.

There are holy pools where people bathe, and one of them is said to never go dry. Steps lead up to the Sun Temple, dedicated to Surya, the sun god. And one of the most interesting things for me: There's a clan of monkeys that lives in the forest around the site, and they're extremely comfortable around tourists. Plenty of Hindu temples are known for having monkey visitors, but Galtaji is *the* temple of monkeys.

Shiv suggests going in the morning. Apparently, the temple hasn't been tended to well over the years, and the lack of restoration and the continuous visits by tourists and locals have left the site a little less pristine than most would like. If we get there earlier in the day and beat the other tourists, hopefully we won't have to see in real time the way modern humankind has strayed from taking care of history.

Mohini sends me in a cab to the temple, which drops her off first ("Don't worry about the fare! Think of it as a shared Uber—I need to go to the market, you need to go to the temple . . . we're both going on our own pilgrimages!"), and I wait near the entrance for Shiv. There's a small fee for visitors if you're bringing your phone in, and I hand the person at the counter some bills.

I don't want to move from my spot before Shiv gets here, since I'm currently somewhere that's easy to find. I feel a little nervous being here by myself as a single girl. Shiv offered to pick me up, but I wanted to feel like I was making the pilgrimage myself, as in ancient times (though, of course, they didn't have taxis back then). I stand up straight. It's broad daylight, there's barely anybody here, a woman is collecting tickets, and I'm dressed in casual Desi clothes, essentially indistinguishable from locals.

I am Archi Dhawan. I don't need a man to see monkeys.

As I wait for Shiv, a few people dressed for prayer walk

by. Someone nods at me but keeps moving, and I realize it's because they think I'm one of *them*, that I belong here. A flush of pride runs through me, as with the guard at Jaigarh Fort. It's such a small thing, the nod from a stranger, but it means so much. I imagine my parents and their parents strolling these very paths, staring out at this same skyline, feeling this same wind on their skin. Would they be proud of me, knowing I made it up here by myself?

I'm distracted enough by these thoughts that I jump when something barrels into my feet. It's panting and it's furry, and it's way bigger and way closer to me than any monkey ever should be. I glance down, and an involuntary smile spreads over my face.

It's a dog. The dog is adorable and fluffy—golden brown, probably something like a lab mix, with the cutest big eyes. I shouldn't pet him—Baba once had to get a rabies shot after being bitten by a stray dog in India—but how can I not? The dog keeps licking my hands as I try to pet him, and when I scratch the back of his head, my fingers snag on a collar. Wait. This dog isn't a stray. Dangling from his collar like a necklace is a small, paper-wrapped cone of wildflowers.

When I look up, Shiv is there. "I see you've met Champ."

I beam at him, hugging the pup. "You brought your dog!"

"I had to come up with a more creative way of delivering your flowers. Now that I've made a habit of it, I think if I didn't show up with flowers one day, it would be an insult."

I laugh, looping my fingers around Champ's collar and unclipping the miniature bouquet. "I would take offense."

"Speaking of . . . what'd you bring *me* this time?" He smiles wickedly.

"I got your ticket." I hand him the little paper. "Are we keeping score?"

Shiv shakes his head. "Never. Honestly, you brought me to Galtaji, which is big enough. I haven't been here in years, either." He pauses. "You're taking me to a lot of places I've been missing."

"You spend a lot of time at work and home, huh?"

"I'm basically always with my family. My sister's a great built-in friend, but . . . it's nice to get out more. Leave the nest, or whatever."

I pause. "What happened to your friends from school or childhood? You mentioned the guy who went to VBIS."

"Yeah. Tushar. My friends growing up are all great. Most of them don't live in Jaipur now, though. I have a few friends starting college abroad and some who live in Delhi and Mumbai. We stay in touch, but you know. I graduated early, so I wasn't on the same schedule as everyone. I was homeschooled for a bit, too. And the palace is full of old people. I haven't been in a setting with a lot of people our age in a while."

"So you're sticking with me by default," I tease. "Because we happen to be the same age."

"Exactly. It's not because you're fun or interesting or make me laugh or pick fun things to do around the city or anything like that."

"Right." I bite my lip, keeping myself from grinning too widely.

Champ begins sniffing my shoes, and Shiv claps his

hands together. "Champ, sit!" And immediately, Champ does, gazing at Shiv with attentive eyes, no longer the fluffball of energy he was moments ago.

"Good boy." Shiv drops a treat into Champ's mouth.

"Are you allowed to have dogs here?"

"Champ has special privileges. He's super well-behaved. He's even allowed on trains." Shiv glances at me out of the corner of his eye. "And I paid the guards a little extra."

"Of course you did." I wonder how much Shiv's gardening salary is if it allows him to bribe temple guards. Luckily, most of the things we've done together have been free or close to it, with the student discounts for tickets to historical sites and the fact that our first official hangout was on the royal family's dime. But I worry it's rude to ask about money, so I don't.

"Plus, Champ will keep us safe from any overly bold monkeys," Shiv adds. "They're cute and friendly until they think you have food, and then the monkeys will straight-up rob you."

"No way."

"Way. I've lost my favorite pair of shoes to Jaipur's mandir monkeys. The ones in the city, you might have seen them from afar. . . ."

I nod. I've seen a few near VBIS, but they're scared of people and never come close enough.

"Yeah, well, they steal clothes right off people's clotheslines."

"Okay, but they're adorable. So they're forgiven."

"Maybe to you. To me, monkeys are menaces." He's clearly joking.

"And yet you still agreed to come here with me. Even though you're not the biggest fan of these monkeys."

Shiv shrugs. "I'm a big fan of you."

I turn slightly, but I can't stop the smile growing on my face. It's amazing how Shiv says things like this so casually, in a way that doesn't feel planned or even flirty. In fact, I've learned to stop reading into Shiv's words. For others, they might be lines, but Shiv simply says what he feels. He's honest. Blunt and to the point, but honest. Like he is a big fan of me, and why shouldn't he tell me how he feels?

And the truth is that I'm a big fan of him, too. I love going on adventures with him and learning more about this city I've already come to view as a second home. And because of our agreement that we'll only be friends, there's no pressure, no stress, no urge to fit into someone else's mold, no wondering if he cares about me the way I care about him—not like there was with my ex.

With Champ leading us, we make our way up the steps carved into the mountainside. Shiv's right—Champ is super well-behaved. He's off leash, but he stays a few feet ahead and waits for us to catch up, as if he's our tour guide.

"It's hard to believe he was ever a stray," I tell Shiv.

He smiles. "I found him when he was a baby, basically." Shiv's eyes light up with fondness at the memory. "I'd adopt every street dog in Jaipur if I could. Champ is just a start."

"He looks like a baby. All dogs are puppies to me."

"I do that, too!" says Shiv. "Senior dogs? Also puppies. They're all puppies. It's cuter that way."

I grin. "You get me."

Shiv freezes in his tracks, and I wonder if it's because of what I said, but then I follow his gaze. We've finally come across our first monkeys.

There's a trio sitting on the wall by the stairs, eyeing us. It's a mamma with her baby on her back, and another monkey that seems pretty young. "Oh my gosh," I coo, stepping forward.

Shiv's hand goes to my back. "Be careful, please."

"I'll make sure to keep my shoes on."

I step a little closer to take a photo with my Polaroid camera, smiling as the monkeys appear to be posing. They're little, smaller than I expected, and they chitter around as I snap pics, replacing the film with a new package so I can take more.

"Don't look the baby in the eyes," Shiv warns. "The moms can get super possessive."

I retreat back to where Shiv stands, eyeing the monkeys suspiciously. "Try having the same love for these guys that you did for Champ," I say.

"Again," Shiv says, "Champ didn't rob me."

"I don't know about that. Didn't you have to pay extra to let him into the temple?"

Shiv humphs. "Touché."

We walk up the stairs, where I take more photos of the monkeys and the view. The temple area really is a sight. There aren't a lot of tourists here yet, but locals bathe in the kunds. Some monkeys even join them in the small reservoir. Although the temple is beautiful, there's litter around the steps, plastic bags that probably had snacks or milk that people like to feed to the monkeys. Parts of the architecture could use more restoration, and it hurts my heart to see such a cool piece of history not be cared for properly. It's the museum girlie in me.

It's a steep climb to the Sun Temple, and as we walk, Shiv points out wild plants that grow in the crevices of the architecture, tells me about the forest in the background. We don't see them today, but apparently there are wild peacocks that roam the hills the way turkeys do in the United States. He tells me more about the last time he was here, when he took off his shoes outside the temple to go in for prayer, and when he got back, they were missing.

"They were *nice* shoes, too." Shiv makes a face. "A gift from my mom for a birthday. And I was panicking, searching everywhere, and then I finally looked up and there was this monkey sitting on the edge of the wall, holding my shoes. I swear he was smiling."

"Hey, maybe he liked your style." I hold up a hand. "Think about it. When do monkeys get to buy their own shoes? He was probably jealous."

He bumps my shoulder. "Of course you're taking the monkey's side."

I grin. "It's more fun that way."

Champ stays close as we check out an archaeological site with eighteenth-century astronomical instruments.

"Whoa." I lean forward to get a better view.

"If you like that," Shiv says, "then you must see Jantar Mantar. It's an observatory, but historical Indian style. It has the biggest sundial in the world, and some of the instruments were so advanced for their time." He pauses. "It's gotten a lot of restoration. I wish Galtaji got that, too."

"Jantar Mantar sounds familiar. I think it's on Mohini's list."

"We should go," Shiv suggests. "We could probably go right after this. It's early enough in the day."

It's only eleven in the morning, and I'm having a great time with Shiv, but for some reason, spending the whole day with him as opposed to a few hours seems . . . like a lot. And a second destination? The angel pops up on my shoulder. *This wasn't part of our plan*, she says. *We planned for one stop.*

But you want to say yes, don't you? the devil interrupts. *You want to spend more time with him. You want to spend* all *your time with him.*

My mind protests. No. That's not true. Shiv and I are friends. We agreed explicitly to be friends. The devil is making things sound romantic. But I set a boundary. I agreed to a plan. We can't cross that.

But don't you wonder if he wants to—wants to cross the line? the devil asks. *He's been getting you flowers, and even your boyfriend didn't do that.*

He's being nice! says the angel.

I've never met a boy that nice, the devil retorts.

Shiv seems to see right through my angst. "No worries," he says before I even tell him no. "You should go with Mohini. I wouldn't want to steal her thunder."

"You're right. She'd be pissed if I went to another spot on her bucket list without her." The tension diffuses, the angel and devil disappear, and we keep walking up the hills.

Near the Hanuman Temple, named for a Hindu deity

who appeared on earth as a monkey, we find a man feeding peanuts to a family of monkeys. He offers some for us to try, and though Shiv declines, he takes photos of me feeding the animals, giggling the whole time as they run up, grab a handful of peanuts, and run back, repeating the actions several times until we're out of food. These photos are going to make for incredible pages in my journal and in the album Whitney sent.

At the top of the climb, which is actually a much tougher trek than I'd imagined, Shiv and I find a place to sit. Galtaji is beautiful, like a secret poking out of a corner of the mountain range. Champ lies down beside us.

"True or false," I say to Shiv: "the monkeys are growing on you."

Shiv laughs. "Maybe true." He nods at me. "True or false: you're having a good time."

"True." I smile. "I like seeing so much of Jaipur. Sometimes in big cities, there's a ton to do but not enough time to do anything. I feel that way in D.C., and I live there. Here I only have a semester."

"A semester is longer than you'd think," Shiv tells me.

"Time seems to be going by faster every year. You know? Like, when I was five, a year felt so long, because it was literally a fifth of my life. Now a year is much shorter, relatively. And it's only going to get shorter and shorter as we get older."

"Doesn't that just make everything in life even more precious?"

I smile. "Yeah. It does."

There's a long pause before Shiv speaks again. "True or

false," he says: "you're going to miss Jaipur when you have to leave."

"Definitely true." I glance down. "Don't make me think about it!" Time marches on, and before I know it, I'll be on a plane headed back home. I'll have to leave India. I'll have to leave Mohini. I'll have to leave Shiv.

I'll miss this city. And my roommate. And I'm going to miss my . . . friend.

And that's when the feelings hit me, really hit me full force, so strong I can't keep denying them anymore.

I like Shiv.

And, yeah, I know what I've been repeating for a month. We're just friends. We agreed. We had a plan. This isn't romantic. This is supposed to be a boy-free semester. But don't I know, better than anyone, that things don't always go to plan?

Here I am, in Jaipur, *because* my plan for London didn't work out. Despite how it all ended with Nick, despite the way he chose to break my heart and cast me aside, aren't I *glad,* in some ways, that our plan for London didn't work out? Aren't I happy now?

What's so bad about another plan going awry?

But logic gets in the way of my feelings again. What's so bad is that it's going to end. Is hanging out with Shiv and getting to know him—getting to like him—only to have to say goodbye in a few more months even worth the trouble? In reality, we don't even get the full semester. I have to be back at Odyssey in May and do all the graduation festivities.

You're going to get hurt, my heart reminds me.

Could Shiv and I, together, be worth the eventual heartache?

When Nick and I broke up, it sucked. It really, really sucked. I hadn't ever been that heartbroken before, the pain in my chest so bad I cried myself to sleep. And he ruined things in a way I never saw coming—the part I refuse to let myself revisit. But somehow, even after all that, I still don't regret dating him. There were good memories in there, before it all fell apart. I wouldn't change those.

And I wouldn't change this either—meeting Shiv, spending time with him—because someday soon, we'll have to say goodbye. I wouldn't want to live life in fear.

I like Shiv. And all this time he's spent with me, could he like me, too? I mean, he's only ever said he wants to be friends. Maybe my plans changed, but his might not have.

I swallow my emotions, my fears, and I change the subject. "True or false," I say, saving the questions for another time: "you're ready to get out of here."

Shiv stands and stretches his hand out. "Let's go."

When we leave, he insists on taking the train back with me. "Champ will be our bodyguard," he says. He puts on a pair of sunglasses as we board the train back to the city.

"Indoor sunglasses?" I joke. "Who are you hiding from?"

He rolls his eyes.

"Don't worry," I tell him, pulling out my Polaroid. "The only paparazzo here is me." I point the camera lens at him, and he covers his face jokingly.

"Wait. You didn't tell me what you decided to do for your Capstone."

"Oh yeah!" I grin and dive in. I tell him my vision,

inspired by the Isabella Stewart Gardner Museum heist and the Greek museum, and his smile grows as I talk.

We get off at the station closest to VBIS, and I turn to Shiv. "You should come visit me at the museum sometime. I can give you a tour. I learned how to do that as part of my job, you know."

Shiv grins. "A personalized tour of MSMS II."

"Well, I didn't say personalized. I only know the standard tour script."

That gets a laugh from him. "Yeah, maybe."

"How about next week?" I'm already imagining the different works I'd show him.

"Uhh . . ." Shiv's face grows serious. He seems uncomfortable. "Yeah, I'll check my schedule. We'll figure it out."

We're at the station, and it's getting crowded as people wait for the next train. Someone tries to come up to us and pet Champ, their phone out to take pictures, and Shiv, normally so cordial, stiffens and moves us out of the way. "Sorry," he tells the young woman. "He doesn't love strangers."

Which . . . is an odd thing to say, considering that Champ seems super excited about strangers. But before I can question Shiv, he turns to me. "You know, I think I need to get home. But we'll talk later?"

I frown in confusion. "Is everything okay?"

"Yeah, yeah." He seems distracted. "I should get Champ home, though. He gets overwhelmed in crowds."

We say a quick goodbye, and I stand still at the station, bewildered.

I've never seen Shiv be so brash, so . . . ungentlemanly.

He was curt to the person taking a photo of Champ, and then he was curt to me. His whole mood seemed to be off. We had a more serious conversation today, and I opened up to him.

Oh god.

Did I overshare? Did I freak him out?

Did Shiv realize that I like him, but he doesn't like me back?

I watch his retreating back and feel my heart rate speed up. He left without even a hug. And it's our first time saying goodbye without making plans to see each other again.

What just happened?

Chapter 11

Having a Crush Can Be So Cringe

I spend the afternoon trying to push what happened with Shiv aside and focus on my time with Mohini.

Thankfully, I have a great distraction in the form of a visit to another historic site, by the palace: Hawa Mahal. Hawa Mahal is the iconic pink castle that shows up when you Google Jaipur, stretching toward the sky in layers of pink sandstone and intricately patterned windows, through which palace women of a certain time were confined to looking at the city, the artistry on the windowpanes hiding their faces from the public. It's like much of history: beautiful in one way, gut-wrenching in another. We take pictures of the dome-shaped chhatris, a quintessential Jaipur architectural element. I immediately send photos of the structures to Baba.

We then head to a cramped coffee shop near campus, where we empty the contents of our backpacks on the table between us. Mohini tells me about a food bank and delivery project she's been volunteering with every weekend.

"The organization does sanitation work, too, but one of its goals is getting more meals to families who can't afford them, especially those who live on the outskirts of the city but don't have great access to transportation. You'll have to come sometime."

"That sounds amazing. Just tell me when."

As we keep sharing our updates, everything I've been trying to push aside comes rushing back to me—the doubt, the confusion, the distracted look on Shiv's face right before he left me on the train platform. So I tell Mohini every detail of my time with Shiv, in case she might have the answers to the questions I've been asking myself over and over.

"It's probably nothing," Mohini says, sipping her cup of masala chai.

"He immediately ditched me! He didn't even walk me back to VBIS! I know I said I don't need a man to get around, and I don't, but it would have been nice."

I feel ridiculous. Mohini's updates are about helping society. Mine are about Shiv.

Mohini takes my story seriously anyway. "Would you have wanted that?"

"Yeah!" I pause. "Well, I would have liked for him to at least offer. Right? He got super weird after we got out at the station. I don't know if it was something I said—or what. He started looking around, and I don't know, it was like he was trying to *escape*."

Mohini snorts.

"What?" I'm indignant.

"For a 'boy-free semester' girlie, you're really getting worked up over a shift in a boy's mood."

"Mood shifts are important!" I insist. "If I had been paying attention, I would have known things were off with Nick."

She jots down something on her homework sheet but otherwise only raises an eyebrow. This, I've come to learn, is code for *keep going.*

"He started brushing me off, planning fewer things, and then boom—we were sitting down at the Cheesecake Factory, and he was breaking my heart."

"The Cheesecake Factory?" Mohini is incredulous.

"The Cheesecake Factory. At least he paid for dinner."

"Why do boys always *take* you somewhere to break up with you? Once, my friend got broken up with on a hot-air balloon. They were trapped up there until they had to come back to land." Mohini snorts.

"Don't laugh! That hot-air balloon story sounds worse than mine!"

She rolls her eyes. "Now I have to see a Cheesecake Factory. Another thing to add to the America bucket list."

"See, this is the problem!" I throw my hands up, and Mohini stares at me, amused.

"Yes?"

"Boys complicate things. I get in my head, and I start getting too invested to the point where I'm overanalyzing their every change in tone, and now he's taking up all my brain space, space I need for the amazing things we could be doing here in Jaipur, or what I could be doing for my final project!

If I keep this up, I could fall behind and fail this semester. I realized I like him like five seconds ago, and it's already this bad. This was supposed to be my *Eat, Pray, Love* semester!"

"I'm pretty sure she finds a man at the end of that. *And* I'm pretty sure you can't fail at studying abroad."

I groan.

"You like Shiv," she says.

In my head, I immediately picture Shiv at the royal garden, Shiv silhouetted against the mountain range, Shiv hiding an amused smile at something silly I've blurted out, Shiv offering me a miniature bouquet. Shiv, Shiv, Shiv. Bright eyes, wide smile, gentle, thoughtful voice. Ugh. Having a crush can be *so* cringe sometimes.

I nod, scowling. "Duh."

"But you're afraid of getting too invested in him."

I nod again, stiffly this time. That's what it is, isn't it? I planned a future around Nick—planning our study abroad, making decisions far in advance, altering my plans so they'd fit his . . . all for him to tell me things were over. That's the problem: when I fall for someone, I focus on them too much and not enough on me. This semester was supposed to be me focusing on *me*.

"Do you want to be with him? Like, do you want him to feel the same way about you?"

"No!" I frown. "I mean. I don't know." I've only just come to terms with the fact that, despite my plans, I have feelings for a boy. A boy who, at the end of the semester, will be on the other side of the world from me. I haven't thought about what happens next. I assumed . . . I don't know what I assumed. "He's avoiding me as it is. So—"

"Is he avoiding you?" Mohini asks. "Or did he really have to get home quickly?"

"Well, he hasn't texted me."

"Have you texted him?"

I frown.

Mohini laughs, like this is all so absurd. "By that logic, you're avoiding him, too. Why don't *you* text *him*?"

"And say what?"

"Anything! You could ask to see him again. There's an underground party happening next week, organized by some other queer Desi influencers. I'm on the list and can bring friends. You could both come to that."

"He did say he wishes he had more friends our age."

"Exactly." Mohini taps my phone, which is face down on the table. "You got this. He's just some guy. The stakes are so low."

"Okay." I take a deep breath and open my phone to type a new message to Shiv.

> **Archi:** Hey! Hope you're doing okay! Are you free next week to see each other again? Mohini was telling me about a party.

And then I try to get back to work.

I spend the rest of the day attempting to focus on my Capstone project and all my homework.

When Kiran-ji told the staff about my idea, they were

interested but had some "concerns." As she expected, their biggest issue was whether anyone would care about an art gallery that didn't actually *have* art.

"People will want a refund if they spend money to see nothing!" Rathore's head archivist, Bhavya, said before giving me an apologetic expression. "No offense."

At the silence after the feedback, Kiran-ji turned to me expectantly.

"I agree," I said, surprising everyone. "We need more than just emptiness. Jaipur is not empty, and neither is its cultural or historical scene. I don't want the gallery to suggest that all our important art is gone. I want it to both critique the theft of artifacts and honor how our culture has persisted, how artists go on despite adversity."

Bhavya's eyebrows went up.

"Since I've been exploring Jaipur, I've seen art everywhere. Yes, in historical sites like Jaigarh Fort and Hawa Mahal, but also in modern spaces, from the artisans at Johari Bazaar to the classic Rajasthani-style saris women here wear daily. I want to show off *that* art. Not only famous art but also the way art exists in every moment here in Jaipur."

"How do you plan on doing that?" our social media and website manager, Madhavi, interjected.

Thankfully, after Kiran-ji's warning, I'd done a lot of thinking about this. "I'll reach out to local artists, but I think we could also do an open call. Ask people to submit their work and make the process of being showcased in a gallery more accessible to anyone and everyone who creates art."

When I glanced at Kiran-ji to see her reaction, there

was a quiet, satisfied expression on her face. "All right. Let's do it."

Now at my dorm room desk, I organize my notes on Jaipur artists I've found through social media, from tailors who design saris to leatherworkers to tattoo artists. We decided on works by ten local artists, and Madhavi put a call out online for submissions. A few have started trickling in. In addition to the open call, I want to source some works myself. I've sent some emails already, and I'm planning on making calls, too.

Kiran-ji set the opening date for the gallery before my final month in Jaipur, a grand finale to my study-abroad experience. It feels simultaneously far away and looming. I need to buckle down if I want the exhibit to be a success.

For the missing works, I run through my list of looted Rajasthani artifacts that haven't been retrieved since the British Raj. There's a painting on paper, bound into a silk album, of two women making floral garlands at a lotus pond. It was probably made in the 1600s around Jaipur, and it's now at the British Museum.

There are crown jewels from when the Mughal Empire ruled over what is now Rajasthan. They were taken to Europe during British rule, but we don't know where they are now. For all we know, they could be in someone's jewelry box. There's the Rathore crown, one of the official pieces from the current royal family in Jaipur. It's currently housed in a private museum outside London, even though it belongs to a Rajasthani family that still exists.

Several miniature paintings are missing, created as far back as the 1500s. According to the MSMS II files I have access to, that's not even the oldest art that's missing. Stone sculptures of deities from around 1000 to 1200 were taken from Rajasthan, too, from temples and forts. Bronze and terra-cotta sculptures dating from BCE are also missing.

It's a particular kind of grief to catalog a history that's been lost—no, not lost, stolen. It's hard to put into words. Which is exactly why a visual exhibit could really showcase the pain and anger. *This* is the work of a good curator: not simply choosing art people should see but choosing art that, when put together, sends a message.

I think back to KAVI, to how her art does that—how it often makes *demands*. On my laptop, I do some Googling and find a website claiming to be run by "KAVI's team," though I don't know if KAVI even has a team. I peruse her art, the frustration and political messaging in each piece. I find that photo of her display outside the British Museum and stare at it for a long time. What if, in addition to showcasing empty frames, I add KAVI-style demands for repatriation alongside them? We could send the demands in a letter to the British Museum, like Mohini suggested, and the letter could be part of the exhibit. If only there was a way to commission KAVI herself for art for the Rathore Gallery. She could get people to take notice.

I'm pulled out of my thoughts when my phone starts vibrating.

I jump.

Is it—?

It's not. It's not Shiv. But it *is* Whitney, her face appearing on the screen as soon as I accept her call.

"*Whitneyyyyy.*" I get up from my desk to lie on my bed. "Perfect timing. I needed some girl talk."

No offense to Mohini, who's out with Chandana, but she would tell me to *definitely* not double-text Shiv, who still hasn't replied. Whitney, on the other hand, is in loooove and thus a bit more of an enabler, especially in the pursuit of a true love story. Sometimes it's better to ask for advice from the person who's going to tell you exactly what you want to hear.

I fill Whitney in on everything.

"Maybe he got really nervous," she says. "Because of how much he likes you. Like, he's so into you that the thought was so overwhelming, and he had to run home and, you know, process."

"That would be the most flattering interpretation of his actions."

"Think about it! He sent you a letter to hang out. You were suspicious he was asking you on a date even then. He's brought you flowers. He's cooked for you. That is the behavior of a guy who *likes* you."

"But that's his personality. He hasn't done anything, like . . . obvious. He hasn't said anything suggesting he wants to be more than friends. And he hasn't tried to, you know . . . hit on me."

"And whose fault is that?" Whitney widens her eyes on my phone screen. "*You* told him you want to be friends. Do you wish he wasn't respecting your boundaries?"

"Well, no. The fact that he's so kind and respectful makes me like him even more."

"Exactly. So he's following your lead, which means you have to make the first move."

"But if he likes me, why hasn't he texted me back? I asked him to hang out!"

"He's probably taking a while to think about the best way to respond. I bet he's drafted a million texts and he's having all his friends vote on which is best."

I think about the friends Shiv said he's still in touch with, even though they're scattered around the world. Has he told them about me? The same way I've told my friends back home about him? "Maybe," I say doubtfully.

"Remind me what he looks like, again?"

I sigh. "I wish I could show you, but he doesn't have any social media. He's an enigma."

Whitney frowns. "There's gotta be *something* about him online. You know me. I'm like the FBI."

"Mohini tried, and even she couldn't find anything."

"Give me a few days," says Whitney. "I'll know everything there is to know about him."

"Wait!" I remember then—"Your Polaroid camera! I took photos on our date."

"Perfect." Whitney holds out a hand as if I can physically give her the pictures. "Let's see them."

I find the album Whitney sent along with the camera and fish my stack of photos out of the pocket on the side. "I still need to arrange these in the album," I tell Whitney, spreading out a bunch in front of me. In succession, I see the past several weeks in images. The bazaar, Mohini, the sunset overlooking Jaipur, the monkeys, and . . .

"Huh," I say, switching over to the back camera so Whitney can see what I'm seeing.

In every photo I took of Shiv, you can't see his face.

Either he's turning away from the camera, or his hand is covering his face like I'm a paparazzo and he's a celebrity off duty, or he just so happens to be hidden by something else in the foreground. I don't have a single clear shot of Shiv.

"God, Archi," Whitney says with a laugh. "You're a terrible photographer."

"Hey! The monkey photos came out amazing."

"Okay, but you couldn't get one good pic of the more important primate?"

I snort. "Dork." But I frown at the photos, none of which have captured Shiv well. I remember joking with him on our date, asking if he was camera shy. "It feels like he's purposefully facing away. I don't think he likes photos of himself."

"That's suspicious. Why? Does he have a girlfriend who can't catch him in photographs with you?"

My heart thuds. "A girlfriend?" Is that why he freaked out at the station? Did he see her? Is that why all our hangouts have been so discreet and far from crowds? The thing I haven't tried to think about since my breakup threatens to bubble back up. A girlfriend.

"Or he's undercover," Whitney says, realizing my panic and trying to backtrack. "Maybe he's a cop. Or a CIA agent."

"We're in India."

"Okay, an agent from the Indian Intelligence Bureau," she amends.

"He's our age."

"Think about it," says Whitney. "He works in close proximity to the palace. He's a gardener, but he was wearing a suit the first time you saw him. That's some James Bond shit."

"Again, we're in India!"

"Right," says Whitney, clearly racking her brain for a Desi reference from the glossary I've taught her. "That's some *Dhoom 2* shit."

I burst out laughing, imagining Shiv as the lead in the infamous Bollywood movie. But I come back to the only plausible fear at hand. "Do you really think he could have a girlfriend?"

"Probably not. From what you've told me, he seems way too nice. And he said he doesn't know many people his age in Jaipur. How could he have a whole-ass relationship?" She leans in closer to the screen. "He really hasn't texted you back?"

"No."

"He will. I'm manifesting it."

"That's what Mohini said. I was hoping you'd tell me to text him again anyway."

Whitney shrugs. "You're going to do whatever you want to do, in the end."

We leave it at that, and then she tells me about how her cousin Becca is starting to discuss where she wants to study abroad and how the new D.C. location of Thierry's family's chocolate shop will be opening soon. Ugh, what I wouldn't give for a bonbon right now.

When we hang up, I'm alone in my room. Mohini's still out, so I'm left to my own devices. I stare at my phone, at my text asking Shiv out going into the void. My skin grows warm, anxious. What if there's a serious reason I haven't heard from him? Maybe not a secret girlfriend, though I probably should also get to the bottom of that. But what if something bad happened? The vibes changed so quickly at the station.

I blow out a long breath. Maybe I should say *something*. He's always been so forward. Why can't I? I'll keep it casual but also get to the point.

I cannot believe that humans used to get fight-or-flight from actual predator attacks in the wild and now here I am, having the same burst of adrenaline because I'm texting a *boy*.

I type quickly, then send it out into the ether.

> **Archi:** It would be fun to see you if you're down, but if you're not interested, no worries! Just let me know.

Before I can even turn my phone off and bury my face in my hands, there's a new message.

> **Shiv:** Hey!

Oh my god. Oh my god oh my god oh my god.

That was *so* fast. I feel suddenly embarrassed at having double-texted him. What if I sounded sooo pushy? I reread my text, then realize he's typing. Oh my god. I put my phone face down on my desk, wait a couple breaths, then turn it over.

I have new notifications.

> **Shiv:** Sorry, I was at a family function! It's been a little nuts.

> I don't know if I can swing the party, but I do want to see you again.

> I am interested.

> Just so you know 😊

I feel like I'm on a roller coaster. He *is* interested. Just so I know. I want to sink to the floor. Maybe scream-squeal.

He's *interested.* But, like interested in *me* or interested in hanging out? That's the question, isn't it? I think of what Whitney said. If I'm going to find out, I might have to make the first move.

I fumble with my phone as another text comes in.

> **Shiv:** Is it time for me to cook chole bhature for you?

My heart flutters, remembering our text conversation two weeks ago, his promise to cook me my favorite Indian dish.

> **Archi:** I could be down 😋

> **Shiv:** Want to go here, on Friday, for dinner?

He sends me an address, and I click on it, finding it on my maps immediately. It's a . . . restaurant.

> **Archi:** I thought you said you'll be cooking for me.

> **Shiv:** Oh don't worry

> I will

I'm delirious, staring at the message. All that anxiety, for him to say he's interested. For him to ask me to dinner. This is why I wanted a boy-free semester. Having a crush on a boy makes me feel so out of control.

But I find myself typing back anyway:

> **Archi:** Okay.
>
> But I can't do Friday. I need to do more planning for my Capstone. Would Sunday work?

It's a little nerve-racking to ask. Whenever Nick would plan something, he'd never let me make adjustments.

> **Shiv:** Of course. Your project comes first.

My heart soars.

> **Archi:** Amazing. Meet you there?

> **Shiv:** At night? No way. I'll pick you up.

SPRING SHOWCASE

ARTIST
OPEN CALL

Jaipur City Palace's Rathore Gallery requests that local artists and artisans interested in showcasing their work submit a portfolio online here.

RATHOREGALLERY.COM

SUBMIT BY MARCH 1

Chapter 12

Finally, Finally, Finally

The morning of my dinner with Shiv, Mohini shakes me out of bed so early that it's still dark out.

"Huh?" I grumble, rolling over.

She turns my nightstand light on, blinding me. "Wake up! You said you'd come with me."

"What's going on?"

"Samudaay Food Bank!" Mohini says. "Remember?"

The memory slowly comes back to me, of my agreeing to go volunteer with Mohini at a food bank. "I don't think I realized it was this early," I moan.

Mohini snaps her fingers at me. "Well, we have to pack and deliver the food by breakfast. Come on!"

I sit up in bed and check my phone to see a text from Shiv, sent last night after I fell asleep.

> **Shiv:** Dress comfortably tonight! I'll pick you up at 7:30.

The text wakes me up properly. Today's the day I'm going to test the friendship boundaries I so carefully set. Today's the day I'm going to make the first move.

"Good girl," Mohini says when I stand up and pull my hair into a bun. "We leave in fifteen."

An hour later, we're in the midst of the action at the food bank, scooping food from trays into tiffins. These packed lunches are filled with roti, a vegetable sabzi, dal, rice, and yogurt for a variety meal. The food bank is a little run-down, based in an old house converted for volunteering purposes, but the volunteers seem to be making do, working together to chop onions, stir pots of dal, and fluff rice with ghee.

Chandana is here, too—she walked over with us when we left Kothari Hall. I watch her and Mohini giggle as they race to pack the most tiffins. I can see the way Chandana looks up at Mohini for her reaction, the way Mohini leans in closer as they talk. I smile and go back to my own work.

There's noise and loud music, so much noise and movement for this early in the morning. I'd guess there are about two dozen volunteers of all ages. Mohini has brought a few boxes of her PR packages to give away, too, clothes and skin-care products.

When the food containers are ready, we stack them in boxes and shuffle into a few cars. Mohini, Chandana, and I get into a car with one of Mohini's new volunteer friends, Gaurav. He's a college student nearby, studying social work, and he borrows his family's car on the weekends for food bank deliveries.

"I saw a video Gaurav posted online," Mohini tells me.

"It was, like, a day in the life of a college student volunteering in Jaipur. And I *had* to message him."

"Thank goodness she did," Gaurav says as we drive to a part of town I haven't explored much yet. The buildings are narrower, more crowded, and the streets are bumpier. The sky has lightened now. People are starting their days, entering and exiting their homes around us. "We really need every hand we can get. Thanks for joining us today."

"I'll be back," says Chandana. "You do this every weekend?"

Gaurav nods. "We'd do it more days, too, if we had the resources."

"I'm posting footage from today on my account," Mohini adds. "I'll include info if people want to sign up to help out."

Gaurav pulls over, and we grab boxes from the trunk. Together, we walk through the narrow streets and drop off food at closed doors and hand tiffins to elderly men sitting on stoops. I watch as Gaurav greets every person, many by name, and Mohini jokes around with people as they accept the dishes. One Uncle teases us, saying he'll have to write a review if the food is bad, and Mohini promises a full refund if the vegetables aren't to his liking.

When we've handed out all our boxes, Gaurav drives the three of us back to VBIS. Mohini glances at me from the passenger seat. "You'll have to let us know after tonight how our food compares to your gardener boy's."

"Gardener boy?" Gaurav asks, oohing.

I feel my cheeks heat up. "It's this guy I met."

"She's in love!" exclaims Mohini.

"I like him," I correct. "That's all."

Chandana joins in. "And you're seeing him tonight?"

"Yeah." The nerves kick back in. I'd been distracted from them all morning, and now they're bubbling up again. "I don't know. I want to see if he feels the same way. But I have to figure out how."

"We can help," Gaurav says. "If you want a guy's perspective, or whatever."

I laugh, and Chandana claps her hands together in excitement. "Okay, let's start from the top."

I'm ready promptly at seven-thirty, dressed down in a sweater and jeans.

I've rehearsed what I'm going to say a million times with Mohini . . . and Chandana and Gaurav. How I'm going to tell Shiv that even though I agreed for us to strictly be friends, I've been doing a lot of thinking, and I know I'm only here for a little while, but—

There was a lot of hedging in the rehearsal. Careful lines, checking to see how he feels without wanting to overstep or seem too attached or—

"Say how you feel," Chandana told me. "Let him sit on it. No need to rush."

"Yeah," said Gaurav. "You don't even have to kiss him tonight. You can talk it out. Be really mature. Take things slow."

I agreed. That's the plan. Slow and mature and careful.

But the moment I see him at the entrance to campus, I don't remember anything I practiced. He's dressed comfortably, too, in a hoodie and sweatpants. His scooter is parked beside him, and a thrill hums through my heart. There's something in me that lights up automatically at this boy. Still, doubt lingers, from my conversation with Whitney and the way he and I last left things. Shiv tensed up. Could I be vulnerable about my feelings tonight and end up falling flat on my face?

"Hey," I say, approaching Shiv. There's a little flower tucked behind his ear, and when I come closer, he picks it out and places it behind mine, tucking my hair and the stem behind my earlobe.

I shiver at his touch, at the greeting beyond words.

Okay, come on. That has to be a sign—friends don't do *that*, do they?

"Hey," he says, smiling. "Are you ready?"

"Mm-hmm." I study him. He hasn't shaved, and scruff lines his jaw. What would it be like to run my fingers over it?

There are so many other questions crowding my mind.

Do you have a girlfriend?

Are you an undercover operative?

Why won't you face the camera in any photos?

Are you afraid to be seen with me?

Clearing my throat, I go for a less terrifying option. "The restaurant link you sent me . . . it says it's closed today. It's not open on Sundays?"

"Do you trust me?" Shiv asks.

I remember his asking that on our first date. I opt for honesty. "I'm figuring that out."

Something falls in his eyes. But he nods.

I try for a joke. "As long as you're not going to kidnap and murder me . . ."

"Damn. I was planning on taking you out to the hills."

I gasp. "I'd kill you before you could kill me."

Shiv snorts. "That sounds like a threat punishable by law."

"Would the king send an army after me for harming the royal gardener?"

There's a pause as Shiv considers. "Do you have diplomatic immunity?"

"Shit," I say. "You got me."

He grins, and I get that gold-star feeling again. It's so easy with him—this banter, this back-and-forth. Our weirdness balancing each other out. Shiv gestures to his scooter. "Your chariot awaits."

We do the little dance of getting on the scooter together, my arms going around him for balance. This time, I keep my eyes open as we soar through the streets of Jaipur, and it's a sight to see. I recognize more of the city now. We pass the market Mohini and I went to, now closed. There's the movie theater where Mohini took me to see a rerun of one of her favorite films. We pass the café that VBIS students frequent to "study," always filled with chatter and the scent of chai. Even at night, the city feels alive, bursting with an undercurrent of excitement. People walk the streets, chuckle through open windows in apartments, clink glasses at outdoor food stalls that line the road.

I want to take more photos to send to Mamma, to ask her if she knows this bazaar, or this food stall, or this restaurant. If she went here when she was a few years older than me. If things look different now than they did then.

Shiv pulls to a stop outside the restaurant he texted me about. The one that is most definitely not open. And yet Shiv parks at the rear and fishes a set of keys from his pocket. He waggles his brows at me, and then he unlocks the door with a flourish and brings me inside. Lights flicker on, and I realize we're in the restaurant kitchen, sparkling and metallic silver and empty.

Shiv sets his keys down and leans back against a kitchen counter, eyebrows furrowed at me. "I'm sure you have a lot of questions."

Oh. So he knows I'm here to get answers.

I position myself so I'm leaning against the kitchen counter opposite him. We face each other. I think of Whitney and decide to launch right into it. Better to get it out of the way, no? "Do you have a girlfriend?"

"What?" Shiv splutters, his eyes wide.

I look at him expectantly.

"No. What? No?"

"You sound unsure." My heart pounds. The thought of having feelings for a guy with a girlfriend—being the other girl . . . nothing would destroy me more. Not after—

"No," he says again, more firmly this time. "Why would you think that?" His voice is soft around the consonants.

"You avoided the camera in all the photos I took," I say. "And you got weird at the train station. *And* we're meeting now at an empty restaurant. I wondered if it was because you didn't want to be seen with me. Like, we had to be secretive because there's someone else."

Amusement flickers across Shiv's face for a second before he smooths out his expression. "Archi, I do not have a girlfriend."

"Boyfriend? Partner?"

"No." His lips twitch as if he's trying not to smile. "I am currently unattached." He pauses, and his eyebrows go up. "Why are you wondering?"

And maybe this could be the moment to ask. To tell him how I've been feeling. What I've been struggling with. But for all my rehearsing, I clam up. I'm not ready yet to take the plunge, to maybe have Shiv say, "Oh. I'm sorry. I'm flattered, but . . . I really meant it when we said we should be friends." I want to enjoy this evening a bit more before potentially losing Shiv, even as a friend.

"I don't know," I say finally. "You were being so weird."

Shiv pauses, as though he's trying to decide what to say—how much to share. "I'm a little camera shy. And I get nervous in large crowds. That's why we met at the garden when it was quiet. And at the temple, before the tourists arrived. When we got into the busy train station, I got overwhelmed. It wasn't Champ who was stressed. It was me."

Oh.

"You're not . . . a secret agent?" I try, knowing how ridiculous it sounds as the words leave my mouth.

"Like . . . you're asking if I'm on a government mission but I'm being distracted by spending time with you?"

I press my lips together to bite back my smile. It does sound so silly. "Or a con artist."

He grins. "That's more likely." But his face grows serious. "I haven't lied to you, Archi," he says gently. "I wouldn't."

There's no way for Shiv to know this, but that's exactly what I needed to hear. After everything with Nick, all the bullshit stories and evasions, all the weird distancing and last-minute cancellations before the truth finally came out, I need reassurance that Shiv won't betray me. The truth is that maybe I do trust him—at least enough to believe he won't try to hurt me. And after everything, don't I owe him some level of trust, too? How can I ask him to lay his heart on the line if I've kept myself behind a wall labeled "boy-free semester" since we met?

I think of the reasons I instated boy-free semester.

I wanted to focus on myself.

I wanted this Jaipur trip to be about learning—about my Desi history and my family history here.

I wanted to grow into myself and not depend on a boy to influence my future or hold my heart in his hands.

But hasn't Shiv helped me to do all that? It's because of him I learned more about this city. Because of him that I felt a connection to the Jaipur of today, and not just the Jaipur of my parents' story. I created my own love story with this city. Because of him, I've learned more about this place, and even brainstorming with him allowed me to dig deeper for my Capstone.

A boy-free semester was meant to guard me from letting a boy pull me away from myself the way Nick did. Because Nick always put Nick first. And he expected me to do the same. Shiv . . . Shiv likes me because I choose *me*. He said so himself. He likes me for what I'm passionate about. When I'm with him, I'm still choosing me.

So I decide, right now, that my boy-free semester is officially over.

"Okay," I say finally, meeting his eyes.

A grin flickers around the edges of his mouth, and I want to press my fingers, my lips, there. "When I said you must have questions, I meant about the restaurant."

"Oh." I tilt my head. "I do, actually. How . . . how are we in here?"

"Would you believe me if I said palace perks?"

I narrow my eyes. "Seriously?"

"The palace owns this restaurant, and when it's closed, I sometimes come by to practice cooking."

"They let you do that?"

"Yeah, I mean. As long as I clean up after myself and don't set the building on fire."

"How? To be honest, that doesn't really make any sense. Why would the royal family let their gardener practice cooking in their restaurant kitchen?"

Shiv looks embarrassed. "I did tell you I sometimes help with food at the palace, since a lot of ingredients come from the garden. The royal family supports my cooking, I guess?"

"Are you, like, besties with the prince and princess or something? Is that what you're not telling me?" I shake my head. "I can't imagine the king and queen being so generous for no reason."

Shiv laughs. "Yeah. It's hard to believe. I guess that's why I don't talk about it much. But I wanted to share this with you. I thought it'd be cooler than cooking in the VBIS dorm kitchens."

I pull a face at the thought. "No, this is definitely cooler. It's also surreal. The royal family really owns a restaurant?"

"They have investments all across the city."

I think back to my excursion this morning with Mohini. How worn down the kitchen in the food bank was. "And this place is closed on Sundays?"

"And Mondays and Tuesdays," says Shiv. "It's a small place, so it's only open half the week."

"Wait." An idea strikes me, one Mohini is going to love. "Have you heard of the Samudaay Food Bank?"

Shiv shakes his head. Frowns.

I grin and jump into telling him about this morning, about cooking and packing food to donate. "If the palace lets you use this kitchen for yourself on days the restaurant is closed, could they let the food bank use it to give meals to people who need them?"

A light comes to Shiv's face. He glances at me thoughtfully. "That's a really good idea. I . . . I don't know how much sway I'll have, but I can ask. I'll suggest it for sure."

"You sure?"

"Yeah. The royal family doesn't have a ton of political power if you'd believe it." He runs a hand through his hair. "Or that much money. I mean, it's a lot of money for one family to have. But it's not like the palace runs the Jaipur economy. So we can use our resources in more limited ways. Helping the food bank expand sounds super impactful."

"*We?*" I say. "*Our* resources?"

He reddens. "It's so easy to fall into the 'royal we.'"

"You and your palace perks," I tease.

"Hey, it's getting you your favorite dinner, isn't it?"

"Thank you, King and Queen of Jaipur!" I call into the empty restaurant, as if they can hear me in the void.

He laughs. "Come on. Let's get the ingredients."

"Oh, am I helping? I thought you were cooking *for me.* I fully planned on sitting pretty."

That gets an eye roll from him. "I'll be doing most of the cooking. But I thought it could be fun to show you some of the ropes." He brings a few boxes of ingredients out from the industrial pantry and fridge, and washes his hands in the sink. "Next time, you can put me to work at the museum."

"Maybe I'll send you on an expedition to recover the stolen artwork."

"I'd do it."

"Or you could track down KAVI and get her to help with my exhibit. That's about as realistic as recovering the original art." I wash my hands, too, standing next to Shiv so I can follow his lead.

He smirks. "As you wish." Shiv taps the counter. "And you know, anything you wish for in a restaurant kitchen comes true."

"Is that so?"

"It's the magic of industrial dishwashers," he says. "Better than any coin in a fountain."

I giggle as Shiv slips an apron over his head and hands me one, too. I watch him tie the apron around his back. He pulls out an onion from one of the pantry boxes and slides it toward me. Then he places two cutting boards and knives on the kitchen counter. "Chole and bhature coming right up."

And so it begins. First, we chop onions until we're both crying, laughing and joking through our tears, as Shiv shows me the correct way to hold an onion, my hand a claw. We prep the produce first, tomatoes and fresh ginger and cilantro for garnish.

Shiv shows me how he already set the dried chickpeas to soak before I got here.

We fold cumin seeds and turmeric into the chole, mixing the chickpeas with tomatoes and onions he reduced. Shiv shows me the whole spices he's adding to a spice bag. Cinnamon, bay leaves, cloves. He holds up a little black seedpod. "Elaichi," he says. "Cardamom. I showed you green cardamom in the garden the first day. That one's used more for sweets. Black cardamom is better for savory dishes. This one's from the garden, too."

After we leave the chole to stew in the pot on low heat, Shiv shows me how to roll dough into perfect circles to fry into bhature. Mine are misshapen, but Shiv doesn't mind. "They'll taste good no matter what."

One by one, he dips the flattened dough rounds into the kadai of hot oil, and we watch as they puff up into spheres, golden and shiny. When the food is ready, Shiv and I sit at the bar in the restaurant, the lights dim around us.

I close my eyes as I inhale my first bite. "God, Shiv, you always outdo yourself." The chickpeas are warm and spicy and delicious, the sauce melting in my mouth. I can't believe Shiv made this from scratch. I can't believe I helped. Chole bhature is one of my favorite meals in the world. It's challenging to make at home because of the work of deep-frying the bhature, so Mamma saves the combo for special occasions. Tonight feels like a special occasion.

I take a photo with my phone. "My parents are going to be so impressed. They've never seen me do anything in a kitchen, much less sous chef a five-star meal."

He laughs, but I can tell when I look at him that he's pleased. Proud. "Oh!" He jumps up to jog to the kitchen.

When he returns, he has two cups of mango lassi in his hands. "I made these earlier. Almost forgot."

I take a sip, not caring about the mango mustache above my lips. "Amazing. You think of everything."

"A good meal needs something sweet alongside it."

"Exactly."

We dig in, and for a few moments, there's happy silence as we scarf down the food, still piping hot, and enjoy each bite. When we're done, we head back into the kitchen and clean up. It's then I realize the night is coming to an end.

"I'll take you home?" Shiv offers. We walk to his scooter, and the evening chill hits me. I still haven't told Shiv how I feel. Still haven't asked him how *he* feels.

My heart drums in my chest as I figure out how to get the words out. Shiv helps me onto the scooter. Seemingly oblivious to my nerves, he tells me about other recipes he's brainstorming on our way back, and I nod along, adding in commentary but worrying all the while whether I'm going to be able to do this. Whether I'm going to be brave.

When Shiv pulls up outside VBIS, he steps off the scooter and helps me off. He unclips my helmet. I don't want this night to end.

But the sky is dark, with the promise of tomorrow near, and reality calls. Classes and responsibilities. I try to remember the lines I rehearsed earlier, the plan for being slow and careful and mature.

Shiv holds my helmet in his arms and smiles down at me. I lift my chin to meet his eyes. He pauses, studying me, then says, "We'll do this again? Or something like it?"

At his earnestness, I forget my lines. I push the plan aside, and I borrow Shiv's boldness. I decide not to be careful.

"Shiv," I say, thinking back to our game at Galtaji Mandir. "True or false."

His eyebrows go up.

"You had fun tonight."

"Very true. Did you?"

I nod, and my hands are getting clammy, my heart is thundering, my brain is going fuzzy. "True or false," I try again.

He waits, patient as ever.

And then I say it: "You like me." I press on before he can answer, and the words tumble out, not at all close to the neat, measured way I practiced them. "Because I know we said we should be friends, but . . . I like you. And if that's too much and not what you signed up for, we'll pretend this conversation never happened—"

"Archi." His eyes rake over me. Spots of pink have appeared on his cheeks. "True." He doesn't look away.

My heart jumps, floats, does a backflip.

"You like me?"

He seems amused. "Haven't I been obvious? I bring you flowers whenever I see you."

I shake my head. "You said you wanted to be friends. And I thought—the flowers were out of habit. Since you're a gardener."

"Partly, yes. I like gifting people plants. And I do want to be friends. But maybe not *only* friends. That day at the garden, I wanted to spend time with you, however that ended up."

The next word comes out of my mouth unbidden. "Why?" I surprise myself at the question. I certainly didn't rehearse *that*.

Shiv cocks his head, his eyebrows furrowing. I've surprised him, too.

"I don't mean it in a self-deprecating way," I explain, twisting my nose ring so I have something to do with my hands. "I'm not fishing for compliments or anything. I just . . . I want to know why."

"You asked me this when I asked you to meet at the garden for the first time, too," he points out.

"I know," I say. "I'm still trying to wrap my head around it. You're . . . you're, like, this amazing guy who works in the royal palace, knows everything about nature and food and this city. You rescued a dog, for god's sake!" He laughs at that, and so do I. "You bring me flowers. You're clearly a romantic, and you're from here, and yet you're interested in a girl who's going to leave at the end of term."

Shiv smiles at me. "Yeah."

"You didn't even know me when we met."

"I think that's how it works when you meet anyone," he says. "You start to know them *afterward*."

I roll my eyes. "Okay, smartass."

"I first sent you that letter because I couldn't stop thinking about you after our run-in on the train, and then when you appeared in the garden, it was as if I'd wished for something and gotten it. I thought, *I want to get to know her.* And I think the best sorts of romantic relationships start off as friendships. A friendship was my initial priority." He pauses. "I didn't know you then. But I know you now. And I do—like you, that is." His cheeks are even pinker now.

"I know you care so much about the work you do," he continues. "The way your face lights up when you talk about art and history and preserving our culture. How passionate you are—it's incredible. I know you were worried about how you'd fit in here, since you're from here in so many ways but you also feel like an outsider. I know you're a good friend to Whitney and Lilyn and Mohini. That you miss your parents, and you're honoring them by studying here." He pauses. "There's a lot more I still want to learn, and I want to keep getting to know you. But that's why I like you. The more I discover, the more I want to find out. You're like a . . . a Wikipedia rabbit hole."

I burst out laughing. "What is that supposed to mean?"

"Like when I can't sleep and I'm scrolling through random Wiki articles, and I keep reading about all this stuff that doesn't have any purpose besides making me happy. And I want to dive deeper and suddenly I'm up till four in the morning learning about feathered dinosaur evolution."

My jaw drops in complete delight. "Feathered dinosaur evolution?"

He blushes. "You think I know a lot about random stuff. Well, this is how."

"You really are something," I whisper, smiling at Shiv in awe.

"Something amazing," he says, grinning, repeating my own comeback from our visit to Jaigarh Fort.

"Shiv." Even though Gaurav and Chandana said to take things slow, I'm high on this moment. On my boldness.

His eyebrows go up, a question.

I push the words out. "Do you want to kiss me?"

Shiv's eyes soften, and his mouth opens. "Yes," he says simply.

So I stand on my tiptoes, pull him close by the front of his shirt, and kiss him. His arm goes around me immediately, holding me to him, and I lift my hand to his cheek, his chin, running my fingers over the stubble on his jaw. His mouth is warm against mine, gentle and careful and yet—all want.

We are kissing. Finally, finally, finally.

I curl my fingers into the hair at the nape of his neck, and the helmet in his hand clatters to the ground.

We separate, Shiv's cheeks pink, his eyes ablaze, reflecting the streetlights around us.

"Oops." I blush as he bends to pick up the helmet.

When he stands again, Shiv shakes his head in wonder at me. I can't get over the look in his eyes. I don't think a boy has ever looked at me like that—like I'm something to *behold*.

Heat crawls up my body. "It was good seeing you," I finally manage.

That gets a smirk out of him. "Likewise."

I grin at Shiv, at this boy who has been a total surprise, and bite my lip. His gaze follows the movement. A current runs through me—electrifying. The feeling carries me all the way back home, where Mohini is waiting, sitting upright in bed, a gleeful expression on her face that tells me she saw it all through our dorm window.

"Tell me *everything*."

Chapter 13

The Heart Is a Delicate Thing

The next week, I'm summoned by Sharmila Aunty and Rajesh Uncle to visit them for the weekend.

I text Shiv and Mohini a photo of the view from the train window, letting them know I made it to the station safely. They both offered to take me, but I insisted that I know my own way. The train out of Jaipur is familiar now, and I get a sense of déjà vu in the train car, barreling away from the city. I started my whole journey on this train, heading toward VBIS after staying with Sharmila Aunty and Rajesh Uncle. I started planning for my Capstone on this train. I met Shiv on this train. Going back is important to me—I'm already a different person than the Archi Sharmila Aunty and Rajesh Uncle met when they picked me up from the airport. I wonder if they'll even recognize this courageous new version of me, the one that understands that sometimes deviations from plans can lead to the best experiences.

For the first half of the ride, I work on my list of local artists. It's been a tougher process than I expected. Many of the artisans sell only in person and don't have online profiles. And for those I managed to get phone numbers for, only one agreed to be featured in the exhibit. The others didn't seem interested in a display, even when I told them we were planning on paying each selected artist. "I don't have time for extra projects," one said, and hung up before I could say it wouldn't take long.

It got so bad that Mohini offered, sympathetically, to ask her parents if they knew any filmmakers or photographers in Jaipur who could display their works at the gallery. I sent her the link to the open call so she could forward it to her mom.

Despite all that, our social media posts *have* reached people. I scroll through the submissions forms, clicking over photos of paintings and sculptures designed by local artists, many of whom found the open call because their excessively online kids told them about it. One in particular strikes me: photos of block-printed quilts, the kind I saw in Johari Bazaar. They're beautiful and naturally dyed, and I zoom in to see the richness of the fabric, the colors bright on every thread. I flag it as an option and send it to Kiran-ji for approval.

When my laptop battery dies, I stare out the window as the towns and landscapes pass by like blurry watercolor images. Relaxation washes over me. It's morning here, which means it's late night in D.C. I pick up my phone and WhatsApp my parents. Soon, their faces are on my screen, smiling brightly and filling my headphones with questions upon questions.

"Kya haal hai, Archi?"

"Did you eat enough at breakfast?"

"How were classes this week?"

"Did you bring something as a host gift to take to Sharmila Aunty and Rajesh Uncle?"

"What are you wearing? No crop tops in front of the aunties and uncles, okay?"

"Do you need anything?"

I answer each question as fast as I can. "I'm good, I did, they're good, I brought mithai, it's too chilly for crop tops anyway, no thank you."

Mamma smiles at me on the screen, leaning into Baba as they battle for who will be in frame. They always hold the camera too close to their faces. Mamma's roots are growing out. Usually, I help her color them with black box dye. Baba is wearing his glasses, which he didn't wear at home before, only at work. I feel a pang of homesickness.

"You look nice," Mamma says. "Glowing. Are you wearing new makeup?"

"No," I answer, flattered. "I actually didn't have time to really get ready this morning."

Mamma picks up on my words. "Didn't have time? Why? Did you wake up late?"

"Only by a little!"

"You could have missed the train! And then Sharmila Aunty and Rajesh Uncle would have been so worried."

"But I didn't miss the train," I respond, trying to hide my smile. This is so Mamma. Worrying about possibilities that never even happened.

"You got lucky, then."

"You seem happy," Baba says, steering the conversation back to our original topic. "That is nature's makeup."

I pause, thinking. "I am happy. I really like it here." I grin at Mamma. "You can say it."

Her eyes sparkle. "I told you so."

"Mothers are always right, aren't they?" Baba jokes.

"Yours is," Mamma tells me, chuckling. "Are you enjoying exploring?"

"Yeah." I push loose hair behind my ear. "I made a new friend. The person I cooked with? I sent you photos of the chole bhature."

"Oh, yes. That looked so good. The friend is from VBIS?"

"No . . ."

Mamma's eyes narrow. "You're meeting strangers?"

"Mamma, everyone here is a stranger to me until they're not!"

"Who?" she demands.

I laugh. "His name is Shiv—"

"Oh-ho!" Mamma says, dramatically slapping a hand to her forehead. "*His* name!"

"A friend, huh?" Baba chimes in. "No wonder she's so happy."

I'm tomato red in the small rectangle on-screen that shows my face.

"How did you meet this Shiv?"

"He works at the palace by the museum." Not a lie. I just don't want to say I met him on the train first. That would really worry them.

"Oh," Mamma says, as if that's an acceptable answer. She is quiet for a moment, and she exchanges a glance with Baba, talking in the secret silent language made possible after decades of marriage. "Be careful, okay?" she says finally. "The heart is a delicate thing."

"You can never really trust anyone," Baba adds quite ominously.

I roll my eyes. "Yeah, yeah. Not even yourself. We get it." I never should have introduced Baba to that meme of the guy pretending to attack his clone. He sends it in the family group chat a little too often these days.

I tell Mamma and Baba about my adventures in Jaipur and promise to send them more photos that actually have me in them, not just the scenery. They're very impressed when I tell them about the volunteering Mohini is doing.

When I update them about my Capstone project, a thought tugs at me. "Hold on. Do you have any pieces of Rajasthani art that mean a lot to you?"

Baba pauses. "That's a good question."

"Does it have to be famous art?" Mamma asks.

I shake my head.

"Then yes. Twenty-four years ago, your father sent me a postcard when he was in America and I was with my family in India. He painted a lotus on it, and he told me for the first time that he loved me."

I pull a face. "He told you he loved you for the first time through a *postcard*?"

Mamma laughs. "We had not been dating for that long when his job took him abroad."

I glance up as the train pulls into my station. "Can you send me a photo?"

The hustle and bustle of the train platform is calming to me.

I feel like part of the background in a busy painting, watching as strangers with full and colorful lives pass by me, our paths intersecting for a brief moment. I snap a photo and send it to Shiv.

Archi: Currently in your worst nightmare.

Shiv: You might as well have sent me a still from a horror movie.

Archi: I love being in crowded places

There's something so anonymous about it

I'm just another one of the many people here

Shiv: I like that thought.

I think when I'm around a lot of people, I feel like they're all watching me. Makes me nervous.

Archi: Don't worry. You're not THAT important.

Shiv: Ha

Archi: To strangers anyway

Shiv: 😊

I tuck my phone into my bag and march through the crowd out of the station to the street, where I immediately see Sharmila Aunty standing by a car. Rajesh Uncle sits in the driver's seat.

"Archana, bachha!" Sharmila Aunty yells when she sees me. "Come, come! Quickly." She gestures at the car. "We are not supposed to be parked here."

I bend down to touch Sharmila Aunty's feet in respect, but she waves me up. "No, no, no time for that. Get in, get in!"

I toss my bag into the backseat and slide in after it as Sharmila Aunty gets into the passenger side and Rajesh Uncle hits the accelerator. We lurch forward, and Sharmila Aunty turns to face me. "Train was good? Food is ready at home. Kids are so excited to see you. Rahul and Reema cannot stop talking about American Archana Didi. They think your accent is so funny."

I can't help but laugh. "Are they . . . home by themselves right now?" Both Rahul and Reema are under ten, unless they've magically aged since I last saw them.

Sharmila Aunty clucks her tongue. "No, no, they are with the neighbors. I could have stayed home, but they have been so loud this morning, I needed a break. Thought I would accompany Rajesh to the station to pick you." Sharmila Aunty prattles on about some street vendor who held up traffic on the way here, and I settle into my seat, relaxing into her story.

When we get to their house, Rajesh Uncle takes my bag despite my insistence that I can carry a single backpack myself. The dusty-pink house is beautiful, set amid a street of terra-cotta-hued houses, two stories with little plots for gardens in the front and access to the roof, where Sharmila Aunty has hung clothes to dry. There's farmland nearby, so the homes here are more spacious, less crowded, than those in the city.

Inside, the smell of ghee and toasted cumin immediately hits me. My mouth begins to water as we approach the kitchen, where Sharmila Aunty instructs me to wash my hands from my travels and sends Rajesh Uncle to grab the kids from next door. I scan the cluttered kitchen and feel at ease.

"You eat everything, yes?" Sharmila Aunty double-checks as she stirs a large pot on the stove. "Today, we have Punjabi kadhi pakora and prawn pulao. You'll eat?"

Uh, yeah, I'll eat. "It sounds amazing." I fish the box of sweets I brought from Jaipur out of my bag. "I got dessert for us."

"Arey!" Sharmila Aunty says, wrapping me in a hug. "How sweet. Kids will love this."

As if on cue, Rahul and Reema run into the house. "Archana Didi!" they yell, calling me "big sister" as they come to inspect the mithai.

It's funny because Sharmila Aunty and her family are not actually related to me. In fact, I don't even totally know how Sharmila Aunty and my mom know each other, except that they go *way* back. Our families have been close for generations. But it's one of my favorite things about Desi culture—how we *are* family even though we're not blood. They picked me up from the airport, sent me food, and cared for me in their home. Is that not what family does?

"Bachhon, haat dhoh," Sharmila Aunty says, and the

kids rush to wash their hands. Rajesh Uncle begins to set the table. "Come, Archi. Guest eats first."

I pile my plate up with hefty portions from every part of the array: a steaming bowl of kadhi, a golden-colored, spiced yogurt–based broth with chickpea flour and fried fritters; a salad of cucumbers and red onions; rice with shrimp and lemon zest; and crispy fried papad with mint-and-lemon chutney to dip it in. We're all quiet for a while as we tuck into the food. Mamma says that silence at the dinner table is the best sign for the chef—it means everyone is so focused on how delicious the meal is they can't even hold a conversation.

And this meal *is* delicious. The kadhi pakora melts in my mouth, and the prawn pulao zings with heat from the fresh chilis and citrus from the lemon and mint.

I close my eyes to savor each bite. Sharmila Aunty laughs at my reaction. "I'll pack you extra to take back to school."

Mohini would love that. *And,* I think, *I have to save some for Shiv.*

"How is your internship going, beta?" Rajesh Uncle asks. "Your mom said you are doing something about lost art for the museum?"

I nod and swallow my bite of rice. "My boss, Kiran-ji, and I are drafting a letter on official museum letterhead to send to museums in England. They have stolen Rajasthani art that should belong to the MSMS II Museum. And they might know where other art that we haven't been able to track down is located."

"You think they will respond?" Rajesh Uncle asks doubtfully.

"No. At least not positively. But we want to send the letter as part of our gallery process. Show that we demanded repatriation, and we'll include any response we receive from them, which will probably be a stiff no. My friend has a big following online, and she's going to post the letter on her social media profiles to get publicity for our exhibit."

"That is very courageous of you." Sharmila Aunty glances over at Rahul and Reema. "Do you hear what Archi Didi is doing? She is bringing our culture home."

After lunch, Sharmila Aunty sets me up in a guest bedroom, and I pull out my laptop to make some final edits to the letter.

When it looks polished enough, I sign my name at the bottom, ready to forward the document to Kiran-ji so she can add her signature, too. A thrill goes down my spine. I can't believe Kiran-ji has allowed me to do this, to develop my own exhibit from start to finish. I'm actually going to make a difference at the museum—actually have an impact on the Rathore Gallery!

I check the letter one last time. There are nine pieces we're naming, pieces we have records of up to the time of the British Raj and no records of since then. Six of those pieces are either on display or undergoing conservation at various English museums.

Six pieces out of countless stolen works. Kiran-ji suggested targeting specific items. It was hard to narrow the list down, but examining it now, I'm proud of the selection I've made. It's part of a curator's job, making tough choices. It makes me feel more legit.

We decided, ultimately, on the painting in the silk album, which was my favorite—art enclosed in a book of ragas, spiritual melodies. Plus two miniatures in traditional Rajasthani Marwar style, one Nihâl Chand painting, the Rathore crown, a woven tapestry from the original palace, and three sculptures, one stone, one brass, one clay. It's limited, yes, but it showcases a variety of Rajasthani art, and I hope the exhibit will pack a punch, KAVI-style.

Just as I press Send on the email to Kiran-ji, a notification pops up on my screen. It's a Google alert for KAVI. Speak of the artist! I click on it quickly, scanning the text.

Oh my god.

It's as if the universe heard my prayer.

When we last saw each other, I told Shiv I wished I could track down KAVI and have her help with my exhibit. And now it's being announced that KAVI is loaning some of her artwork to the grand reopening of a Jaipur art studio that was damaged in a fire. Her art will be there for a week. I read further, scanning the article quickly. The studio is run by two members of the Hijra community, which includes transgender and intersex people who are officially recognized as India's "third gender."

I learn from the article that the art studio was created as a safe space for queer Rajasthani youth and adults to express their creativity in a supportive environment. It was partially destroyed in a fire last year—the cause is still unclear—though people suspect it could have been an attack fueled by hate. The article also mentions that the Hijra community in India was treated with greater acceptance before British colonization, after which gender fluidity became more taboo.

This studio is exactly the kind of thing KAVI would support. I'm filled with something fierce, reading the article and learning about another community in India made more vulnerable by British occupation. I'm *proud* of KAVI for taking a stand in support of Hijras.

But there's another thing. I don't think I've ever seen KAVI's art showcased *indoors.* Now it's happening in the city I'm in? Does this mean KAVI is coming to Rajasthan to visit?

My shock turns into a massive smile as I keep reading.

If KAVI's willing to loan her art to an art studio in Jaipur, what's to say she wouldn't loan a piece to the Rathore Gallery as well?

OPEN LETTER RE:
STOLEN RAJASTHANI ART

Art is culture, is history, is identity. And it should not, without the consent of its caretakers, be taken and appropriated for display. The British Empire, during its colonization and occupation of what are now India, Pakistan, and Bangladesh, picked apart and shipped back to the UK countless South Asian heirlooms and cultural artifacts. This was theft. Many of these artifacts have now been lost to time, likely stored away in attics owned by the descendants of imperial families, long forgotten and discarded, or sold for more wealth to such a long series of people that the final destinations can no longer be traced.

But this is not true of every artifact. British museums, *especially* the British Museum, have looted and hoarded tangible histories of the peoples the empire invaded and occupied. In the halls of these museums, archaeological treasures from other countries remain on display, "owned" by the British. This theft, displayed with pride, is colonization persisting.

From the thousands of bronze sculptures British troops stole from the Kingdom of Benin (now part of Nigeria), which are held in museums throughout the West but notably not in Nigeria, to Egypt's Rosetta Stone, to Chinese paintings from the Tang dynasty, to Ethiopian textiles, to Easter

Island's moai, to the literal human remains of Indigenous peoples, uprooted from their homes. The people want our art returned. We want our history returned. We want our *ancestors* returned. No, we demand it.

During Occupation, British troops stole Rajasthani artifacts belonging to Jaipur's City Palace. Thus, the Maharaja Sawai Man Singh II Museum demands that the following artifacts be returned to their rightful home:

1. The nineteenth-century silk album of Jaipur's ragamala paintings.
2. Two Rajasthani Marwar miniatures.
3. The Nihâl Chand work held in London.
4. The Rathore crown.
5. The Rathore palace tapestry.
6. The stone, brass, and clay sculptures of Hindu goddesses, currently stored in conservation.

We call now for these nine stolen artifacts, nine out of countless that rightfully belong in Jaipur's City Palace. The British Museum has a history of offering stolen art on loan to their former colonized people, to hold its power over their heads, to remind them that any grace shown by the empire is temporary.

We reject any offers of return on loan. Further, we demand that the empire begin the permanent repatriation not only of Rajasthani art, not only of South Asian art, but of every stolen artifact British occupiers laid claim to through violence and oppression.

These works are our heritage. And we will—one day—bring our history home.

Posted by: @moremohini
11.6k likes
458 comments

Caption: Read this letter by my brilliant friend @archidhawanpov and the Maharaja Sawai Man Singh II Museum!

Chapter 14

Gold-Star Smile

The week of the art studio's reopening, I burst into my dorm room after morning classes, holding my phone above my head as if it's a trophy.

"I got us tickets!" I screech. "To Gharana Art Studio!"

Mohini turns away from her desk with a sheepish smile. "Umm. So did I."

My eyebrows go up. "What do you mean?"

"Chandana and I got timed-entry tickets for tomorrow."

"Oh." I tap my phone. "Mine are for tonight."

"I would totally go twice," Mohini says, "but I'm kind of excited to see it with Chandana. She hasn't been to many queer spaces in India, and I think this will mean a lot to both of us, you know?"

I smile. I get it. The sense of belonging Mohini's talking about is what the art studio is *for*. "That sounds awesome. Do you know anyone who will want my extra ticket for tonight, then?"

Mohini gives me a look. "Come on, Archi."

"What?"

She smirks. "You know what. Take Shiv."

In the common room, I open my text chain with Shiv. It's been over a week since we last saw each other, even though we've been texting nearly every day. I've been so busy with my Capstone and with catching up on my classes. Would he want to come to the studio with me?

Last time I mentioned the museum, he panicked and became evasive. That was at the train station. But based on his explanation, he was acting weird because of the crowd. Though there's probably going to be a crowd at the studio, too, considering the positive press the reopening has been getting, not to mention KAVI's popularity. It's amazing to me that of all places, even of all places in India, KAVI chose Jaipur, right while I'm visiting. But the art studio—it makes *sense.* It fits what I know of the artist. I always wondered whether she was Indian. Could she be *Rajasthani*? The universe really does work in mysterious ways.

Still, the tickets are timed entry, so there can't be *that* many people. I formulate a text, and before I can overthink it any more than I already have, I hit Send.

> **Archi:** Remember I was telling you about KAVI? You won't believe this, but her gallery debut is today at Gharana Art Studio HERE in Jaipur!!! I have two tickets for tonight. Want to come?

I attach a photo of the tickets so he knows the entry time.

Shiv's reply comes while I'm eating lunch in the dining hall and working on a discussion post for class.

Shiv: Let's do it. Dress code?

I beam at the message.

Archi: No hoodies this time

While Mohini naps, I quietly pick out my outfit and smooth my hair. I pin half of my hair back and let the rest waterfall over my shoulders. And then, without Mohini's or Lilyn's help, I manage to pick out a red dress and a lightweight brown coat. I thread a red ribbon through my clipped-back hair, fix my makeup with a touch of powder, adjust my nose ring, and spritz some of my favorite perfume—a gift from Mamma, which has notes of bergamot and saffron—before slipping out the door.

VBIS is only a ten-minute walk from the studio, and Shiv is meeting me at the campus gates. When I see him, my body relaxes instantly. He eyes my outfit as I do the same to him, taking him in. He's dressed *nice,* in tan slacks and a navy button-up with gold embroidery, an Indo-Western combo that's utterly striking on him. His silhouette in the early evening light is gorgeous, and as I walk closer, I can see the golden flecks in his brown eyes, the perpetual smirk of his slightly upturned lips, lips I've *kissed,* the little scar on his chin, his hair curling over his ears. I want to mark every observation with a kiss.

"You look . . ." Shiv smiles. "You look amazing."

I beam, unable to contain my smile. "You clean up well, too."

"You haven't seen me in formal attire since the train, huh?"

"I'm not saying the gardening uniform or the sweats don't suit you, too."

"But which do you prefer?"

I nearly melt at the tenderness in his eyes. *Shirtless, probably,* I want to say, but I don't want to sound too bold. "I like both."

"That's cheating."

I grin.

He grins back his gold-star smile.

Before he can say anything else, I fish out a pocket-sized book from my purse and hold it out to him. "This time," I say, "I brought *you* flowers."

Shiv's eyebrows go up, his eyes wide. "This is a book."

"A cookbook," I say. "I found it while thrifting with Mohini the other day. Well, it's less a proper cookbook and more a family recipe book. All the recipes are handwritten inside. They're in Hindi. I can't read them, especially with the handwriting, but Mohini can. She said there's some really good recipes in there. We don't know how old it is, but it seemed like something you'd like." The words rush out of my mouth. I'm almost embarrassed to give him a gift, like it's a sign of how much I like him, materialized.

His mouth drops as I keep talking, forming a surprised O. "Archi," he says.

I blush. "Open it."

He does, and inside the front cover, he finds the flowers I got him: pink hibiscus and desert rose, pressed paper-thin in the book, dried to last. When Shiv's eyes meet mine, his expression can only be described as *delighted.* "Archi," he repeats, and I glow at the sound of my name on his tongue. "This is perfect."

"You've done so much nice stuff for me." I'm suddenly shy. "I wanted to do something nice for you."

He shakes his head as if he can't believe the thought would even cross my mind. "I brought flowers, too," he says finally. "A little different this time." Shiv has a tote—a classy one, worn brown leather—slung over his shoulder. He reaches inside and pulls out a small box. When he opens it, facing me, I gasp.

"Oh. Wow."

The box contains mithai, Indian sweets made of condensed milk and sugar, but they aren't ordinary mithai. They're delicate dessert bites dyed pale green and lavender, shaped carefully into . . . flowers. I stare at the sweets in awe, at the edible shimmer and dried rose petals pressed into the dough.

"New recipe." Shiv ducks his head.

"How am I supposed to even eat these?" I say in wonder. "They belong in their own art gallery. I can't . . . I can't ruin them."

Shiv rubs the back of his neck. "I can always make more."

"Shiv," I say. "You are such a surprise." It's really the best way to put it, isn't it? After all, the best things come when you least expect them.

"I could say the same about you." There's something so

warm in his eyes. Something so fond. "I'm pretty sure I have."

I tuck the mithai box in my bag, and we start walking in the direction of the gallery. "Did you take the train here?" I ask him.

"Car," he says, and I understand him to mean a taxi. "Just got dropped off here."

"Do you live far?" I realize now I don't have any idea where Shiv spends his time when he's not in the garden or the kitchen. Where is home to him?

"Uh. Near the palace?"

"Oh, that must be convenient for work." When he laughs, I glance up at him. "How's your family? You don't talk about them much."

"My parents are always busy. We try to have dinners together when we're all free."

"When you're not running around Jaipur with me?"

He nods. "Exactly."

"I hope I'm not keeping you away from your family too much." I frown. Shiv and I have only hung out a few times, but still.

"No," he assures me. "I told you, I don't really spend a lot of time with people outside of work and home. It's been a long time since I've met someone on my own." He bites his lip, and I want to kiss him right then and there, but I hold myself back. "Most of the people I meet nowadays are because my parents are introducing me to them, when we have people over or something."

"So what you're trying to say is, you like me because your parents don't know me?" I tease.

Shiv snorts. "What I'm trying to say is, I like spending time with you because I got to choose this myself. I like you because *I* like you."

I'm afraid I'm going to melt into the ground. "Does your family know we're spending time together?"

"My sister does," Shiv says, scratching his ear. "Is that okay? If I'm to admit something . . . the truth is, my parents and I don't really talk about personal stuff that much. I usually go to my sister for that."

I grow warm at the thought of him telling his sister about me. "Your sister the artist?"

He nods. "The very one. So, of course, she approves."

"I'm no artist."

Shiv looks me up and down and shakes his head. "That's debatable."

"All right, all right. Come on."

We're at the studio now, and we pause for a second to take it in. The sign flickers in multicolored lights: GHARANA ART STUDIO. It's written in Hindi and English. I did some research, as any good curator does, and learned that gharanas are intentional all-Hijra communities, found families of a sort. They can often be secluded, as refuge from the discrimination Hijras face throughout India; the studio hopes to be a more public but still safe space.

I present our tickets at the entrance. A small crowd is gathered outside, some press, too, and I remember how Shiv feels around crowds. "You okay?" I whisper to him.

"I'll be better when we're inside," he whispers, offering me a smile.

Instinctively, I reach for his hand and squeeze. He

squeezes back. Inside, the difference is stark. There are still people here, ambling around, but the space is colorful and open—welcoming. Everyone is focused on the art, not one another. The studio is cool, air-conditioned, which I know must be expensive. Community donations, which I heard poured in during the rebuild, as well as the paid tickets to see KAVI's art, are probably helping with the bills.

On either side of us are more private studio spaces, for classes like pottery, weaving, and painting. Sign-up sheets are posted on a wall. Additional community resources are highlighted nearby, including a free-lunch initiative for students. I bet Mohini is going to get Samudaay Food Bank involved once she sees this. It's cool how one wall of postings can be a reminder of how all these different struggles—social, economic, cultural—are connected. A giant banner hangs at the end of the hallway: THE WORLD OF KAVI.

I squeeze Shiv's hand again, which I'm still holding. I don't want to let go. "It's there!" I whisper excitedly.

He appears amused at my eagerness. "Straight there, or do we save it for the end after checking out the rest of the studio?"

"Good idea. I want to build up to it."

"Lead the way."

The studio has a gallery display of both traditional and modern art, created by its artists. At the entrance to the exhibits are two faces I recognize from the article about the grand reopening: they're the owners, Laxmi and Madhu. Like many Hijras, Laxmi and Madhu present in traditionally feminine ways and have selected traditionally feminine names for themselves. Online, they refer to themselves as *sisters* and use feminine pronouns. Today, they wear saris, and their graying hair is long and adorned with flowers. Their eyes are lined with kajal, and their noses are pierced with ornate jewelry.

Shiv and I greet them. "Welcome," Laxmi says as she clasps my hands. Madhu takes Shiv's.

"Your studio is beautiful," I say. "This reopening seems like a huge success."

Shiv bows his head to Laxmi and Madhu. "Thank you for creating this space. Jaipur is so lucky to have you and this studio."

Madhu grins. "Thank you. We hope you enjoy."

With their blessings, we enter the gallery section. As Shiv and I walk through the exhibits, I fully nerd out the way Shiv did when he was teaching me to cook. I tell him about the different eras of modern and postmodern art, the styles emerging in the current art space, the way art has always been used for politics, but every now and then there's a pull away, to see art as itself, without any messaging or agenda, and how that all might fit in with the studio's vision. We take a long look at a wall of pottery painted in a delicate hand.

"My sister has a collection of pottery in a similar style," Shiv remarks, gazing at the display.

"Is she in college? Your sister?" I'm curious to know more about Shiv, more about his family, about the people who made him who he is. I've been wanting to respect his privacy, and now that I can feel him opening up more, I'm ready to ask him the questions I've had since we met.

"She did two years of college, and now she's taking a

gap year. She'll go back next fall." He smiles to himself as if he's thought of a private joke. "I'll have to introduce you two."

"What's her art like?"

"You know, maybe this studio is the perfect place to show it to you. She did this painting of Champ for my birthday last year." With his free hand, he reaches for his phone.

When he shows me the screen, I squeal in delight. On Shiv's phone is an image of a painting in purple, green, and orange, each paint stroke a hair on the dog's fur, a neon portrayal of Champ with his tongue lolling out, his eyes happy.

"That's incredible!"

"One of the best birthday presents I've received, for sure."

I study the painting. The colors and strokes in the image are warm, familiar. They seem to be inspired by something I should be able to name. I meet Shiv's eyes. "When do you turn eighteen, again?"

Shiv narrows his gaze at me. "If I tell you, you have to promise not to do anything for it."

I tap my fingers together. "So it's soon, then."

"My family already makes a huge deal out of my birthday. The best birthday present for me would be spending it as if it's any other day."

"What's the date, Shiv?" I ask, grinning.

He mimes zipping his lips shut and tossing the key over his shoulder. "It's soon. I'll tell you exactly when some other time."

Always a man of mystery. I pout.

"I promise," he says, tucking a piece of loose hair behind my ear.

Now we're at the end of the hallway, where KAVI's painting stands. I take a deep breath.

"Ready?" Shiv asks.

I nod. "As I'll ever be."

We walk into the final showroom, and suddenly, all the other people melt away. In the center, against the back wall, roped off, is a massive painting, as big as the largest presidential portraits in the National Gallery of Art back home. It's a brand-new, untitled piece, never been seen before. An original KAVI. A real painting by *the* KAVI, right in front of me. I didn't know when I'd ever see her work in person, since it's usually spontaneous.

This—this is different. The piece feels . . . personal. I recognize the vision right away. It's a blow-up of a traditional Rajasthani miniature painting, but pop-art style. It's a portrait of a feminine-presenting person, facing the right of the canvas, her long, sharp nose protruding and decorated with an extravagant nose ring. She could be a Hijra. She could be any Desi woman. Her eyes are dark and expressive, lined with black kohl, flicked upward. Her skin is a warm brown, darker and brighter than the faded ink on the miniatures in the Rathore Gallery. She is the archetype of Desi femininity. She is stunning.

And I realize now why it made so much sense for KAVI to choose India for her next installation. I know it because I know this art. Because I can imagine the artist behind it. KAVI is Desi, like me.

This painting, labeled *Untitled,* is different from KAVI's usual in-your-face style, but it still feels as if it sends a message: this young Desi person, her chin held up, her spine straight, not looking at the audience, and yet commanding our attention. *Look at me,* the portrait says. *I am here.* In the Gharana Art Studio, the message is crystal clear. This subject deserves to be here, to take up space. The Hijras do, too. The choice to make a miniature painting style *big* isn't lost on me, either. KAVI has paid homage to tradition while also making a grander statement. It is history and contemporary—it is then and *now.* The art is personal and political. And this is exactly what I want my exhibit to show.

I stagger back, and Shiv catches me. I have chills. I shake my head and gaze at him, amazed. "This . . ." My eyes feel like they're going to well up with tears. This day is unreal. I don't know how to explain what it's like, seeing the painting up close, especially in this particular studio. The work feels, somehow, like a mirror. I nudge Shiv. "Can you believe we're standing in front of an original KAVI painting?"

"Hardly." Again, his smile is amused, as if he's laughing at a secret joke.

I reach for the Polaroid camera in my bag and take a photo, then another. I angle the camera enough so that Shiv is in it, though he can't tell. I want a photo of him in my album. One for me to remember, at least. And maybe a candid is the best way to do it, since he's so camera shy.

I wave the Polaroid in the air as it develops, gazing at the painting with a dreamy sigh. I am so overwhelmed with emotion, standing here. And I am so lucky to be sharing this once-in-a-lifetime moment with Shiv. It could not be more perfect.

Well.

I face Shiv. "Can I admit something?"

He nods. "Only fair."

"Sometimes," I begin, a blush creeping up my cheeks, "when I'm trying to make a decision, I imagine a little cartoon angel and devil talking me through my options. It helps me figure out what I want and whether it's a good idea."

Shiv leans forward, close. "What's the devil telling you to do now?"

Goosebumps appear at his voice low in my ear. "To cross past the ropes and touch the painting for one second. I know it's so wrong. I just . . ." I sigh. "Wow."

Shiv laughs into my ear, and the sound makes my stomach do a flip. "If only. What's the angel saying?"

I shift to face him. "To kiss you."

His eyes soften. "Here?" He gestures, and I'm reminded there are other people also taking in the painting, that it's not just Shiv and me, suspended in our own moment of time. "In front of this painting?"

"What?" I tease. "You don't like it?" Because, okay, silly or not, PDA or not, getting to kiss my dream guy in front of a KAVI painting? Like . . . that's the stuff of fantasy.

Shiv laughs again, another private joke. "No, I just . . ." He looks around for a moment, then pulls me around a corner into an alcove where nobody is watching. There he pulls me into him, his fingertips splayed across my spine, grazing my skin around the straps of my dress. "Come here," he says, and then he kisses me, and I'm soaring, floating, separating from my body, and watching this moment happen to me in real time.

This moment.

Now it couldn't be any more perfect.

Chapter 15

The Power of "Yes, And"

I'm sitting in Kiran-ji's office for our phone meeting with Laxmi and Madhu, Gharana Art Studio's owners.

I told Kiran-ji I wanted to reach out to the studio to try to get KAVI's contact information and to see where the painting was headed after being on loan to the studio for its grand reopening, and Kiran-ji said, "Let's do it."

Whitney loves theater, and she taught me a rule of improv: to make a scene better, to make the story progress, when one person suggests something, you must say, "Yes, and . . ." Kiran-ji has been "yes-and-ing" all my ideas, and now I can see how our story is progressing. We've secured eight artists for the modern section of the gallery, from our submissions form and from the calls I've been making to persuade people who have never thought of putting their work in museums—because they were focused on making a living—to give my idea a chance.

The exhibit opening is coming up, and Madhavi has been putting out email and social media blasts. We have physical flyers, too, because unfortunately, the MSMS II Museum doesn't have a *ton* of online followers, but we're advertising every way we can. There's still a lot to do, and that in itself is exciting. But for now, we have to focus on seeing if we can get KAVI's painting for our exhibit.

Jassi from the info desk is sitting in on this meeting. She taps her fingers excitedly on Kiran-ji's desk.

"Okay," Kiran-ji tells the two of us. "I'm about to make the call. I'll put Laxmi and Madhu on speaker. You both can listen. Ready?"

Jassi and I nod vigorously, and Kiran-ji dials the number. After a few rings, the line connects.

"Salaam, Laxmi-ji and Madhu-ji," Kiran-ji says.

The three of them exchange pleasantries before Kiran-ji continues. "Congratulations on your reopening. I took my daughter yesterday. She asked a million questions, because she loved the space. We'll definitely be back."

"Oh, yes, I remember you two!" Laxmi exclaims.

Kiran-ji beams. "Here at the Rathore Gallery, we are planning an exhibit about lost and stolen Rajasthani art," she explains. "That's the real reason for this call. We want to incorporate some modern art elements into the show as well. We know KAVI has been quite involved in political messaging with her artwork, especially around stolen historical artifacts. I saw her display outside the British Museum online."

I glow with pride. I showed Kiran-ji that to demonstrate how much publicity MSMS II could get from our event.

"Anyway, we're reaching out to ask about the possibility of speaking with KAVI's team about transferring the untitled piece you debuted in your studio to our exhibit. It seems from your website that the work is only on loan to the studio for opening week, so we were wondering where it's going next."

"Nowhere," says Madhu. Her voice is raspier than Laxmi's, and I can distinguish the speaker over the phone. "It is a temporary installation, yes, but it was a complete surprise. KAVI's team reached out to us, said the artist admired our work, and asked us if we would want to put up the painting. Of course, we said yes. The tickets helped us raise record-breaking funds."

"When did this happen?" Kiran-ji asks, clearly curious.

"Just a few weeks ago. It was a very fast turnaround. Luckily, KAVI gets so much media and online attention that we were able to announce it and pull it off quite quickly."

"Clearly, it worked." Kiran-ji sounds intrigued. "Are you able to share the details of KAVI's team so we can set up a meeting?"

There's a crackle on the other end, and my palms start to sweat. This is beyond a pinch-me moment. I am going to be *in touch* with KAVI's team! I can't wait to tell Whitney.

"Interestingly," Laxmi says, "we were told that the palace museum might reach out to inquire about the painting. KAVI's team said that if the Majaraja Sawai Man Singh II Museum asks about the painting, we have permission to transfer it to you for your installation."

I drop my own phone in shock, and it clatters to the

floor. Kiran-ji gives me a sharp look, covering the phone mic, and I pick up my phone sheepishly. Jassi hides a smile and reaches over to squeeze my arm.

HELLO???

What alternate universe am I in?

Is this the power of *yes, and*? Did I *manifest* KAVI? I think back to my wish at the restaurant with Shiv. He promised me the industrial dishwasher magic was more powerful than coins in a fountain, and he was right. I have to tell him my wish came true.

Adrenaline rushes through me. *This* is what I came to Jaipur to do.

"We'll send along paperwork and the contact details for KAVI and her team," Laxmi continues, oblivious to our shock. "You'll likely hear from her legal team soon. Our exhibit goes on for the whole week, but after that, we can plan on transferring the painting to the Rathore Gallery. Does that sound all right to you, at least tentatively?"

Even Kiran-ji is speechless. She pauses for a moment, as if collecting her thoughts. "Yes, that sounds lovely, thank you."

"Wait," I blurt out, surprising myself. We're on speaker, so my voice carries to Laxmi and Madhu.

"Sorry," Kiran-ji says quickly, "this is our intern, Archi Dhawan. She . . . has something to say?"

I make an apologetic face at Kiran-ji. "Laxmi-ji and Madhu-ji," I begin. "It was a total honor to meet you both on opening night. Your studio is so impressive, and such a crucial space. Would you be willing, at all, to allow any of the studio art created by your community to be on display in our exhibit as well? I would love to acknowledge the Hijra community in our gallery. I especially loved the pottery wall in your studio, and we don't have any modern pottery for our exhibit yet."

When I glance over at Kiran-ji, she's wearing the proudest smile.

After the phone call is over, Kiran-ji, Jassi, and I stare at each other and scream in excitement. "I can't believe this is happening!" I yell.

"In all my time in curation"—Kiran-ji shakes her head—"nothing has been so easy."

"Archi, you're a good-luck charm!" Jassi wraps me in a tight hug. "And you got approval for even more local art? You killed this!"

"I feel like I need to run a marathon," I tell them. "I'm sweating and fired up and . . ." I trail off. "Oh my god. I can't *believe* this."

"KAVI's your favorite artist, right?" Jassi confirms.

"Yeah, like, beyond anything and anyone else. Do you guys think . . . could she be *from* Rajasthan? Maybe she's . . . from Jaipur originally? I had a hunch she was Indian, but now she could *really* fit the exhibit description."

Kiran-ji considers this. "You know, I guess I always thought KAVI was an acronym for something."

Jassi snorts. "Like what, Kitschy Artist Via India?"

"Or Karma Always Vindicates Idealists," I offer, and Jassi oohs in appreciation.

"I was ready to make an exception for a possibly non-Indian artist as a political statement to the exhibit," Kiran-ji explains. "She seems to have her hand in so many different projects across the world. I thought it might help with publicity."

"I always had the sense she was Desi." I grin at Kiran-ji. "So what now?"

"Now we put the final touches on the rest of the exhibit." She claps her hands together. "Why don't you go down to meet with the archivists, and you can plan how you want to set up the empty frames and what information you want to share about each piece. And find one more artist for the modern selection. Do you think you can do that in a week? KAVI's painting is great, but we want artists whose identities can be public for the local selection. Yes?"

I'm up with a jump. "Yes!"

On the way to the basement offices to meet the archivists, I merge Whitney and Lilyn in a group video call. It's ridiculously late in D.C., but they both pick up right away. They're clearly in the same room, and Whitney mutes herself so when Lilyn talks, there's no echo.

I recognize Lilyn's family room on the screen. "We're watching *Ready or Not!*" Lilyn says. "You saved us from a scare. What's up?"

I can't even say hello. "KAVI'S PAINTING IS COMING TO THE RATHORE GALLERY!" My voice is so loud that it carries through the stairwell as I make my way to the offices, but I don't even care.

"You're kidding." Lilyn's eyes get huge.

Whitney's face pops up next to her, so now I'm seeing double.

"*The* KAVI?" she yells.

"*The* KAVI."

"Girl, you are living the dream in Jaipur. Killing it across the board," Whitney says.

I literally pinch myself. "I don't even know how any of this is real."

"It *is* real!" Lilyn responds. "You've worked so hard on this project."

"Okay, yeah, but KAVI basically just fell into my lap."

"But the rest of it," Lilyn says, "*you* put together. Maybe KAVI heard about the theme of your Capstone exhibit through the grapevine, and she was, like, 'This sounds like exactly the kind of thing I'd want to work on.'"

I shiver at the idea of *the* KAVI hearing about *me* through a grapevine.

"Have you told Shiv?" Whitney asks, practically singing his name.

"Not yet. I will, though."

"How are things going with you two?" she goes on, ever the romantic.

"Good, I think. I mean. He said he likes me. We've kissed, twice. We haven't talked about a label or anything, but things are going well? I hope."

Whitney laughs. "I'm so glad you broke your boy-free-semester rule. Jaipur just sounds so wonderful. And besides, I'm glad you didn't let Nick ruin future romances for you. He doesn't deserve that much headspace."

"Exactly!" says Lilyn. "You're doing *way* better now. Dating a hotter, cooler, more attentive guy."

"Well, we haven't seen any photos of him," Whitney notes. "So we can't say for sure on the hotter part, but everything else sounds great."

"Yeah. He's really . . . kind of perfect."

Lilyn snorts. "Okay, I mean he definitely sounds better than Nick, but no boy is perfect. You just haven't figured out his red flags yet."

"I don't think he has any. Is *that* a red flag?"

"Uh, yeah," says Lilyn. "Because that's impossible."

"Everyone has red flags," Whitney insists.

"What are mine?"

She laughs, studying me. "You can be a bit of a control freak. It's the Virgo in you, but you sometimes get rigid about your plans. We love that you have goals and big dreams, but sometimes I worry you're not flexible enough when it comes to things changing."

I scowl. "Okay, okay, thank you! I wish I hadn't asked."

"No." Whitney sighs. "The thing is, it's not even a classic red flag. It's a complexity. Something about you that can be good but might also complicate things for you."

I sit with what she's said and . . . she's right. Plans are good—they keep me on track—but I *am* glad I've strayed a little from the path I set in Jaipur. I'm glad that I opened the exhibit up to new and old art. I'm glad I let Shiv—the ultimate surprise—into my life. I smile, recovering. "When did you get so wise?"

"Maybe when I fell in love," Whitney says, and swoons.

"Gross," says Lilyn, and we all burst out laughing.

"Thierry says hi, by the way!" says Whitney.

"Bonjour to him, too."

After the call, I text Shiv the news. He's probably at work. I try to keep the message calm, but I can't contain all my exclamation marks. A girl's gotta be real!!!

Then I meet up with Bhavya, the Rathore Gallery's

head archivist, and her assistants to go over our plans for the empty frames. Since they have all the information about the historical pieces, they're going to help me write up paragraphs for the plaques that go beside the frames, educating viewers on the art that's missing. We work on the Rathore coronation crown, one of the statues, and the album. I write out my notes in my journal, and Bhavya oohs and aahs at my doodles while we work. This exhibit is total teamwork. Once, it was a small idea in my journal on a train ride into the city. Now it's grown into something real, concrete. And slowly but surely, it's coming together. Organically.

We have a spotlight on the stolen art, a section dedicated to local creators, including Hijra artists, and a loan from *the freaking* KAVI. There's something else missing. Something personal.

"Wait," I say toward the end. "My mom sent me this postcard my dad gave her when they were dating." I show them the image, which I printed out and glued into my journal on an earlier page. Alongside Baba's doodle of a lotus are two sentences.

"I was wondering . . . what if we used this postcard as the backdrop for the pamphlet visitors will get at the exhibit?" All the exhibits at MSMS II have a foldable flyer with details about the works on display and photos of highlighted sections, like a playbill for the museum. "My parents met in Jaipur. In its own way, it's modern art about Rajasthan, like the open call we've put out. And we've been advertising the showcase, but we haven't given it an official title beyond 'New Exhibit at MSMS II.' So we could give it a splashy name, like . . . *Ready to Return Home!*"

Farheen, one of the archivist assistants, grins. "Like the stolen pieces."

Bhavya adds, "Sounds amazing. Tell Kiran-ji. She's going to love it. And Madhavi, so she can get it on our socials right away."

When I leave work, on an absolute high, I get a call from Shiv in lieu of a response to my text. I pick up, giddy.

"Congratulations, Miss Dhawan," he says right away.

I giggle. "What's with the formalities?"

"You're a big-shot curator now. I have to refer to you with respect."

"I could get used to that."

"I'm proud of you," says Shiv, and the words make me sparkle. He's proud of me. And, moreover, I'm proud of me, too. "Can I take you out to dinner to celebrate?"

My smile stretches across my face. What is there to say but *yes, and* . . . how's tomorrow?

To: Archi Dhawan <archi.dhawan@odyssey.edu>
From: Komal Dhawan <komalkhannadhawan@gmail.com>
Subject: Baba's Postcard
Attachment: 1 Image

Komal,

I love you.
I am ready to return home.

Ravi

Chapter 16

I Love Denial

The next day, I leave work early to head to Johari Bazaar.

An idea came to me this morning for our final piece of local art. I told Kiran-ji about it, and she told me to get on it quickly.

So now I find myself back in the crowded pink bazaar, with traffic and honking in the middle of the street separating the shops on either side. Street dogs wander the sidewalk, and I take photos to send to my royal gardener.

> **Shiv:** One day, I'm going to adopt them all.

I trace the path Mohini and I took the first day we came to the shops, passing the jewelry and sari dukaans. The staff at the sari store present garments one by one to seated customers. Salesmen call from the shops as I pass by, telling me they have the perfect things for me. But today, I know where I'm headed. When I spot the store, I take a deep breath and hope for good luck. I've gotten better at my spiel, and hopefully this shop owner will hear me out.

When I step inside, the woman at the counter lights up. "I remember you!"

Around her are traditional Rajasthani puppets, kathputlis, in dazzling colors. The puppets are made from mango wood, dressed in miniature outfits in the style of Rajasthani phad paintings, the kind we have at the Rathore Gallery. The paintings are a folk style on religious scrolls, with the characters clothed in bright, colorful garments. The kathputlis reflect the style, and their painted faces are expressive and bold.

I beam. "You do?"

"The American. You asked me so many questions."

"Sorry about that." I wince. "I love learning about art."

"I like questions. And I liked that you immediately thought of the puppets as art and not souvenirs or toys. That's why I remember you."

A warm bubble grows in my chest. "Well, that's exactly what brings me here today." I suck in a breath. "I'm an intern at the Maharaja Sawai Man Singh II Museum in the City Palace. We're creating an exhibit to showcase local art, both traditional and modern. Rajasthani kathputlis are so emblematic of local art, because they combine several things: the painting style of the puppets' features, the fabric design of their clothes, the performance art of the puppet shows, and the history from the stories the puppets tell."

The woman, who I remember not only owns the store but also hand-crafts the puppets, raises her eyebrows.

I take this as a sign to go on—at least she hasn't interrupted me yet to tell me my idea is ridiculous. "I really admired you when we met, both because of your talent in creating these puppets and because of how knowledgeable you were about the history of Rajasthani puppetry. We've been looking for local artists to be a part of our showcase, and I would love to have your kathputlis in the museum."

When I finish talking, the woman's eyes are bright. "Really?"

I nod. "We'll pay a fee to host your art, and if the exhibit goes well and you'd like the piece to remain at the museum after the showcase ends, we're willing to buy it for permanent display. I really think the exhibit will draw in new visitors, and we've already got a lot of amazing artists. You'd be in the best company." I'm breathless as I go through the spiel, and then I realize I forgot the most important thing of the intro. "I'm Archi, by the way. And you are?"

"Sheiza," she says, and her face breaks into a grin. "Thank you so much for the offer. You didn't have to go that hard with the persuasion, honestly. You had me the moment you started."

I laugh. "I've had a hard time convincing other people."

She shakes her head. "I've spent a decent amount of time convincing others that what I do is art, is important, isn't child's play of the past. Why a college-educated girl would go into puppet-making has been beyond many people I know. So this . . . this opportunity? I never thought it was a possibility for me. It sounds wonderful."

My smile widens. "So are you in?"

"Yes!"

At home, I call Lilyn to help me pick my outfit for tonight. I'm still on a high from this afternoon.

Sheiza is our tenth local craftsperson. Our collection is complete. And now I can turn to the excitement of the evening: my celebratory dinner with Shiv.

"Now that you and Shiv are, like . . . together," Lilyn says, "have you thought about what that's going to mean for the rest of the semester? Or when you're back in D.C.?" She makes a face at the sweater I hold up. "Definitely no."

I put the sweater down. "I mean, we're not officially together."

Lilyn raises her eyebrows.

"And you and Whitney are the ones who told me to live in the moment! To stop planning ahead so much."

"Touché. Though, technically, Whitney's the one who said that. *I* think that as long as you're open to things changing, it's okay to consider the future." She sighs. "Whitney wants you to go for this whirlwind romance because she met the love of her life in Paris. She's in love, and she wants all of us to be, too, but be careful, okay? There's a difference between being cautious and being inflexible. You know?"

"Yeah. But I'm not ready to think about it ending yet," I tell her. "It's too early."

"Sounds like someone's in denial."

"I love denial." I set my phone down on my desk and shimmy into a flowy black halter top. "This, with jeans?"

"Where are y'all going, again?"

"Unclear. He said dinner. He's going to pick me up again."

"Ever the gentleman. The denim is okay, but maybe too casual for dinner plans?" A rustling sound comes from her end. "Hey, did you figure out his red flags yet?"

"I haven't seen him since we last talked!" I pull off the top and drag the few dresses I brought out of my closet. "I wore this red one to our last date. And I'll ask him about his red flags tonight."

"Oh, right, because boys are so open and honest?" Lilyn narrows her eyes. "That red dress *is* really pretty."

"Well, I can't rewear it."

"Guys never notice what you're wearing."

"Trust me, he noticed."

Lilyn *ooooooh*s. "Okay, so let's back up. What is going to happen when you leave the country?"

"I don't know, Lilyn! He could visit. We could video call."

"You could break up over the phone."

"Hey! Whitney and Thierry are making it work, aren't they?"

"Well, Thierry has a reason to be in the U.S. sometimes, so that helps. And what if you aren't as lucky as them?"

"Aaahhhhh," I groan. "Why do you have to be so negative?" But I hear what she hasn't said. Shiv could meet someone new, someone in Jaipur. He could pick someone else, because I'm on the other side of the world. He could tell me she's better for his future.

Nope. I push away the thought. I don't want to think about that. I don't think about the *real* reason Nick and I broke up.

"I'm trying to brace you for all the possibilities. You need to know your options before you commit, right? How is he going to afford that international travel as a gardener?" She waves a hand at the screen. "Not the pink dress. It's more daytime. Go for a jewel-toned color."

I humph.

"If he asks you to be in a relationship, what are you going to do?"

Say yes.

At the same time . . . what would be the point if our relationship has an expiration date? It's not statistically likely that high school couples will stay together long-term. Then again, crazier things have happened. Like the fact that KAVI's painting is going to be in *my* curated exhibit. Putting faith in myself has worked out so far. Why deny myself good things from the start because they *might* someday end?

I look Lilyn in the eye. "I'm going to do whatever I think will make me happy."

She smiles, acquiescing. "I can get behind that. I just care about you a lot, you know? I want everything to be okay for you."

"I know. And I love you for that."

Lilyn points to the dark green dress in my hands. "That's the one."

An hour and a half later, I've taken my "everything shower," and I'm scrubbed fresh, hair washed and blow-dried, legs shaved, and eyebrows tweezed, smelling like rose hip oil and coconut conditioner.

I do my makeup in front of the full-length mirror behind our dorm door. Mohini is having dinner with her parents, who are visiting this weekend from filming in Andhra Pradesh. Even though I haven't seen their movies, I felt like a nervous fan girl meeting them when they came to pick her up.

Tonight, my dress is forest green, long-sleeved, and hip-hugging. I switch out my nose stud for a ring and hook a pair of matching gold mini jhumkas into my ears. After I smack my glossy lips in the mirror, I take a selfie to send to Lilyn, Whitney, and Mohini. They text back immediately with heart and flame emojis.

Confidence renewed, I grab my purse and head out the door.

I really could get used to the sight of Shiv waiting for me to come down the steps. He's dressed in a sage-green sweater with slacks, and my heart flutters the moment my eyes catch him. His hair is ruffled in that perfect accidentally-on-purpose way, and I can smell cloves and cologne as I get closer. We both dressed nice on our date to the gallery so that our outfits fit the vibe of the art. This time, we're dressed nice for *each other*.

"Someday, I'll have to come pick *you* up for a date," I tell Shiv, grinning.

"Now, where's the fun in that?" He sweeps me in close.

It's the first time we've touched like this at the beginning of a date instead of waiting until the end for a sweet kiss goodbye or a breathless make-out in a gallery corner.

I wrap my arms around his neck and gaze into his warm, sparkling eyes. "I don't know, you always come to me. I should go to you for once. Equality, feminism, et cetera?"

"Doing nice things for you feels like feminism to me." He smirks and then leans in. We kiss for a moment, and I'm aware we're out on the public street in Jaipur and the sun hasn't even set. I make myself pull away before we're fully making out on the sidewalk. My stomach is liquid, and my cheeks flush with heat.

"What are we doing today?"

Shiv takes my hand in his. "Dinner."

"So you've said! What's with all the secrecy and surprises, Shiv?" I tease.

His eyebrows go up. "I thought you liked surprises."

"Mmm." I bump my shoulder with his. "I'm still curious."

"Ah." Shiv presses a kiss to the top of my head, and I swear, it trickles all the way down to my toes. It's so casual, just as we're walking down the street, our hands in each other's, him bending to kiss me. There's something so intimate about it, the kiss on the top of my head. I don't know how to explain it. Maybe because it's a gesture that's all giving. It's the kind of gesture you do when you care about someone, like, *really* care about them.

Shiv smiles at me, oblivious to how much I'm hyper-analyzing his every touch. "Curious girl."

I bite my lip as the smile grows on my face. "No flowers today?" I ask jokingly.

Shiv rolls his eyes. "Patience, please. I never set up expectations I can't exceed."

After a moment, I realize that we're heading toward the palace. "Shiv," I say, eyeing him. "Are you taking me back to *work*?"

"Do you want it to be a surprise or not?" he asks me teasingly.

Before I can answer, someone calls Shiv's name, and we turn to the speaker. There's a woman, maybe in her early twenties, walking toward us, her short hair windswept around her face, her eyes dark and dramatic. She's tall and limber.

"Hey, Vidya," Shiv says. His hand doesn't leave mine.

"Don't 'hey, Vidya,' me," the woman responds. She strides up to us, and I take a better look at her. She's dressed in overalls and a black shirt, and a septum ring glints from her nose. She's carrying a large tote bag with a rolled-up canvas sticking out of it, and immediately I realize who this is. Vidya is Shiv's older sister.

"You missed the conference this morning," she tells Shiv. "Papa's not happy."

"I told them I wasn't going." Shiv squeezes my hand. "And please say hi. This is Archi. Archi, this is my sister, Vidya."

"Hi," I say. "It's really nice to meet you."

Vidya considers me. "Hi." For a second, her gaze softens, but then it's fiery again as she returns to her brother. "Shiv." Her voice is a warning. "Are you being careful?"

Careful? Does she mean about *us,* the same way Lilyn was giving me advice?

"Yes," Shiv huffs. "This isn't the time, Vidya."

"Yes, it is. Today, of all days?"

He sighs. "Let's talk when I get home. We're headed to dinner."

Vidya's eyes find me again, and I flush under the intensity of her stare. "I've heard a lot about you," she says finally. "You work at Rathore Gallery, right?"

"Yes." I don't know whether I should expand.

"I heard you're doing an exhibit on stolen Jaipur art and palace artifacts."

So Shiv really has talked about me with Vidya. I stand up a little straighter, and now I'm able to string more than a few words together. "I am. I heard you're an artist. I saw the painting you made for Shiv's birthday last year. It was amazing."

Vidya makes a short sound, nearly a laugh. "You should have seen what I did for his birthday *this* year."

"I'd like to," I reply. "Wait. Already?"

Vidya seems surprised, then amused, a mirror image of her brother's face when he smiles at me. "You haven't told her?" she asks Shiv.

I frown, knowing better than to say "Told me what?" right now.

"I'm planning on it. Vidya, you're ruining my surprises."

"We've also been collecting new local art for the gallery exhibit." I try to steer the conversation to something I can contribute to. "We've finalized most things, but there's still time for updates. I'd love to have some of your artwork as part of our showcase."

Vidya exchanges a glance with Shiv, eyebrows up, then comes back to me. Now she smiles for real. It's gentle. Sisterly. "Thank you. Maybe I'll take you up on that."

I nod, pleased. I couldn't guess what kind of impression I'm leaving on Vidya. I can only hope it's positive.

"I'm sorry for being brusque," Vidya says, her voice kind now. "I've been under a lot of pressure lately. You seem lovely. My brother has only said positive things. I tend to be suspicious when I meet anybody."

Shiv laughs at that. "She does. Vidya once ran a complete background check for her best friend on a guy before she met him. He's now an ex."

"It wasn't complete enough," Vidya says wryly. "Or else we would have figured out much earlier that he wasn't worth her time."

"You're a good friend," I tell her.

"The best. Anyway, we'd better go," says Shiv. "Dinner awaits."

Vidya nods. "I'll tell Mummy and Papa you'll be home late." Then, to me, she says, "I hope you have a nice time. Obviously, I want you to be good to my brother, but hopefully he's good to you, too. If he ever does anything to hurt you, I'll kick his ass on your behalf."

A snort escapes me. "Thank you."

As if Shiv isn't standing literally right here, Vidya leans in conspiratorially: "He seems happy. Happier than I've seen him in a while. I hope you both get to know each other in a real way." It doesn't escape me that her words, while a compliment, also have an ominous hint. What does she mean, *in a real way?*

Vidya flicks Shiv upside the head and rolls her eyes. "Go. I'll cover for you."

"I'm sorry," Shiv says when Vidya is out of earshot. "She

can be . . . a little intense." He makes a face. "A lot intense," he amends.

I laugh, but it's uneasy. "Does she not approve of me?"

"No, that's not it at all. She's just . . . She always tells me to be careful with my feelings. Sometimes, she says, I wear my heart on my sleeve."

"I can see that. Why does she need to cover for you with your parents?"

Shiv sighs. "Our parents put a lot of expectations on us. Vidya thinks I have all these duties to our family, and obviously that's true. I missed a family meeting this morning."

"The conference?"

"We're dramatic with our word choices. Runs in the family. I think she wants to make sure I'm serious about the decisions I make, whether I'm skipping family things or dating someone."

"And are you?" I whisper, peering up at him. The street is quiet. A car hasn't passed us in a few minutes. We're near the palace museum, past closing. It's not busy.

"I'm serious about you," Shiv answers, taking my hand and placing it on his heart. "As serious and as steady as my heartbeat."

"I don't know." I smirk, even though electricity is zapping through me. "I think I felt it skip a little."

Shiv rolls his eyes. "Shut up." He grins. "Cheesy girl."

"Look who's talking." I grin back at him. "So. Cheesy girl, impatient girl, curious girl," I list. "Any other words you'd use to describe me?"

Shiv leans in, tipping my chin up so he can kiss me. "Hmm," he says against my lips. "Mine?"

I press up against him, kissing him back. "Let me think on that." Because while what Shiv said about his family makes sense, I can't lie—I'm a little thrown off by meeting Vidya and by the mystery around Shiv in general. I'm suddenly reminded of every time he has evaded questions, unwilling to fully open up. But I've decided to give this thing a real try, and that means trusting him, even if he isn't ready to share everything quite yet. After all, I do want to get to know the real him. And I have time tonight, and the rest of the semester, to do exactly that.

Shiv smiles into our kiss. "Come on. Let's go eat."

Chapter 17

Red Flags

When we arrive at the palace museum gates, my eyebrows furrow.

Shiv reaches into his pockets, retrieving a key card and a set of old-fashioned keys.

We approach a uniformed guard with a thick mustache and beard, and Shiv shows the man the key card. "Salaam," he says.

"Salaam, ji." The guard immediately opens the main gate as if this is completely normal. Do I have access to the palace after hours since I'm an employee, too? I definitely don't have the key ring Shiv pulled out, but maybe that's because I'm only an intern.

Shiv takes me through the gates over to the bronze museum entrance door, which, to my awe, he opens with one of the fancy keys. And then we're able to go through the set of sliding doors with his key card. Just like that, we're inside the museum. Shiv flips a switch, and low lights flicker on—mood lighting.

"How are you doing this?" I narrow my eyes. "And don't say palace perks."

Shiv bites his lip. "But what if it *is* palace perks?"

"Why don't I get these kinds of perks?!" I scan the museum floor, taking in the peace and quiet. "Are we *Night at the Museum*–ing this?"

Shiv's face tells me I'm right.

"No way," I gasp. "How the hell did you pull this off?"

"I've been working for the royal family a lot longer than you. I've cashed in some favors."

"And you're using them all on me?"

He shrugs. "You're worth it."

I shake my head. I don't even want to know how he's pulled these strings. I mean, I do, but also . . . there's a certain magic to this mystery. "Are you going to tell me what the plan is now?"

Shiv holds out his hand to me, and I take it. "The plan is what I told you. First, we're having dinner." He leads me to the side of the museum where the café is located. But when we get inside, Shiv opens a door in the back, and we're in the kitchen. The scent of warm spiced food immediately washes over me, causing my mouth to water.

"I made biryani and lamb." He scratches the back of his neck. "It's ready, but I thought we could make dessert together. Let it chill while we eat?"

This thoughtful boy. My heart sings. "That sounds perfect."

Excitedly, Shiv pulls ingredients from the fridge, one

after another. "You said once that you like kalakand. It's one of my favorite mithais, too. And, it turns out, it's super easy to make."

"For you, maybe. You're a star chef."

Shiv bumps my shoulder. "I'll teach you. And then you'll be a pro in no time, too."

While he lays out the ingredients—whole milk, sugar, ghee, milk powder, cardamom pods, pistachios—I find an instrumental playlist on my phone and hit Play on low volume. "Are we seriously the only ones here?"

"There are guards outside," Shiv says. "They know we're here. But beyond that, yes. Is that okay?"

I'm alone with Shiv. I'm going to be alone with Shiv for the night. "Of course. I just want to text Mohini, so she knows where I am."

Shiv nods, and I fire off a message.

> **Archi:** HOLY SHIT I'M AT THE MUSEUM WITH SHIV.
>
> HE LIKE . . . BOOKED IT FOR OUR DATE? I THINK WE'RE GOING TO SPEND THE NIGHT HERE.

> **Mohini:** Oh MY GOD????
>
> OKAY
>
> HAVE FUN. BE SAFE

I heart the message, then turn back to Shiv. "Show me the ropes."

While indie Hindi music plays, Shiv teaches me the recipe. We heat up the milk on the stove, add lemon juice when it's boiling so it'll curdle, then strain it through a cheesecloth. The whole time, Shiv touches me gently whenever he gets the chance, his fingers grazing my elbow when I'm stirring the milk, his hand on the small of my back as he moves around me to grab ingredients. My stomach flutters. Every. Single. Time.

While the paneer sets, Shiv shows me how to use a mortar and pestle to grind cardamom pods and pistachios into a crumbly powder. Then we add the finished paneer, sugar, milk powder, water, and cardamom back into the pot, stir it until it forms a thick batter, and place it into a lined pan. We garnish with crumbled pistachios, and Shiv lets me lick the spatula before putting the pan into the freezer to chill.

"Good?" he asks, smiling.

I kiss him so he can taste the sugar on my lips. "You tell me."

"Cheeeeesy." Shiv pulls me in by the waist. "Come on."

We leave the café and walk toward the dining area, but Shiv shakes his head, guiding me in the opposite direction, toward the galleries. "But those are—"

Shiv grins. "I know."

When we round the curve, my mouth falls open. In the center of the hexagon-shaped tapestry gallery is a little table with two sets of plates and cutlery, trays above tiny candles keeping the food on top warm. In the middle is a bouquet of flowers in a vase. So that's what he meant when he said he'd exceed expectations every time.

As always, he has. I'm speechless for a full minute.

"Okay, so we weren't *totally* alone," Shiv says, grinning. "I had a friend set this up while we were cooking."

"You are really something." I finally regain my words. My voice comes out thick. It's a callback to one of our early dates. Something amazing.

But Shiv doesn't say that. Instead, he responds, "'Jo bhi hoon, tera hoon yaar.'"

I gasp, startled out of my awe. "Did you just quote Bollywood to me?"

"You set it up perfectly." And I remember that I thought about using the line the first time he said it, too. It just wasn't time, yet.

"Who are you, Karan Johar?" The movie he's quoting is a Bollywood blockbuster by KJo, one of the biggest rom-com directors ever. *Whatever I am, I'm yours.*

"What if I said he's a family friend?"

I snort. "I'd never believe you."

Shiv grins. "I love the classic Bollywood tropes."

"Favorite one?"

"Chasing after the love of your life as she boards a train." His reply is immediate, which makes me think he's thought about this a lot. "Running through a field of mustard flowers."

I giggle. "I love the wedding switch-up."

"Oh, you mean when the main character is getting married to the wrong guy, and the wedding is fully set up, and on the day of, she realizes she's actually in love with the love interest, and they go ahead with the wedding but with him as the replacement groom?"

"That's the one."

Shiv laughs. "That one is so wild. The original groom's whole family is there, and now they have to watch somebody else's wedding?"

"Shhh." I press a finger to my lips. "It's all for the plot. I do love the train one, though, too. *DDLJ* is a classic." *Dilwale Dulhania Le Jayenge* is one of Mamma's favorite movies from when she was a teen. We've seen it together about a million and one times.

"You know," Shiv says, "I've been thinking about your gallery. You said you have everything finalized, right?"

"Basically. Why?"

"Do you have room for maybe one more thing?"

I raise an eyebrow. "Vidya's art?"

"Besides that."

"What are you thinking?" I have no idea where this is going, but I'm intrigued.

Then Shiv blushes, seeming almost shy. "You told me once that you'd put me to work at the museum."

"And this isn't enough?" I gesture to what he's set up for dinner.

He grins. "I guess I wanted to do even more."

"Okay. . . ."

"I've seen palace events that have floral entrances. I was in the garden the other day, and we have a ton of jasmine and marigolds. Would you . . . like a garland over the entrance to your showcase? To make it stand out from the other exhibits?"

I nearly melt right then and there. "Shiv, how am I ever going to get you back for all your kind gestures?"

He smirks. "I don't think that's the kind of thing you have to get someone *back* for."

"You don't have to do all this for me. Really."

"I know," he says. "I do it because I want to."

"Okay." Honestly, I might cry. "But you'll get a little placard for your art, too. The garland will be part of the display. I'm not letting you do this without any credit."

Shiv nods. "Deal."

My stomach rumbles then, and Shiv laughs. "Oh yeah," he says. "Dinner." He lifts the covers on the trays in front of us, and the steam rises from the biryani and the rack of lamb topped with pomegranate seeds. It's a sight to behold, like something I'd expect at a Michelin-starred restaurant, not that I've ever been to one. But who needs to when Shiv's cooking for you?

When I take my first bite, I close my eyes and sigh happily. "I shouldn't get used to this. VBIS dorm food is going to *suuuck* in comparison."

Shiv's blushing. I can tell he's proud that I like his food. His cooking means something to him. As we eat, I think about how perfect this date is. How perfect Shiv has been. And I remember Lilyn saying perfection doesn't exist. And I need to find out his red flags.

"So," I say, "what was the family event you missed this morning?"

Shiv swallows his bite of rice. His eyebrows furrow. "It was just a thing." He waves a hand. "My parents planned it."

I pause, frowning. Another nonanswer. I know Shiv can be guarded; I've seen it in the way he took a bit of time to open up about getting anxious in crowds. I don't want to push him to say more than he's ready to, but I also want to get to know him. And his sister's words have made me nervous. I don't want Shiv to be so guarded that I never see the real him.

"What did your sister do for your birthday this year? And when—"

"Another painting. But it was a bit more complicated this time."

This answer is short. Not a lot of information.

Taking a deep breath, I try again. "You aren't super close to your parents, right?"

"Not nearly as close as I am to my sister. But we have a good relationship. They don't talk a lot about themselves, at least not their personal lives. I don't know much about them as people, you know? I know them as parents."

I frown, thinking of how Mamma and Baba talk to me like a friend. I love hearing their stories, especially about their lives before I was born. It makes me a little sad to know that Shiv and Vidya's parents keep their kids at a distance.

It's maybe the first real thing Shiv has said since I started my line of questioning. Is it a red flag that he keeps so much to himself? Is it a red flag that his sister essentially warned me about getting to know the *real* him? Or is he simply as nervous about being vulnerable as I am? Because there's something I haven't told him yet, either. And even though I like this boy, I don't know if I'm ready to. So maybe if I want to know Shiv, want him to trust me, maybe I have to open myself up more, too.

"Your sister . . ." I'm not sure how to bridge the next topic. "She said . . ." I pause. "Have you dated a lot before?"

A smile crosses Shiv's face. "What's a lot?"

I blush. "I don't know."

"I have dated," he says. "Here and there. One relationship, over a year ago. And some smaller situationships that never went anywhere."

"Ah." I wonder if he's been burned before, too. Maybe he has his own Nick, a relationship that made it difficult for him to open his heart again.

"You?"

I take a sip of my water. "Only one person." I don't know how much context to give, what to tell him. I know that if I want to hear more from him, I have to give something myself, too. But I don't know if now is the time—if I want to turn this moment into something more serious, something heavier. I'm starting to realize maybe that's why Shiv was being minimal in his responses, too.

Maybe it's not a red flag that Shiv is guarded. Maybe this is simply a hurdle that's natural in any relationship, something we'll both figure out as time passes and we get to know each other better. Slow and steady. We're building toward something. The rest will come when it comes. So I change the subject. I ask how Champ is doing, and we finish our dinner. We spend so much of it talking, telling each other about our childhoods, our favorite pop culture moments, embarrassing stories. Shiv doesn't say more about his parents, but he tells me about the games his sister used to make up for the two of them when they were younger, scavenger hunts she'd plan around their home. He tells me about the subjects he struggled with in school (geometry, geography), and we joke about "the geos."

I tell him more about home in D.C. I share stories

about Whitney and Lilyn, times we've snuck out and come home through our windows after a night of driving aimlessly around the D.C. area, getting fast food from drive-throughs and gossiping for hours. I tell him about my first homecoming dance and tripping in my heels, leaving out the part where Nick asked me out with a swarm of balloons filling my bedroom after my parents let him in to set up while I was at Lilyn's. I tell him about my first time getting drunk, in Whitney's living room when her parents were out of town and we drank beers until we were tipsy. How they tasted disgusting, and I thought I'd never drink alcohol again.

The conversation flows so naturally, I don't even know how long we're there. I know it's gotten late, but that's okay, because we'll be together until tomorrow. And the time between now and then seems infinite.

Back in the kitchen, when we're done eating, Shiv grabs the chilled kalakand out of the freezer, and we cut it into squares. "So," he starts, "I promised you I'd tell you when it was my birthday."

I narrow my eyes. "Yeah. You did. And yet you dodged the question when I asked you about your sister's gift."

Shiv reddens. "Well. It's today."

I pull out my phone immediately. "Shiv! It's eleven-fifty-six p.m. What is the *matter* with you?"

He grins. "I told you I don't like to make a big deal out of my birthday, but I promised I'd let you know, and I don't like breaking promises."

"So you wait until your birthday is basically over?" I cross my arms over my chest.

Shiv shrugs. "I'm a humble guy. What can I say?"

"You can say what we can do to celebrate in these last four minutes! You asked me to dinner tonight to celebrate my exhibit, but we should have been celebrating you!"

Shiv shakes his head and takes my hands in his. "This is exactly how I wanted to spend my birthday."

"Was . . . was the family thing this morning for your *birthday*?" I demand. "Did you skip hanging with your family to come hang out with me?"

He sweeps my hair off my shoulder. "No, no. I mean. It was related to my birthday. But we're having a proper party later this week. My parents insisted, even though they know I don't like parties. You know me."

I check my phone again. Three minutes. "Shit." I let go of him and run around the kitchen, opening cabinets and drawers.

Shiv watches me in confusion. "What are you doing?"

"They've got to be here somewhere. Come on, come on." Even in a museum kitchen . . . and then I find them. A half-open box of mini candles. They're worn, and some appear used. Still, they'll work, and incredibly, there's a lighter beside them. I bet the staff have kept them on hand for each other's birthdays. I thank the universe, then rush back to Shiv and the kalakand.

"Here." I stick a candle in the cake pan, light it, then hold up the kalakand to Shiv. "One minute."

Shiv grins. "You really are something, you know."

I don't say the Bollywood line back. "Yeah, yeah, I'm annoyed! Resourceful, too. And, lucky for you, also forgiving.

Next time, I want to know the important dates weeks in advance." I push the cake pan in Shiv's face. "Now make a wish."

Shiv looks me right in the eyes as he blows out the candle. "Wish granted," he says quietly.

I pick out a piece of kalakand and hold it to his lips, and he takes a bite. Then I pop the other half of the mithai in my mouth. "You're ridiculous."

"Yeah, but you like it."

"I like *you*," I tell him. "Despite how much you vex me."

"Vex you?" He grins.

"I said what I said."

Shiv sets the dessert down. "Okay," he says. "I'll tell you these things in advance from this moment on. Okay?"

I nod.

"Good, because you can't be mad at me on my birthday."

"Oh, so now you want to cash in your birthday?" I hold my phone up to him. "Too bad it's past midnight."

Shiv takes my hand again and gestures around us with his other. "This is me cashing in for my birthday."

Oh. His birthday, and yet he picked . . . a gift for me. I throw my hands around his neck and press my cheek to his chest. "Happy belated," I say, his heartbeat echoing in my ear.

His arms encircle me. When I pull away, I keep my arms around him. "What did you wish for?"

"For this," he says simply. "For us to have a perfect night."

I smile. "If you could wish for something else, what

would you ask for?" I think I know his answer, and I think I'm ready for it. Ready for him to ask.

He pauses, bites his bottom lip. I want to kiss it. "Archi," he says. "Would you be my girlfriend?"

My heart swells, my answer coming out before the angel and devil on my shoulders have a chance to say a single word. "Yes. I will."

When we kiss, I remember what I told Lilyn. I'm going to do whatever I think will make me happy. And maybe I don't need to know the answers to every single one of my questions yet. Maybe I don't need to know how this will end to figure out whether I should give it the chance to start. I only know that saying yes right now is making me happy. And that's what matters most.

After we tidy the kitchen, Shiv takes me to one of the smaller galleries, where he's laid out cushions, comforters, and piles of blankets all over the floor, like we're having a sleepover. Because . . . we are. Shiv hands me a big sweatshirt—one of his, I presume—and when he turns around, I change into it like pj's, and he changes, too. There's an empty wall in front of us, where the museum usually projects informational videos about the history of Jaipur, but Shiv fiddles with a remote, and he turns on a Bollywood movie I've seen a million times—a classic from when I was a kid.

He flops down on the bedding and reaches out for me to join him. When I do, his arm goes around my waist as if it belongs there, and I settle into his side. "Do you think the artwork is going to come alive tonight?" I whisper to him.

"*Night at the Museum* style?"

I nod.

"If so, we'll have a great story to tell tomorrow."

Luckily, I already do. I lean into him, and we kiss and kiss, and then, as they always do at the beginning of Bollywood movies, the credits start to roll.

Chapter 18

Breaking News

In the morning, Shiv walks me back to VBIS.

I guess this is what people call a "walk of shame," but I don't feel ashamed. I feel giddy, warm, and bubbly—but also tired. Shiv and I stayed up late chatting and watching movies, and we had to wake up early to ensure that we left before the museum opened.

Even so, this date has been perfect. Shiv holds my hand as he takes me back to campus, sunglasses and a hat shielding him from the morning sun. I'm wearing sunglasses, too, to be fair. We pause outside my dorm building, and I glance up at Shiv. "Thank you."

"For what?"

"For this." I gesture at the space between us, trying to prompt my sleep-deprived brain to come up with words. "For yesterday, for everything."

Before Shiv can reply, I press up on my tiptoes and kiss

him. His arms wrap around my lower back, and he kisses me, too, but the kiss is brief. Sweet. I hear a click as we separate, and when I glance to the side, there's someone with a big camera across the street. The lens is pointed directly at us.

I blush. Oh no. I don't want to be on one of those Instagram pages. "Humans in Jaipur" or something. *A young couple kisses goodbye at the International School.* Despite my love for museums, *I* am not a specimen.

Shiv follows my gaze, and his jaw tightens. He looks as if he's about to say something.

But a yawn escapes me. "Sorry about that," I say. "I guess it's time for a nap. I have a long shift at the museum later this afternoon. I'm giving tours today."

For a moment, his eyes seem conflicted, but after a slow, sleepy blink, I see his expression is soft once again. I must be even more exhausted than I thought if I'm seeing things.

Shiv clears his throat, drawing my attention back to him. "Get some rest," he says, giving me a smile.

When I wake up from my nap, Mohini is standing over my bed, staring at me.

"I just got back from class!" she says, the moment my eyes flutter open. "Thank goodness you're awake. I want to hear all the details."

So I tell her, from start to finish, and she oohs and aahs in the right places, nodding thoughtfully when I tell her about the things Shiv seems to be more guarded about, squealing excitedly when I announce that Shiv and I are now official.

"Archi! Way to bury the lede! You should have started with *that*."

I giggle. "I wanted to build up to it!"

"Wow. He really is like a Bollywood guy, huh?"

"I can't believe it's real most days," I admit. I hop out of bed, stretch my arms over my head, and grab Whitney's photo album from my desk. "Here, come check out some of the Polaroids from our last few dates. I still have to add some of them into the album. Want to help?"

"I need a semester romance," Mohini says as she helps me glue Polaroids onto the album pages.

"What happened to Chandana?" I frown. "I thought you two were going out."

"Going out as in going *outside*, yeah. She doesn't want anything romantic. She got out of a relationship a while ago, and her parents don't know she's into girls. She's figuring stuff out, and it doesn't seem like the right time." Mohini sighs. "We're still friends, obviously. But it isn't going to be more than that, at least for the time being."

"Damn. That's a bummer, Mohini." I reach out and give her a hug.

"It's hard finding someone to have a crush on," she says quietly. "And it's hard to know if my crushes are into girls, because people aren't as open about it here as they are in America. And even if they are, they might not be ready for a relationship, because of their parents or what they think other people around them might say."

"I'm sorry." I squeeze her hard. "I wish things were different for you."

She sighs. "It is what it is. It's one of the reasons I care so much about changing things. The world should be a better place to live in."

I nod. "It will be, because of you."

"And you." She sniffs, then holds out a hand. "Anyway. Let's get back to scrapbooking?"

"Whatever you want." I smile and give her a few more Polaroids to help me stick in the book. We work in silence for a couple minutes, and then Mohini gasps.

"What?" I turn to her.

She holds out a Polaroid. "This."

"Yeah, isn't it beautiful?" It's KAVI's debut painting from the Gharana Art Studio. "It was so incredible to see it in person."

"No," Mohini says. "I mean, yes, it's beautiful, but that's not what I'm talking about." She points to the corner, where I finally got a glimpse of Shiv's face in one of my photos. "This is . . . ?"

I laugh. "Yeah. That's Shiv. I never get him in pics, but I managed to take that one without his noticing. I think he was mesmerized by the painting, too."

But Mohini's face has gone pale. "*This* is Shiv?"

"Yeah . . ." I frown at her. "Are you okay? What's—?"

She jumps up and grabs her laptop, bringing it back to the floor to open a Google search. "There's no way," she mutters to herself. "I guess I didn't see him well when he showed up as I was taking a shower, so I wouldn't have known. I didn't have my contacts in. And the whole privacy-policy thing—there aren't a lot of photos of him around, or at least, there weren't. Until his eighteenth birthday, so now he's *all* over the news." She prattles on, talking mostly to herself. "But then again . . . the palace, the high-budget dates on a gardener's salary, the favors from the royal family—"

"Mohini," I say. There's a pit in my stomach. "What are you going on about?"

"It was Shiv's birthday yesterday?" she confirms.

"Yeah, I was so mad he didn't tell me till the last minute."

Mohini types furiously on her laptop, then turns the screen to face me. "There's a *lot* he hasn't told you, Archi."

There, on Mohini's laptop screen, is a blown-up photo of Shiv. Though it's not even just a photo—it's a portrait, a painting, like the portraits of members of the Rathore family in the MSMS II Museum. The webpage is of a news article from yesterday by the *Times of Jaipur,* and my eyes lock onto the headline:

RAJKUMAR JAIDEV SHIVAM RATHORE TURNS 18; ROYAL FAMILY INTRODUCES SON TO PUBLIC NOW THAT HE IS OF AGE

The subhead states: Prince skipped morning press conference but will be at palace party later this week. It takes me a minute to process what Mohini is suggesting. Shiv is a prince? Like, *the* prince? Of Jaipur? A buzz goes through my stomach. I've been hanging out with a royal. Without meaning to, I get a rush like I've met someone famous.

Is this not a classic fanfic fantasy—for the regular-schmegular girl to end up with a celeb? Like *The Princess Diaries*, except I'm not the secret heir to the throne . . . he is. But that's all fantasy. This is real life.

"No. That can't be. This is a mistake."

"The prince turned eighteen yesterday. How old did Shiv turn?"

"His name is Shiv Kandari," I say. "He told me."

"The painting looks a lot like this Polaroid," says Mohini. "And the prince's middle name is Shivam. Like . . . Shiv."

I shake my head vehemently. "That has to be a coincidence." But I lean in to examine the painting again. "He's a gardener. No, no, no way. That—" My brain is spinning. Even though I'm seated, I feel as if I'm losing my center of gravity. "No."

Mohini turns the laptop back to her and types away again before showing me another article. It's dated a few years ago, about the king and queen's wedding anniversary. "Kandari," Mohini whispers quietly. "It's the queen's maiden name. He must go by that, too."

I hold on to the side of the bed to steady myself.

"Archi," Mohini says quietly. She's trying to gently break the news I'm clearly not ready for.

But everything is coming together now.

Shiv's reluctance to talk about his parents. The family "conference" he missed yesterday morning. His sister warning me about knowing the *real* him. His discomfort in crowds, and with photos. How secluded our dates were. His constant proximity to the palace. The keys and access card he has. The visit to a private restaurant owned by the royal family. The reason he was able to schedule two dates, without guards, on palace grounds. The way he was in the first-class car on the train when we first met, the way he was wearing a suit. A pocket square. The fact that his parents tried to get him into polo when he was a kid, and how embarrassed he got when I pressed him on it. The palace flag flying high when Shiv was working in the gardens.

The photo the stranger apparently took of us kissing by the dorm doors.

No. It can't— *He* can't— He couldn't have been lying to me about something this big. I told him I wanted to get to know him. I told him I wanted him to tell me real things. He said, last night, after he made his birthday wish, that he'd tell me important things in advance.

But that wasn't the truth. Shiv lied.

For a second, I let myself imagine what it would have been like if Shiv had told the truth. If he'd told me who he really was. Would we have lived out a royal love story? Would we have gone to balls and dressed up and met dignitaries from other countries? Could we have used that royal power he spoke of to do something good for the wider Jaipur community? Not only donated meals but maybe created more job opportunities for people who needed them, projects to clean up the city and make it more accessible, even a *real* initiative to get back stolen artifacts with the power of the crown?

Maybe there was a world in which we could have had all that, but in that world, I wouldn't have been caught off guard. I would have known Shiv for who he really is.

It's wild because in another life, this could be the coolest, most exciting news. Who wouldn't want to date a literal prince? But I know the cost of ignoring lies to keep a relationship going. And I know the hurt of trusting someone and finding out they were keeping something from you the whole time.

What was Shiv thinking in hiding his identity? Was this some sort of joke to him? Messing around with the new girl who didn't know anything about Jaipur, didn't know anything about the royal family, wouldn't suspect him of lying? Using me while I was here? The naïve American transplant.

And that's the truth underneath this mess, isn't it? I should have known better. I've spent the whole semester so far thinking I was finally fitting in as a local, but I didn't even do research on the family at the center of the city. I should have looked them up, should have tried to dig beyond the royal privacy policy. I should have asked him more, pressed instead of letting him dodge questions. But I didn't.

I think of Shiv's kind, warm eyes, his gentle voice with his soft, rounded words, which I can now place as an upper-class Indian accent, and I feel sick. His joke about Bollywood director Karan Johar being a family friend. Was he baiting me? Trying to see how far I'd let him go with his tricks?

I remember learning about the royal family's insistence on maintaining their children's privacy until the prince turned eighteen. Is that why he didn't want to tell me about his birthday? He knew the truth would come out yesterday. What, did he hope I wouldn't be paying attention? And the truth is, I probably wouldn't have been.

Mohini is way more clued-in to current events. I'm too focused on examining the past, I guess.

My heart is warring with my mind. Shiv lied to me: this much is clear. The devil is back on my shoulder, telling me to be angry, so angry. To feel betrayed. And I do. I feel taken advantage of. But the angel is there, too, reminding me of the careful way Shiv's fingers felt on my chin when he tipped my face up to kiss me. The flowers he brought me on every date. His excitement when I told him about my Capstone project's progress. It all seemed so genuine. *He* seemed so genuine. Sincere. Like he really, truly cared about me. But how can you claim to care about someone and then lie to them about something so important?

This whole time, I've been wanting to get to know Shiv better. And I never even knew his real name.

I bury my face in my hands. "Oh my god, oh my god, oh my god."

"Archi, I—" Mohini says. "He really never said anything?"

"No," I groan, and I can't tell if I'm going to burst into tears or throw up all over our rug or both. In the end, my body does nothing, succumbing to the emptiness of shock. My fingers are shaking. "I can't believe this."

"This . . ." Mohini runs her fingers through her hair. "This is certifiably bonkers."

"I'm . . ." I trail off. "He's . . ." I don't even know what to say. "Shiv? My Shiv? How . . ." I can't breathe. My heartbeat is a sharp staccato. "I said yes to being his *girlfriend.* This—" I switch tabs on Mohini's laptop so we're back on the *Times of Jaipur* page that shows the royal portrait of the prince.

The royal portrait of Shiv.

"It's him," I say simply. "How is this real?"

Mohini eyes me with concern and then says the words I've been unable to utter. "Archi. I think you've been dating the prince of Jaipur."

Chapter 19

Told You So

I sleep fitfully, my dreams a barrage of warped images of Shiv in a crown.

I called in sick at the gallery yesterday, and Mohini ultimately put me to bed last night with a mug of tea and a "Sleep on it. Don't do anything just yet" warning. So I turned off my phone and tried to go to sleep.

Now, as the sun streams in through our curtains, I sit up in bed and reach for my phone. Mohini is still asleep, eye mask on and earplugs in. When I power my phone on, the notifications start barreling in, one after the other after the other. I have my usual texts from Whitney and Lilyn, who remain peacefully oblivious to the news I received. But my WhatsApp is overflowing with new texts, from Mamma and Baba, from Sharmila Aunty, from relatives I only speak to on birthdays.

And I have two missed calls from Shiv, along with a simple text:

I open my group chat with Mamma and Baba next. They've forwarded me a message from a family friend in Rajasthan. It's short and sweet.

Attached to the text are a few photos, and I click on them so they'll download. A second later, the images appear on my screen. The first is a photo outside VBIS of me and Shiv, from yesterday morning. I recognize my outfit, my arms around Shiv's neck, our faces together. The next photo is of us separated, me smiling at Shiv, him smiling at me. The third, likely taken a moment later: I'm facing the camera, frowning. This must have been when I heard the click of the shutter.

The last image is a screenshot of a tabloid headline.

NEWLY IN-PUBLIC RAJKUMAR JAIDEV "SHIV" RATHORE CAUGHT WITH FLING, IDENTIFIED AS VBIS STUDENT, AMERICAN ARCHANA DHAWAN

Oh my *god.*

The photographer. He must have asked around at VBIS to see if any classmates could identify me. And I thought it was someone taking note of our PDA. I didn't want to be a specimen then, as an example of anonymous PDA, but this is more than that. Now I'm a *headline,* not for anything important or cool I've done but because I'm with a *boy.*

Before I can begin to process, a new text notification pops up, this time from someone I haven't spoken to in months.

> **Nick:** Hey. I've been meaning to reach out, and then I saw you go viral. Just have to ask—is it true? Are you really dating a prince? You moved on fast.

My stomach clenches. Has *everyone* seen the news? Nick reappearing was nowhere on my study-abroad bingo card. Then again, neither was finding out that Shiv is a prince. Nick's text only fuels my anger, and I stare at it with fire in my eyes, wondering whether I should respond, and what I'd even say.

Option 1: *SCREW YOU!*

Option 2: *Who are YOU to talk about moving on fast?*

I pick Option 3. I click the button next to his contact, scroll down, and press Block. And then I delete his message from my phone and my life. Nick is gone. Deleted. Irrelevant. All things he should have been a long, long time ago. He was never worth my time, and this thing with Shiv is at least a good reminder of that.

I return to the headline about me, my mind a swarm of buzzing, needling bees. All the information is coming in too fast, and somehow not quickly enough. I do a quick Google search and find the whole article, as well as a few others with similar headlines. When I scroll through, I gasp at the line after my name.

"The *Star* reached out to the palace for comment. A

representative for the prince only said, 'We do not know of any romantic relationship the prince is involved in. He unequivocally denies any and all dating rumors. The image circulating is not of the prince. The young lady is unknown to the royal family.'"

My stomach knots. "A representative for the prince." That means Shiv knows about the article and denied any dating rumors. He denied me.

After all, I am a nobody. I am an unknown to the royal family. I am just Archi Dhawan, a regular girl from Washington, D.C. And Shiv is a liar.

I don't know why the palace statement hurts the most. That he has publicly scrubbed me right out of his life, distancing his image from mine. As if all the moments that were so important to me, the moments that made my semester special, meant nothing to him.

The angel appears on my shoulder.

Don't, I tell her.

I told you so, she says anyway. *You were supposed to focus on yourself this semester for* exactly *this reason.*

I close my eyes and press my fingers to my temples. She's right. I was supposed to be careful to keep myself from getting hurt. The moment I gave in to my emotions instead of logic, things unraveled.

The angel gives me a sympathetic pat. *You need to tell him how you feel. Communication is key.*

The devil scowls. *Maybe so, but he didn't communicate with* you. *End things. Hurt him the way he hurt you. You deserve better.*

I scroll through my phone app and call Shiv back,

holding the phone close to my ear and cupping my hand around my mouth so that when I talk, it won't be loud enough to wake Mohini. Shiv picks up right away.

"Archi," he says breathlessly. "I—"

I cut him off. "We need to talk. Central Park, in an hour." I pick a public place in the city. "They're doing landscaping, so the walkways are blocked. Nobody else will be there. Sneak past the boundaries. I'll meet you by the fountain."

"Archi." Shiv's voice is a plea.

I grit my teeth. "I'll see you there."

After I hang up, I throw on a light jacket and pull my hair back. I tie a silk scarf around my head, covering much of my face, grab sunglasses to complete the disguise, and text a reply to Mamma and Baba before putting my phone in my purse.

> **Archi:** Not what you think. I'll tell you more later.

I ignore the messages from Sharmila Aunty and my other relatives and turn off my notifications. Then I write a note on a Post-it and leave it on Mohini's nightstand, letting her know I'm heading out to see "Shiv" but that I'll be back in an hour and that I'm going to be okay.

With that, I head out. In the hallway, I see Anjit, the RA. His mouth opens to say something, but suddenly I get nervous he's read the post about Shiv, too, and he's going to talk to me about it, so I turn and walk to the exit in the opposite direction.

My chest tight, I dodge people the rest of the way out of campus, knotting my scarf under my chin. When I'm out in the streets, walking to Central Park, I suck in fresh air in large gulps, my lungs expanding. I keep walking. It's extremely unlikely anyone will recognize me. I was only in one tabloid, and the Jaipur general public has no idea who I am. On these busy streets, I thankfully fade into the background.

On the walk, I brainstorm what I'm going to say. The questions I'm going to ask. I think about how I plan on staying calm and cool and mature, despite it all. How I intend to tell Shiv that I can't be with someone I can't trust. How I am not going to let myself cry.

I haven't yet. Cried, I mean. Mohini mentioned the stages of grief last night. It was obvious I started out with denial. I couldn't believe the news—it didn't make *sense*. Now I know I'm in the anger stage. My skin is hot, my heartbeat fast. I walk with purpose down the street, and when I get to the enclosed park, I check both ways before ducking under the fencing. We're clearly not supposed to be here, but there's not a chance in hell I'm going to meet Shiv in public again. And besides, if we get in trouble, his father—the *king*—should be able to get us out of it.

Scowling, I make my way through the grassy area toward the fountain, which I've sat at with Mohini before. I like Central Park; it's a generally calm spot in Jaipur. But right now, I'm bringing my anger here, disrupting the otherwise serene space. When I make it to the fountain, Shiv is there already, wearing a hat. He's seated at the edge of the fountain, but he stands as soon as he sees me.

"Hey," he says, his eyes running over me. There's a crease between his brows.

"Hello, *Prince Jaidev.*" I bite out the title.

Shiv's face falls, and he chews on his bottom lip. "I'm guessing you saw the photo. I was hoping you hadn't."

"No shit, I saw the photo. My whole family did," I snap, then try to collect myself. "But it's more than that. You *lied* to me. You're . . . you're not a gardener. You're the son of the royal family!"

"No," Shiv insists. "I'm so sorry it came out this way. I didn't mean for any of this to happen. But I never lied to you. I just didn't bring it up."

"Oh, a lie of omission? You should be a lawyer, Shiv, not a prince."

"I didn't *choose* to be a prince," he counters. "And I didn't lie to you. I couldn't tell you the whole truth, even if I'd wanted to, not really."

"What? Why?"

"Because I would have had to get you to sign a bunch of legal documents and a nondisclosure agreement, and it would have gotten so formal right away, and we probably wouldn't have hung out at all."

"Yeah, because maybe I wouldn't have wanted to once I knew who you really were!"

Shiv appears pained. "It's been difficult meeting people outside my family's circles," he says. "You were one of the first people I've met in years who didn't know of me, didn't know who my parents were. I wanted to keep it that way."

I'm in no mood to listen to him. "You manipulated me so you could keep your little illusion."

"No. I was protecting myself. And my family. My dating life has always been complicated, especially because sometimes people want to date me because they've dreamed of being a princess. I don't get a normal life. These are the concessions I have to make. I have to be more private." Shiv runs a hand through his hair. "But I never lied to you. Never. I promise."

I scoff. "You and your false promises. You told me you'd share the important things in advance. On your birthday. But you didn't tell me any of this."

"I was going to! I was going to tell you the next time we saw each other. I wanted to enjoy that day, though. I always knew that once I turned eighteen, my life would turn upside down. The little privacy I had before—the chance that at least most people in public wouldn't immediately know who I was—would disappear. I wanted to put that off while we were together. I didn't think the news would get so much attention that quickly, especially since I didn't even go to the press conference. I hadn't realized how much people might still care about a mostly defunct royal family. I thought we still had time before things would blow up."

"You saw the photographer that morning."

"I reached out to the family publicist right away. I thought we could get it pulled before it went online. But we were too late."

Family publicist. God. Does he not realize how utterly ridiculous he sounds?

Shiv reads the expression on my face. "I should have told you sooner."

"You think?" I shout. "The whole world found out yesterday. And I had to find out from my roommate." I swallow back a lump in my throat, trying to wrap my mind around how fast things have changed between us. "You knew this was coming—you knew your life would change at eighteen. You had time to prepare for things to go public. But you still couldn't take the time to let me know. Beyond that, you denied it—me—to the press."

"Because..." Shiv's voice wavers. "I technically shouldn't have been dating you in the first place. My parents would have forbidden it. My sister knew, and I was able to pull some strings at the museum and garden without my parents being aware, but if they knew, which they do now, the lawyers would get involved, and the publicist would get involved, and everything would change. That's what happened with this article, too. I didn't talk to the press. I didn't go to the press conference my parents set up for me. I didn't mention the photos of us. Someone else from our staff must have spoken to the tabloid. I didn't have say over that."

"But you had a say over this. Over *us*. Why did you date me at all? You chose to do this. You chose to risk our relationship. You put me through something I didn't even get to agree to! I didn't want to be in the limelight like this—as *gossip*." Yes, there were times I imagined being in the news, headlining papers . . . but those dreams were of notoriety for my work, for curating art and showcasing history. Not as the random American making out with the prince of Jaipur. Not as someone reduced to nothing after being labeled as an unknown by Shiv and his family.

"I told you. I wasn't planning on dating anyone. You caught me by surprise, and I couldn't help feeling connected to you. I wanted some normalcy. I wanted you to know me as Shiv."

"But I don't really know you at all." Even though my voice breaks, I will myself not to cry. I won't cry. I can't.

"That's not fair," Shiv says. "You know more about me than most people. You know me beyond my title."

I clench my jaw and meet his eyes.

"Archi," he pleads, pausing to take a shaky breath before continuing. "I'm sorry. I should have handled this differently. I didn't know what to do, but I clearly handled it wrong. Our lives are polar opposites. It would have put me at a lot of risk to tell you who I was. If you tried to take advantage of it, or if you told other people . . ."

Something about his words—the way it sounds like he's now turning this on me, as if I've done something wrong, even hypothetically—rids me of the semblance of self-control I've been working on.

"If *I* took advantage of it!" I gasp out. "You're right, Shiv. We are not the same. You have a publicist and lawyers to handle bad press for you. You have the backing of the royal family. The palace. I'm here as a student, without my family, without my home. I don't have the resources you do, but my face and my name are out in that tabloid, too. What about putting me at risk? I'm not a public figure, but you've made me one, in the most embarrassing way. Doesn't that matter, too?"

"Of course it does," Shiv stutters. "That's not what— Please. Let me explain."

"Save it," I say. "I trusted you. I agreed to be your *girlfriend*. But I didn't even know who you were. I got out of a relationship a year ago because my ex lied to me. He made me change my plans for him, but he lied to me about *his* plans. He'd keep from me where he was spending most of his time, and finally, I found out from one of his *friends* that he was hooking up with a college freshman from a nearby university. He had the same excuse as you when I confronted him. He'd never lied to me. He just hadn't been fully honest." This is the real reason London never happened. Nick wanted to focus on his future, on his college applications. That included hooking up with the girl who was advising him about apps. It meant leaving me behind.

"Archi." Shiv's voice is filled with regret.

I push on anyway. I don't want Shiv's pity. "He betrayed me. And so did you. You're all the same, all of you guys. You use girls, and you manipulate us, and you take advantage. You were afraid of my taking advantage of Your *Royal Highness*"—I spit the words out—"but you took advantage of my ignorance. You knew that I didn't know you, and so you decided I was a safe target to pass the time."

"No." Shiv shakes his head, lifting his hand to reach out to me before thinking better of it and letting his arm hang limply at his side once again. "That's not it at all. I liked you because you were special. You stood out to me. And I wanted you to like me for *me,* too, not for my title. I was scared. I didn't want it to affect our relationship."

I grit my teeth. "Well, it has. Because now we don't have one."

Shiv flinches as if I've hit him.

"I thought you were such a good guy," I whisper, and now the tears do fall, streaming down my cheeks. "I really, really did. But you only care about yourself."

"No," Shiv says. Tries.

I shove the article on my phone screen in his face. "Yes. Because after all, I am unknown to the royal family."

I don't know for sure, but it looks like there might be tears in Shiv's eyes, too. "I didn't say that. I promise."

"You're not at fault for anything, huh, Shiv? Oh, sorry, I mean Jaidev." I scrunch up my face. "You want me to believe you're a prince without any power."

I'm hotheaded now, spiraling, crying, and spewing my anger over being so gullible again. "You hid the truth from me, you let my private life become public, and then you denied to the world that you knew me. You can keep your royal privacy, Shiv. I'll deal with the fallout on my own."

"I'm so sorry, Archi," Shiv tries again.

"Too little, too late," I say with some finality as my heart splinters. "I deserve someone who will always choose me." And that's what it is, isn't it? I chose Nick over the first boy who asked me to the dance. I chose Shiv over my plans for a boy-free semester. But neither of them chose me. Nick chose the other girl. And Shiv chose his secrets. "I deserve someone who will be honest—fully honest, not technically. I deserve someone I can know completely. Someone I can trust. And someone who will pick me in front of everyone else."

"I would." Shiv sounds so, so sincere.

I shake my head. "You had the chance to and didn't. Please don't contact me again. As far as I'm concerned, the royal family is unknown to me, too."

Chapter 20

I'm Archi Dhawan

To Shiv's credit, he doesn't contact me.

In that sense, he keeps his word. Two days go by. I block his contact, then delete his number. I cry myself to sleep. I skip classes. I tell Kiran-ji that I'm still sick and can't come in to do my shift, even though I know preparations for my Capstone exhibit are ramping up and Kiran-ji probably knows the real reason behind my excuse anyway.

The truth is that every single thing I worried would happen if I broke my boy-free semester rule has come to pass. I'm letting a boy distract me from school and my Capstone project. I'm wasting my time in Jaipur thinking about some boy when I could be learning about myself, my family, and my culture. I'm falling apart again. And somehow it hurts even more the second time around.

But I guess I did learn one thing about myself through all this: I was right to be rigid. It never hurt me the way this unplanned relationship has.

I call Whitney and Lilyn and tell them that the world's shortest relationship is over: not even forty-eight hours long. As I cry, feeling ridiculous, Lilyn says exactly what I want to hear.

"Screw him!" she yells. "Guys suck. Lying princes, especially." She makes a face. "I can't believe he said you were 'unknown to the family.'"

"That's kind of the worst part. Like, adding insult to injury. Rubbing salt in the wound. Or whatever they say."

Lilyn nods. "But at least now you can say that you've *dumped* a prince. That's pretty iconic."

"Yeah," says Whitney. "You turned down a *prince*. Who gets to say they've done that?"

My mouth twitches. "I guess that's a win."

"Did he sound sorry?" Whitney asks.

"He apologized. But was still trying to justify the fact that he hadn't told me. He only seemed sorry he didn't tell me sooner, like he was sorry the news broke before he could get to me. But he didn't seem sorry for not telling me right off the bat." I sigh. "I feel silly. I thought he was so *good*. That's the thing, you know? I thought he was this great guy, perfect. Always the gentleman. Someone who always brought me flowers. Someone who critiqued the royal family's politics. But it turns out he's one of them. He's not the guy I thought he was at all. He's someone totally different."

"I told you to look for red flags," Lilyn says a little sadly. "Sounds like you found them."

"Nobody's perfect," says Whitney. "You thought he was. Now you're realizing he's not. Imperfection is okay if the person works to fix things, though, right?"

"The world saw him kiss you, and then he told everyone he has no idea who you are," Lilyn counters. "I'd say that's pretty hard to fix."

Whitney raises an eyebrow. "You've got a point. So that's two strikes. He kept something huge from you, and he burned you in public."

"Yeah. I guess I just have to keep my head low. People keep giving me weird looks in the halls and on campus. I feel like I'm the butt of an inside joke everyone else knows. I don't even want to go to class. I skipped *work*. And you know how much I love my internship."

"Screw him," Lilyn says again. "This is *your* semester. Your time abroad. You can't let him ruin that for you. You're Archi Dhawan."

I pout.

"Say it with me," Lilyn says. "I'm Archi Dhawan."

"I'm Archi Dhawan," I echo quietly.

"Louder!" Whitney demands. "Screw the boy. You are here to do something *big*. Your project. Your goals. Your life. There's more than a month left before you return. Let's get you back on track."

I blow out a long breath, and it pushes my messy hair out of my eyes. Then I sniff and clear my throat, wiping my damp face. "I'm Archi Dhawan."

When Mohini gets home, she sees me still in bed, exactly where she left me when she went to class.

This time, at least, I have my laptop open and my term books scattered around me. I have work to catch up on.

"Feeling any better?" she asks. "It's good to see you not crying."

I snort. "Thanks. Yeah, I think so. I've decided to forget about Shiv and go back to my initial goal for this semester. To focus on me, my work, and my time here in Jaipur. I don't want this to ruin that."

I expect Mohini to cheer, but she frowns.

"What?"

"Well." She pauses, then swings her legs onto my bed and sits down diagonally across from me, holding one of my pillows to her chest. "I'm glad you're feeling better. And glad you want to get back to focusing on your work. But do you think you want to forget about Shiv entirely?"

My eyebrows scrunch up. "What do you mean?"

Mohini sighs. "You smiled more when he was around. You got to focus on Jaipur better around him. And you seemed more excited about your work and your Capstone after you would talk to him. Do you really think he was taking away from your goals? It seemed like he was helping you connect more to Jaipur, to be honest."

I frown. "Are you . . . taking Shiv's side?"

"No!" Mohini holds her hands up. "Never. I am always on your side. But being on your side means thinking about what will really make you happy, right?"

"Well, he can't make me happy anymore. He lied. And then he made a fool of me in public."

"I'm not denying that," Mohini says. "He was wrong. But . . ."

"But what?" I'm shocked Mohini is being sympathetic toward Shiv. She seemed ready to kill him for upsetting me.

As if reading my mind, Mohini waves a hand in the air.

"Don't worry, I will still castrate him for this if you say the word. And I will hold a grudge against him forever, even if you forgive him. I'll never forget any way he messed up. But . . ."

There it is again. "But?"

"I've had to deal with some of the same stuff he has. Not to the same extent, obviously, but my parents are famous. I've had people try to be friends with me because of who my parents are or start acting weird when they learn who I am. So I kind of get it, you know?"

I wait, listening.

"It's really possible he wasn't legally allowed to tell you who he was. It could have gotten *you* in trouble. And who knows what sort of legal rights you'd have if you'd signed anything—or if you hadn't signed something, since you're on a student visa. It could have gotten really complicated and technical."

"Then he never should have hung out with me, if it would have been so complicated to do it the right way."

"Do you really wish he'd never hung out with you? Would you take back all the times you spent together?"

I pause, because I don't know if I would.

"He might have been scared. It sucks when people try to take advantage of you. He was probably trying to be careful."

"Well, he did it wrong. He had every chance to say something on his birthday, and he didn't."

"I agree. He did it wrong. I understand it's messy, but maybe it's not unforgivable?"

"I don't know." I close my eyes for a beat. "Right now, I

don't feel like I have any reason to forgive him. He hasn't done anything to fix the mess he created."

Mohini nods. She takes my hand and squeezes it. "You're right. He'd have to do some massive grand gesture to make it up to you. Not just give you another damn bouquet of flowers."

"I doubt I'll ever hear from him again. I told him not to contact me."

"Well," Mohini says, "they made an announcement in class today. The prince's birthday party is this weekend. It's supposed to be a huge event, and . . . every VBIS student has been invited."

My jaw drops, and Mohini grins, waving two golden invitations at me.

I hesitate. "I can't . . . I can't . . ."

Mohini clucks her tongue. "You can. You don't have to talk to him. You don't even have to look at him. You can, however, get tipsy on palace champagne, eat palace hors d'oeuvres, and call that your reparations. The palace owes you hella. Might as well take their money when you can."

Even despite my hurt, I laugh. And maybe Mohini's got a point. The palace *should* owe me for the way they described me to the press. And why should I have to miss a once-in-a-lifetime opportunity because of a broken heart? That *really* would be letting a boy get in the way of my meant-to-be boy-free semester. I should go. Because the Archi who arrived in Jaipur on day one would go. Because the Archi who planned for an ambitious, adventurous semester would go. Because even despite everything with Shiv, the Archi I've grown into deserves not to miss out.

Taking a deep breath, I nod and grab an invitation.

"Good." Mohini leans back and twists a coil of hair around her finger. "Because, really. Who can resist a ball?"

Everyone, and I mean *everyone,* from VBIS ends up going to the prince's birthday party.

Everyone, including me.

The palace clearly wanted to fill the space with people approximately the prince's age, and since Shiv, as he told me often, doesn't have many of his own friends nearby, they had to outsource. I don't know what he's been up to since we last spoke a few days ago. I've been avoiding news of him online, even with my entire extended family texting me about him every other minute.

Part of me can see now why Shiv kept his identity private at first. Everyone seems way too interested in him. I don't think he and I could go to a temple or the train station or even walk down any street in Jaipur now that most people know who he is and what he looks like. I catch myself feeling a little sorry for him, but then my anger quickly returns.

I remember running into Shiv's sister, Vidya. She's a princess, and she's older than Shiv. How was she able to be out in public when we first met? I tell myself it doesn't matter. I'm not here for that. I'm here for . . . well, I don't really know. Maybe to get my reparations in the form of free drinks and snacks, like Mohini said. Maybe because part of me, a part I don't want to think about, misses Shiv and wants to see him again, even though it hurts.

At the entrance to the palace, which is decked out with lights and floral garlands, Mohini and I wait in line. When we get to the front, we show our invites, our VBIS IDs, and our government IDs before we're allowed to go through metal detectors and a pat-down.

"Damn," Mohini whispers to me.

After security, we're ushered through a hallway, where I can hear buzzing music and chatter, and then we're in the ballroom, which is crowded with dancers, guests, and servers carrying mini bites on wide metal trays.

It's overwhelming, and my eyes sweep around right away, hoping to find Shiv. I'm afraid to see him again, even in this crowd. But I don't see him, Vidya, the king, or the queen. I only see people I know from school and other guests.

"I think they'll make a formal appearance later," Mohini says, reading my mind. "They're probably waiting for everyone to arrive before they do their grand entrance."

I nod, and a tightness in my chest releases. I can enjoy the magic of the royal ball, which under any other circumstances would be straight out of a fairy tale, without worrying about running into Shiv.

The ballroom is giant, with tall, curved ceilings and so many chandeliers. I've never been to this side of the palace before. It's not open to the public. It's the residence, which means . . . Shiv *lives* here. I brush the thought out of my mind and try to take in the sights so I can tell Mamma and

Baba about them later. They'd have been horrified if I'd passed up the opportunity to visit the residential palace.

Everyone is all dressed up. Mohini is in a purple anarkali, and I'm wearing a gold lehenga with a shimmery blouse and a long cream-colored skirt that has thick gold embroidery and a bejeweled design. My hair is wavy and down, and I'm wearing a larger nose ring than normal, dangly jhumkas, and a thick necklace. I catch my and Mohini's reflections in a window we pass and wish I had the Polaroid camera to take a photo. I settle for selfies on my phone and take some shots of the interior of the palace as well. Mohini is stunning, as usual. I only wish I felt as good as I look.

An hour passes without incident. Mohini makes me dance with her and Chandana. We clink glasses of champagne—the drinking age in Rajasthan is eighteen, so I'm only a few months away, and really, the servers aren't checking.

The food is, unsurprisingly, stellar. There are small pakora bites, skewers of tandoori chicken, chutneys of every type, kathi rolls with paneer, and glasses and glasses of lassi. There are deep-fried puris filled with sweet yogurt shrikhand, a fancier way of serving the classic dish. I can see green and black cardamom pods in one of the kadai, and it's ridiculous, but I turn away, reminded of Shiv showing me the cardamom growing in the palace gardens, of him teaching me the difference between the two types while he cooked. I make Mohini check my food for any elaichi pods before I eat—they're annoying to bite into on their own (every Desi knows the pain of shoveling in a huge bite of biryani and accidentally biting down on a piece of cardamom), but now I really can't handle the bitterness.

Just as I'm finally beginning to relax, to feel okay being here at Shiv's home—at his *birthday* event—the music quiets. A spotlight comes up on the stage at the end of the ballroom, and all eyes shift that way. There's a door and a backstage area, roped off and guarded by security. And then, to booming applause, an older man in attire that can only be described as *rich* comes on stage, a man I recognize from my Google searches over the past few days. Shiv's father. King Aditya Rathore.

"Welcome, everyone," the king says to the ballroom audience, and everyone stills. Some people lift their phones to take photos, and the king smiles graciously. "Thank you all for joining our family on this very special day, to celebrate my son's coming-of-age. We are so grateful to share today with you."

The king says how proud he is of Shiv and tells an anecdote about Shiv as a kid, but his words go over my head. I cannot believe or process that any of this is real. Shiv's mother, Queen Yaamini, follows, wishing her baby boy a happy birthday, and then a young woman appears on the stage.

She is beautiful, and it takes me a minute, even as the queen introduces her as Vidya Kavita Rathore, to place her. She is *Vidya*, the princess. And now I know why she was able to be out and about without anyone recognizing her. Onstage, she is fully decked out, an alter ego. She has extensions in, and her hair is long and luscious, trailing in curls and intricate braids dangling down her back, embedded with jasmine flowers. Her eyeliner makes her eyes seem massive, and she has dotted beauty marks around her face with makeup. She's as gorgeous as she was the day I met her, when she was covered in dried paint and her hair was cropped into a pixie cut, but I can see how she wouldn't be easily identified in public.

She shares a story about a time when she would get nightmares and Shiv insisted on sleeping on her bedroom floor to protect her. It's hard to keep my heart closed to the adorable memory, but I manage, and Mohini sends me a look of solidarity.

I can't do anything but hold on to Mohini's arm when Vidya wraps up: "So please join us in saying happy birthday to my brother, Jaidev Shivam Rathore!"

Shiv walks onto the stage dressed in a kurta and sherwani. The gold collarless shirt matches perfectly with the luxe coat. His hair is artfully windswept. He smiles at the crowd and holds up a hand to wave, but—and I can't tell for sure from this distance—the smile doesn't seem to reach his eyes.

"Namaste," Shiv says into the microphone after the clapping and the cheers of "Happy birthday" die down. "Bahut shukriya," he continues, thanking everyone. "This is a big milestone in my life, and I appreciate everyone coming here tonight to share it with me. I want to thank my parents, my sister, our entire extended family, and every staff member who made tonight happen, and also anyone who shaped me as I grew up in this palace."

Mohini glances my way to make sure I'm okay. I nod

at her. Still, it's so weird to see him like this. Shiv hates crowds. I notice him clenching his fist at his side, but his smile remains constant.

"It's been strange growing up under these circumstances." He takes a breath. "I know it's a privilege to get to complain about how I grew up, and I don't take any of that for granted. But I also know that because of my position, I've had a more difficult time making friends and maintaining relationships with people. It's been hard to grow into myself when barely anyone knows the real me." He scans the crowd, as if he's searching for someone.

"There's a lot of responsibility that comes with being the son of a royal family. A lot of privacy that needs to be maintained, especially as a kid. Now that I'm of age, I have more say in my life but also less control over who gets to see me, have opinions about me. For a long time, I've wondered if the price of being royal is too high."

The audience is quiet, listening to Shiv's speech, which doesn't seem celebratory whatsoever. On the left side of the stage, his parents frown as they notice the shift in Shiv's tone. Vidya has her eyebrows raised.

"We have wealth but little political power. History but little impact on the future. We can try to exert our influence in the ways we can, but in the end, this title of being a prince, of being a Rathore, doesn't really mean anything, does it?"

I see the king try to step forward, maybe to interrupt, but Vidya holds her father's arm and whispers something in his ear. The queen grimaces.

"Now that I'm a prince in the public sphere, I want

things to be different. The palace will be instituting programs for public assistance, including shelter, food, and loan programs, as well as social programs for students and for people impacted by gender violence. But I won't be the face of these. I will be working behind the scenes as much as possible to do what I believe is our duty as members of the Rathore family, as people who had the sheer luck to be born within these palace walls. Beyond that, I want a life outside the limelight, and I think it's okay for me to ask for that. I didn't choose this life, but I can choose what I do with it."

Mohini elbows me. "What the hell is he saying?"

I, like everyone else, am transfixed on Shiv, hanging on to his every word. I can't imagine how nervous he must be right now. If I were there with him, I'd kiss him for luck. But I'm not. And he doesn't deserve that from me.

"A couple months ago," Shiv goes on, "I met a girl who showed me what that life could be like."

Mohini gasps. "Oh my god," she says.

My mouth falls open.

"I got a glimpse of what life could be if I got to make my own decisions. If I got to spend my time as I wanted to, if I got to do things that were worthwhile and meaningful to me, and beyond me." He pauses, swallows. "But I messed up. I kept too much from her. I wanted to show her the real me, but I ended up hiding the other parts of me that are important, too."

"Archi," Mohini whispers. "Is he . . . ?"

I'm stunned. Unable to move, unable to reply.

Shiv keeps talking. "This past week, tabloids reported

that I had been seen with a girl at VBIS. Our publicist, without my knowledge or approval, issued a press statement denying that I even knew the girl. But that's not true. And it doesn't protect me to lie or not be faithful to who I am, to what I want—or who. That *was* a photo of me. And the girl is Archi Dhawan, my biggest surprise this year. My favorite surprise this year."

Chandana, who has been standing beside Mohini, oblivious this whole time, lets out a tiny shriek and turns to me, her mouth covered. A few heads turn, and then some whispering begins, rippling through the crowd.

"Archi, if you're here somewhere in this overwhelmingly large crowd, I am so sorry that I hurt you. I am sorry that I lied, even by omission. I am sorry I didn't correct the article sooner. I know you said you didn't want to hear from me again, but I got VBIS students invited to this event in case you might show up."

Mohini clutches my arm. "A grand gesture," she chokes out. "He's doing. A. Grand. Gesture."

I find my voice. "And it's not flowers," I mumble under my breath.

"I know you love old Bollywood movies," Shiv says into the mic. Now he's speaking just to me, ignoring the audience. "In your favorite, the guy messes up. He messes up *several* times. But when he falls in love, he fights for the girl. He crosses a continent for her. He crashes her wedding for her." At that, there are some titters from the crowd as they recognize the movie. "I might not crash your wedding," Shiv says, "but I hope I don't have to. I hope I can make this up to you tonight. I want to say I'm sorry, and that I care for you so much. More than care. I promise I won't mess this up again. I hope you'll give me another chance."

My brain short-circuits.

Mohini elbows me, but aside from flinching, I don't move. "Archi," she says under her breath.

I'm stuck staring up at Shiv. And before I can control it, my eyes well up with tears, which spill over and down my cheeks.

"She's right here!" Mohini yells then, waving her hand in the air. Every single face in the ballroom turns toward us.

Shiv's eyes go wide, and he staggers a little onstage when his eyes lock with mine. For a moment, we stare at each other, my eyes glassy with tears. He takes a step forward, off the stage, leaving the mic. He calls out to me. "Archi. At the museum, when you played music, I wanted to dance with you. But we got carried away with our conversation, and I thought we'd have plenty of time to dance together later. So now I want to ask you, will you dance with me?"

And, as if on cue, my favorite song from the cult classic *Dilwale Dulhania Le Jayenge* starts playing. It's an orchestral version, *Bridgerton*-style, and it's utterly, absolutely romantic. Shiv is looking at me. The whole crowd is looking at me. The *king and queen* are looking at me.

I can't deal with everyone's eyes on me. I'm vulnerable in a way I've never been before. And I don't know what to do.

For once, my angel and devil don't appear.

My eyes are locked on Shiv's, his mouth opening like he's about to speak again. I don't know what to say to him, not in front of so many people. I have no idea how I'm supposed to feel. With the spotlight on me, I can't think properly. My heart is racing. It's so overwhelming—especially with everyone in the crowd waiting for my answer.

But I don't have one.

So I spin around, dragging Mohini by the hand, and run for the exit.

Chapter 21

Just What I Needed

It's Monday morning, and I'm trying to keep myself together for my shift at the museum.

After I left the birthday ball, I decided the best option would be to pretend nothing happened. I answered no questions. I didn't bring it up. I didn't journal about it.

As a new week begins, there are other things I need to focus on. Getting back to work. Catching up on classes. Regulating my emotions again. I can't let this past week get in the way.

Before I leave my dorm, I ring Mamma, whose calls I've been dodging since the news about Shiv broke, with texts assuring her I'm okay and it's no big deal—lies. It's late in D.C., but Mamma picks up on the second ring. She always does.

"Archi, kaise ho?" She sounds worried, and my guilt trickles in. She's probably been stressed.

"I'm okay," I say automatically, then pause. "I don't know, Mamma. I really liked him."

"Oh, beta. Sab kuch bata doh."

So I tell her everything, from the beginning. She knows a lot of the details about my dates already, but I tell her the things I realized in hindsight—why Shiv was so private, why he avoided certain places. I tell her that he asked me to be his girlfriend and I said yes, but after the news came out, I ended things. Finally, finally, I tell her what happened at Shiv's birthday party.

Mamma sighs. "He *DDLJ*-ed you?"

I nod and laugh through a few stray tears. "He *DDLJ*-ed me."

"How do you feel, bachha?" Mamma's voice is gentle and comforting and reminds me of home, and I wish so badly, for a moment, that I was there in our house in D.C., wrapped up in blankets on our couch, watching movies with my mom.

"I don't know. I was upset that he lied and that he denied knowing me. And then he apologized in front of everyone for both of those things. He might have chosen me in front of the world, but I have to choose me too, don't I?"

"You do," Mamma confirms. "But choosing yourself doesn't mean you have to push other people away when they make mistakes." She takes a breath. "It will be up to you in the end what you decide to do. You have to protect your heart, yes. But you also have to follow it."

"I miss you," I say quietly.

"I miss you too, bachha. You will be home soon. Make the most of your time while you're still there."

And so I try. I get dressed. I do my makeup. I brush my hair. I head to the MSMS II Museum. To the Rathore Gallery—the gallery named after Shiv's family.

Jassi greets me at the door, twisting her long braid around her finger. "Hi. Good to see you." Concern flashes on her face, but I appreciate that she doesn't ask me any questions or mention Shiv, though I'm sure she knows. "We're meeting with Kiran-ji in a few. Do you want any coffee? I'm going to pick some up."

I smile, wave her off. "I'm okay. I have some final touches to the exhibit planning I want to go over before the meeting."

When Jassi returns, she brings me a drink anyway, and together, we step into Kiran-ji's office, me holding my files and my journal close to my chest. I'm not going to lie—I'm nervous. I hope she's not thinking it's going to be too difficult to go through with the exhibit because of the bad press that *I've* been receiving. (Social media did get a kick out of me running from the ball, according to the barrage of WhatsApp notifications from relatives.)

But when we walk in, Kiran-ji glances up at me from her seat with her brows furrowed. "Archi," she says. "How are you doing? Is there anything we can do to support you?"

"I'm doing better. I want to focus on work, honestly."

Kiran-ji smiles broadly. "Good. Well, let's hit the ground running. Archi, we have two important meetings today. We're signing the final paperwork to get KAVI's painting here in time for the opening. And we received a reply from one of the English museums." She waves a hand. "It is, as expected, a gracious *nope*."

I roll my eyes. "Not surprising. What are the meetings?"

"The first is a phone interview with a reporter." Kiran-ji scans her calendar. "We'll both be on it, but I think she wants to speak with you in particular."

I gulp. "If this is about the whole—"

"Then I will put a stop to it immediately," says Kiran-ji. "But the inquiry was about the exhibit, and it might be nice to drum up some publicity."

My heartbeat quickens. "And the other?"

"That one is for you. As your internship is coming to an end, a member of the museum board has requested to speak with you."

"Why doesn't that sound good?" I ask, frowning. A member of the board? Am I being punished for leaving the prince hanging?

"Archi," Kiran-ji says, "breathe. I don't know what it's about. She's my boss, so I had to say yes. And I'm your boss, so you have to say yes, too."

"Drama drama," Jassi says, and Kiran-ji clucks her tongue at her.

"Don't scare her." Kiran-ji sighs. Then she turns to me. "It's going to be fine."

I nod, but I'm worked up. Boy drama in my personal life, and now possible drama in my work life? Just what I need.

We have half an hour until the interview, so until then, Kiran-ji, Jassi, and I prepare talking points and go over leftover to-do list items for the exhibit. We have a little over two weeks until opening night, and luckily, Jassi and Kiran-ji did a lot of narrowing down already for the local artists. I have to make the final choices as—Kiran-ji tells me with a smile—the lead curator for the *Ready to Return Home* exhibit.

Lead curator. The words are a thrill.

Eventually, the phone call comes, from a journalist at the *Times of Jaipur.* Instantly, I am relieved. This isn't a tabloid. It's serious. We introduce ourselves on the call.

"I'm Mira Khan," the journalist says. "I do the Arts and Entertainment column at the *Times,* and I've always had a personal interest in the concept of postcolonial art repatriation, so I'm fascinated by this new exhibit. What can you tell us about it?"

There's a pause. I don't know who's supposed to answer.

"I'll let our lead curator on the project go for it," Kiran-ji says, nodding at me, and I dive in, unable to contain my grin.

"I'm Archi Dhawan," I say, and if the journalist recognizes the name, she thankfully doesn't say anything. "I'm a study-abroad student here at VBIS, and I've been working with the curators and archivists at the Rathore Gallery these past months. When I learned more about the pieces of art and history that used to be in the palace's possession but were lost—well, stolen, really—in the years of British imperialism, I had the idea to do an exhibit that discusses the missing art. A sort of study on absence. I thought it could be interesting to show the empty spaces where our art should be."

"So it's going to be a gallery of lack," Mira Khan says.

"Only partly," I clarify. "We're definitely going to highlight what's been taken from Jaipur's history. The concept is inspired by places like the Isabella Stewart Gardner Museum in the United States and sort of in parallel with the Acropolis Museum in Athens, which was designed to show the lack of sculptures from the Parthenon that were taken by a British lord and were never returned. In a similar vein, we'll show the empty spaces to really convey that visceral reaction to cultural grief and loss. At the same time, we don't want to suggest that Jaipur is a place that's *lacking.* The city is a rich and artistic hot spot, and our goal is to highlight how artists have held on to and built off of history despite having so much stolen. The exhibit will also showcase local contemporary art that continues the tradition of Rajasthani artistry."

Kiran-ji gives me a thumbs-up as I speak, and the rest of the interview goes smoothly, focused entirely on the exhibit, on my work. I feel proud in a way I'm not sure I've ever felt before. I'm so close to realizing a vision for an idea I came up with and getting to own and share it with the world. Opening day can't come soon enough.

At the end of the interview, Kiran-ji checks the clock. "Oh, Archi, it's time for your next meeting. I'll walk you up."

My pride and excitement instantly melt into nerves. If I tell the board member about the interview, she'll be happy, right? Good publicity to outweigh the bad? I could try to stave off any potential firing in my last month.

Kiran-ji squeezes my shoulder reassuringly. "You'll be fine," she tells me, but then again, even Kiran-ji doesn't know the reason for the meeting. "It could be to congratulate you on the exhibit!" she suggests, but I doubt that's it.

We head to a more corporate side of the building and take the elevator up to the third floor. It's a narrow section of the palace grounds, not visible to tourists. On the third floor, we walk down a hallway to a door at the end. It's an unmarked conference room, and I can see a shadow of a woman inside through the frosted glass.

My palms sweaty, I take a deep breath. Kiran-ji smiles. I prepare myself for all the possibilities, then open the door, eyes wide to whatever's inside.

The one possibility I didn't consider stares back at me. At the end of a long conference table sits Vidya Rathore, the princess of Jaipur.

Chapter 22

Are You Surprised to See Me?

Vidya doesn't stand.

She gestures at me to take a seat across from her, but I'm frozen. Do I curtsy? Do I bow and touch her feet as a sign of respect? Do I call her Princess Vidya now?

She's dressed as she was the first time I saw her—in casual clothes, her hair short and wavy. Vidya raises an eyebrow. "Sit down," she commands, and now I do, because what else do you do but listen when a princess is giving you orders? "Are you surprised to see me?"

I clear my throat. "You—you're on the board?" And then I remember something Kiran-ji said about the art gallery having a more gender-diverse staff because the princess insisted on it.

"Obviously."

I frown. I have no idea what I've been called in here for, especially now that it's Vidya who's staring me down.

Is she here to tell me off for rejecting Shiv publicly at his *birthday party*? Oh god. I bet from her point of view what I've done is unforgivable, especially after seeing how protective she was of Shiv when we first met. She probably hates me. My cheeks heat up in shame. I haven't checked online, but I'm certain my running away did not look good for Shiv or for the royal family. I heard from Mohini that his speech made waves, particularly the commentary on royalty and his freedom. It made me proud, but I'm strong enough to separate my feelings.

But now that Vidya is here, another wave of guilt creeps in. I was so self-righteous about my anger toward Shiv, and I still am. He lied to me. He made a fool of me in public. Online. I don't regret cutting things off. But now, thinking of what the aftermath must have been after I left—after he confessed his feelings for me.

"Are you going to fire me?" The words tumble out of my mouth before I can save them.

Vidya does the unexpected: she laughs. Laughs!

"What?" I touch my face self-consciously.

"No, Archi. I heard you got us a feature with the *Times of Jaipur.* I am not going to fire you. Besides, I'm not in charge of employment or internships."

"I'm sure you'd have some sway," I mumble as my heart rate tries to return to normal. "So . . ."

"I wanted to meet with you," Vidya goes on, "to talk about my brother."

"Oh." Of course this is what she wants to talk about. "I'm sorry for ruining the birthday party. I shouldn't have gone."

Vidya studies me. "He wanted you to."

"Yeah, but I should have realized that it would make things weird. I didn't know he was going to say that. I'm sorry I embarrassed your family. I really, really am." And it's true. Vidya and her parents didn't need to be collateral damage for my breakup with Shiv.

"He put his heart on the line for you. In front of everyone."

I pause. "I know. But . . . I didn't ask him to."

"Fair." Vidya sighs. "He said you're not returning his calls. So I thought I'd be the meddlesome older sister, as always."

"Wait—his calls?" I frown. "I . . . I blocked his number."

The princess crosses her arms. "Well, that makes sense. But you should know, he's heartbroken, Archi."

A certain level of defensiveness rises up in me, even as the weight of her words hits me hard in the chest. "So am I," I manage. "He hurt me, too, you know."

Vidya nods. "I know. I'm not going to defend him. But I thought maybe I could add some more context."

Now that I know I'm not being fired, I lean back in my seat and wait for her to continue. But then again, Vidya could change her mind about not firing me at any time. I don't want to piss her off.

"Before I start," she says, "I want you to know that any article that mentioned you has been taken down. The photos, everything. We have a powerful PR team, and I knew—Shiv knew—you wouldn't want those to stay out there. We managed to report the posts on social media, too."

My eyes go wide. "So if I Google *Archi Dhawan . . .* "

"All you'll see, once it's published, is the article about your exhibit."

My eyes brim with emotion. "Thank you," I manage.

Vidya launches into her story. "We grew up with a lot of restrictions," she begins. "Shiv said it best—nobody wants to hear a royal complain about how hard life is. So I'm not doing that. Shiv and I didn't get much of a chance to be our own, individual people. Me especially, since I'm the eldest and a girl. Maybe because of my position as a figurehead, not despite it, I grew up really interested in politics. Indian politics. Global politics. But because of who my parents are, I was never allowed to say anything publicly. We are not permitted, really, to get involved in political issues—to endorse anyone in elections, to make opinionated statements. I had to do that through my art."

She goes on. "Shiv had similar restrictions. He didn't care as much about voicing his opinion. He wanted to be more involved in the Jaipur community. He snuck out all the time when we were growing up—got really good at it. He would befriend the guards, bribe them if need be, and leave and return without our parents' ever realizing it. Before we turned eighteen, it was very difficult to even find our names online, so he was less at risk of being 'discovered' by the public. But there was always a chance, especially as he got older. Especially in the weeks leading up to his eighteenth birthday. The risk that someone would recognize him, whether it was a staffer, someone who had met him at a gala, someone who had found the mostly hidden info online, or someone who realized he and our parents resemble each other. Or how he and I do. Even I, when I go out now, dress fully down so I'm unrecogniz-able. I'd say I'm disguised, but I think as you saw from Shiv's birthday, *that* was my disguise."

I nod. But still, I don't say anything.

"He really took a risk with you," Vidya continues. "I've never seen him spend so much time with anyone outside the palace grounds. He told you his real name, too. Shiv. It's what we all call him at home. He could have given you any name. He even could have said Jai, for his first name. That's what our family's social circles call him. But I knew he liked you when he told me you called him Shiv. And he even let you meet Champ. Shiv's not online, but Champ is. He has a whole Instagram account and everything. People might have recognized *him* the day you two went out together."

My heart skips a beat.

"After Shiv skipped the press conference that was sup-posed to announce him to the world, my parents were pissed. They'd given him a lot more freedom than I'd had, which is why he could work in the garden and do his restaurant stuff and even have a scooter, but I think they expected in return that he'd at least be there for his coming-of-age ceremony. And then the news broke about you. God, the house was on fire for days after that."

The house. "You mean the royal palace?"

Vidya laughs. "Yeah."

"What happened?" I shouldn't care. I shouldn't. But I do, of course I do.

"My dad was off-the-walls upset. He thought Shiv was screwing around, in his rebellious era, whatever, and they got into this huge shouting match."

I frown. I can't imagine Shiv—calm, collected Shiv—shouting.

Vidya laughs like she knows exactly what I'm thinking. "Yeah. I'd never seen him raise his voice. I don't know that the common person would call it yelling, but for Shiv it was. He told our dad it was about time he got to make his own choices. Our dad was, like, 'Haven't you been doing that already?' And Shiv said he didn't want to be himself only in secret anymore. They argued for a while. By then, my dad had already had someone on the press team put out the statement about Shiv not knowing you. I guess they were hoping they could pass off the guy in the photo as somebody else, not Shiv, which is so ridiculous. Nobody fell for it."

I bite my bottom lip so hard it hurts. "Are your parents still angry with him?"

"Well, after his stunt at his birthday, they were ready to be pissed off again. But I think they saw Shiv's reaction—the way he called out to you. It's hard to be mad at someone you feel bad for. He's been holed up in his room since then, watching sad movies in bed." Vidya cracks a smile. "It's so cliché." She sighs. "But he made a deal with my parents. He said he'll come to all the royal events that they want him to as long as he's not a spokesperson against his will, and he gets to make all his other choices. To live where he wants, to go to school where he wants, to meet and be with whomever he wants."

My breath catches in my throat. "Did they agree?"

Vidya watches me carefully. "They did. But the first place he decided he wants to live is Delhi."

"Delhi?" I repeat.

"Our grandparents on our mom's side are there. He said he wants to live with them a while. Experience the real world in a normal way." Vidya pauses. "He has some friends there, but I honestly think he wants to be away from here. At least for a while."

"How long?" I ask, unable to stop myself. "Is he already gone?"

"Until May." Vidya's voice drops. "His train leaves today."

May—when I return to D.C. Shiv is leaving Jaipur because of me. In that moment, it hits me. Shiv *chose* me, at his birthday party. And I chose myself, too, didn't I? With my Capstone? With my ambitions this semester, with the goals I set and achieved. I *didn't* give up everything for Shiv, the way I'd feared I would. Could I have both?

Shiv isn't perfect. Hasn't been. But then again, as Whitney has said, everybody has complications. Even me. I'm hotheaded, impulsive. I run from things that scare me, things I can't control. I ran from Shiv.

He put his heart on the line for me, and I bolted. He asked me for a chance. A dance.

"He did a grand gesture for me," I say to Vidya. There's a lump in my throat. "I hurt him, but I didn't mean to."

"He didn't mean to hurt you, either." Vidya runs a hand through her short hair. "I'm biased toward him because I'm his sister. But I'm also on your side, because we're both artists. And you should know, his party wasn't the only grand gesture he did."

I look at her, confused, at the flecks of paint on her shirt, at the slight uptilt of her lips, the smirk she's giving me. It's as if my brain does the math—finally.

Vidya Kavita Rathore. "Kavita," which means "poetry."

Her work as an artist. The ease at which a painting I'd wanted forever suddenly showed up at the Gharana Art Studio. The promise that it would be delivered to the Rathore Gallery. Shiv asking me to make a wish. Vidya saying she outdid herself for his birthday this year.

My jaw goes slack. Because sitting in front of me isn't just Princess Vidya. Isn't just Shiv's older sister. Isn't just a member of the MSMS II board.

It's KAVI.

Vidya smiles as she realizes I'm having an epiphany. "Surprise," she says with halfhearted jazz hands.

"You? You're . . . ?" My eyes go wide, and I feel like I'm going to burst into tears. "He got your art into my exhibit for me?"

"Don't worry. I wouldn't have agreed for just anyone. I saw what you were planning. I decided it was worth it. *You* convinced me."

But I'm not even thinking about that. "He used his birthday present on *me*?"

Vidya presses her lips together. "He's been doing these things for you the whole time."

She's right. I was mad at Shiv for not choosing me. But he had been. He always had been, unlike Nick, who only chose me when it was convenient for him—only reached out after our breakup, when he saw that I was seeing someone else. Shiv has always chosen me. Even on his birthday, even over his princely duties. I stand up quickly, and tears blur my vision. "How long until his train leaves?"

Chapter 23

Do You Want to Get Out of Here?

Vidya takes me to the train station—she gets a palace car, which makes me feel immediately fancy and also as if I'm at the center of a Bollywood movie again.

But this time, I'm the one chasing the hero and trying to win him back before he boards his train. In *DDLJ*, there's an infamous scene where the heroine is leaving by train after saying goodbye to the hero. He's missed his chance to tell her how he really feels about her. But as she walks to board her train, he thinks to himself, *If she loves me, she'll turn around. She'll glance back.* The word he uses is *palat*. It means "turn," but it also means "to capsize," and right now, I feel like my heart is a boat in rough waters, about to flip.

On the way over, Vidya drives fast—way too fast—weaving in and out of traffic. "There's only one train leaving this hour. We have about ten minutes. But it takes eight minutes to get there from here, on a good day."

She sucks in a breath, and we lurch forward again. I'm not going to lie—I'm a little scared for my life in Jaipur traffic. If I thought D.C. drivers were bad . . .

But I'm not about to critique a princess. Especially not one who's driving fast so I make it to Shiv on time. She glances at me as she floors it. "I'll kick his ass if he ever does anything to hurt you again. I already did last week, before he went into heartbreak hibernation. So I can tell you he won't. He may be dumb as hell sometimes, but his word means everything to him. And he promised, at his birthday, not to fuck up again. He meant it." She grins. "But don't think that means I won't also kick yours if you hurt him."

I smile. "Deal."

When we arrive, Vidya pulls up, and I bolt out of the car before we've even come to a full stop. "Go, go, go!" she yells, and I heed her advice. I haul ass. I run through the station entrance, which is crowded and busy, past the ticket sales office, all the way down to the tracks, following the signs. Train to Delhi in one minute.

Sweat beads at the small of my back, but I run anyway, my lungs straining, my calves aching with effort. I stumble past a group of people onto the platform, my eyes searching for Shiv with his bags, about to board.

Palat, palat, *palat,* my heart calls.

But I know from the moment I push past the people waiting that I'm too late. Because at the end of the tracks, pulling away into the tunnel, is the train Shiv's taking to Delhi.

I bend over, grabbing my knees and heaving from my

sprint. I'm panting, but I can barely focus on my body while I process that Shiv has left Jaipur and he won't be coming back. My heart breaks, again and again and again, and tears begin to well up in my eyes. This time, they spill over. I gasp out a breath or maybe a sob, not caring that I'm in public. That's when I realize that—wait. I'm in public. I'm at a train platform. But it's quiet—unnaturally so. It's almost as if the platform has gone into a hush.

And then I hear my name, "Archi," in the softest and most achingly familiar voice.

So I turn around—I *palat*.

And there, standing in front of me, is Shiv. I run my gaze over him, and my heart stutters. No wonder the crowd went quiet. Everyone is taking Shiv in. He stands tall, dressed comfortably but nicely. His hair is tousled; his eyes are bright. His lips curl up in a hopeful smile, his chin dimpling above his scar.

"Shiv," I say, and he opens his mouth to say something back, but I'm running again. Except this time, I'm not running away. I practically leap into his arms, throwing my arms around him, and he lifts me up for a moment, holding me closer, closer, closer to him. I hear the clicks of people taking photos, but I don't care.

I'm here. Shiv's *here.*

"Archi." He's bewildered. "I—"

But I kiss him, drowning out the train of thought, pouring my every emotion into the kiss, into the way my hands make fists of his sweater—is that *cashmere?*—the way happy tears streak down my face, and I taste the salt in our kiss. And Shiv must, too, because he pulls away.

"Oh," he says so gently, and sets me down, eyes carefully scanning me. I bite my lip and look at his reddened mouth. Shiv brushes a tear off my face with the pad of his thumb. "I'm so, so sorry, Archi." He takes me in like he's never seen the sun and I just peeked out on a cloudy day. "I can't believe you came."

I make a noise that's somewhere between a laugh and a sob. "I thought I'd maybe let you suffer enough."

Shiv's eyes soften. "You believe I'm sorry?"

I make a show of thinking about it for a moment, and then I see the worry in Shiv's eyes. I nod. "I talked to Vidya." Then I pause. "I can't believe *you're* here. Your train—"

"Vidya texted me. She told me missing it would be worth the wait."

"I'm sorry I ran out at your birthday." I duck my head into Shiv's chest, and he lifts my chin with warm fingers.

"I'm sorry I was an idiot," he says. "I messed up big time. I knew you were special. I should have told you more from the beginning. I should have trusted you."

I suck in a breath and take him in, this boy. This prince. *Mine,* my heart says. "As long as you promise to tell me everything from here on out. Honesty, no lies by omission."

Shiv wraps his pinky finger around mine. "Promise." He rubs his stubble. "I got the scar on my chin from a time Vidya and I broke into a weapons room in the palace and tried playing with swords. They weren't real weapons, more like preserved art, but they still cut like a bitch."

I laugh, but my eyebrows furrow at the change of subject.

Shiv presses a kiss to the tip of my nose. "When I was ten, I had a nightmare so bad I made the guards stand in front of my closet the whole night to keep the monsters out." He kisses my forehead. "I had a crush on a family friend's daughter in year seven, but she told me she didn't want to be a princess, she wanted a real job, and so she couldn't be with me, and I cried for three days straight."

Another giggle escapes me. "Your villain origin story."

"She changed the trajectory of my life. Now I want a real job, too." Shiv kisses my cheekbone, holding my face in his hands as if it's something precious, and I close my eyes to his touch. "The first time I dated a girl, it was a friend of a friend. When I went to the bathroom, she took photos of every square inch of my room and posted them online. And when I came back out, she was gone. She only wanted to be inside the palace." He grimaces, then shakes his head.

"I started being homeschooled in year eight," Shiv tells me. "It's also when I started sneaking out. The first time I tried, the guards carried me all the way from the garden to my room like I was a baby." Another kiss. "I wet the bed until I was seven. I used to have an imaginary friend named Count Barfi. I named Champ Champ because I thought it would bring good luck." A kiss. "I've always been embarrassed I can't handle spicy food like a real Desi person should. When I saw you in the train that first day, my heart started beating so fast. I was nervous, and I had no idea why. I knew something was about to change. I—"

"Shiv," I say finally, my eyes fluttering open after another sweet, lingering kiss. "Why are you telling me all this?"

He quirks an eyebrow. "I thought you wanted me to be honest and tell you everything."

My laughter vibrates between us, and I reach up to pull him closer to me. "Okay, maybe not *everything* at once."

When we step apart, I remember the crowd at the train station. For those moments in Shiv's arms, it felt as if nothing else mattered, like we were the only two people on the platform—in the world. I look around, and Shiv's gaze follows. He squeezes my hand. "Do you . . . want to get out of here?"

A grin threatens to break my face. "Yes, please."

Chapter 24

Not All Our Heirlooms Were Stolen

On opening night of the *Ready to Return Home* exhibit, Mohini and I get dressed before meeting Shiv outside VBIS.

I'm wearing a sari, one of Mamma's. In the mirror, it flows delicately around my hips in swaths of silky black fabric with gold accents. The blouse is tight, corset-like. Mohini's wearing a sari, too, in butter yellow. She looks ethereal.

"It's the big day!" she squeals from beside me. "How do you feel?"

"I can't believe it. I designed an art exhibit. I curated it. And it includes an original KAVI." I shake my head. "If you'd told January-Archi that any of this would happen, she'd have thought you were delusional."

"Delusional or manifesting?" Mohini asks. She adjusts the fabric at my shoulder. "You are now *friends* with *the* KAVI."

I fake a swoon. "Almost more outrageous than the fact that I'm dating a prince."

Speaking of, my phone buzzes with a text from Shiv, saying he's here, and we make our way down the dorm stairs. Outside, there's a car waiting at the curb, and Shiv stands by the door, leaning against it. Seeing him stops me in my tracks. He's in a blue-black kurta, a dupatta draped artfully over his shoulders. He looks royal. He looks gorgeous.

Mohini greets him first. "Sweet ride." She lets herself into the car, not-so-discreetly giving us a moment outside.

"Hi," I say softly.

"Hi," he repeats.

How is this my life? I want to bottle this moment and hold on to it forever. Shiv pulls something from behind his back. It's a thick gold box with a ribbon wrapped around it. Attached to the ribbon is a soft white lily. "You look beautiful. But I wanted to bring you some accessories."

"Oh yeah?" I smile up at him.

"Tulips aren't in season yet," Shiv says shyly. "But next week, they'll be growing all over the palace garden. Just for you."

I resist the urge to stretch up on my toes and kiss him. Am I lucky, or what? "So, lilies, for now."

"Mm-hmm." Shiv holds the box out. "And a little glamour."

I carefully open the box. When my gaze lands on what's inside, I gasp. The box contains a thick golden choker with a droplet of a ruby red pendant that resembles a pomegranate seed. It's lavish and sparkly. I don't even want to know how much it cost.

As if reading my mind, Shiv grins. "It's on loan for tonight. From the palace." He catches my eye. "Not all our heirlooms were stolen."

I gape at him. "This is—"

"A crown jewel. One of the Rathore rubies."

"And I get to wear it?"

"If you won't, I will," he jokes.

I bite my lip to keep my grin from taking over my face. Shiv raises an eyebrow. "May I?"

I nod and turn around, and delicately, gently, Shiv lifts my hair up and to the side, his fingers brushing the back of my neck. I close my eyes, and he clasps the necklace. Then, carefully, Shiv extracts the lily from the ribbon and pins it into my hair. "Flowers and jewels. Fit for a museum curator."

I smile.

Shiv opens the door to the car, which is professionally hired by the palace, and I'm about to step in, but then I stop. "Oh," I say. "I forgot Whitney's camera!" I grin up at Shiv. "Now that everything's out in the open, I can finally take some photos with your face in them."

He nods. "Go ahead."

I run back upstairs to grab the Polaroid, and then we get in the car, and my heart is beating so fast from adrenaline and excitement. We are going to my first gallery opening night. The first of hopefully many more to come.

At the entrance to the MSMS II Museum, a line is already forming with attendees, and my cheeks get hot from seeing how many people are interested in coming to see something I've put together. I, Archi Dhawan, have an audience.

Kiran-ji greets us at the door after the valet takes away the car. "Archi, welcome."

Jassi is right behind her, and she gives me a hug.

My breath catches the moment we walk into the gallery. "Oh. It's perfect."

Shiv's jasmine-and-marigold garland—traditional, like the kind Indian women wear in their hair—drapes the entrance. Beside it is a sign with Shiv's name: RAJKUMAR JAIDEV SHIVAM RATHORE. He's an artist, too. I squeeze Shiv's hand, and he squeezes mine back, and then we're on to the exhibit I spent all semester curating.

Beyond Shiv's garland is a blown-up image of Baba's postcard to Mamma and a sign in gold naming the exhibit: READY TO RETURN HOME. Mamma even mailed me the actual postcard, and it's inside as part of our modern Jaipur collection. Brochures contain information about all the pieces of art, stolen and present, and I grab one before heading into the hallway. The first room contains the local art— pieces on canvas, fabric tapestries with rich illustrations of temple scenes: women collecting water at ponds; bright, lush sunrises. There's pottery from Gharana Art Studio, with a placard containing information about the studio and about Hijras in Rajasthan and in India more generally. Brassware and idols of gods and goddesses. Leatherwork and prints from a Jaipur tattoo artist's portfolio. Miniatures in the Rajput tradition. Block-printed quilts. Photographs from one of Mohini's local contacts. And, of course, Sheiza's Rajasthani puppets, dangling from a bamboo stage. I have to do a slow spin to take everything in.

The second room is dim. It's largely empty, except

for the center, which holds the blown-up "miniature" by KAVI. The intentional blending of traditional miniature and contemporary pop-art style is emblematic of the way I want to curate art through my career: honoring the past while creating a future. The space the woman in the painting takes up fills me with determination, too. She is the Rajasthani woman of today, the Desi woman of today. She is bold, complex, bright. Though she's inspired by history, she stares ahead, into tomorrow. She's still untitled, but her presence says something anyway: *I matter. Yesterday matters. Where we go from here does, too.*

The portrait seems to watch us with a knowing smile as we navigate the room. *You did this,* it says to me.

I did, I say back.

Shiv touches the small of my back as we walk through the gallery, and finally, we are in the last room, which is dramatic, with intricate gold wallpaper and velvet carpeting, as if it holds something special. But on the walls, where the art should be, and on the stands, where the statues should be, are empty spaces, framed in gilt metal. Beside each empty frame is a placard with the information about what each spot should hold, where each piece currently is, and when the work was last in Rajasthan. At the entrance to the room is a pinned-up photocopy of the letter the British Museum mailed back to us, denying our request for repatriation. It is an indictment alongside the missing art.

Shiv and Mohini flank me.

The rest of the evening is a glorious blur. I take Polaroids with Mohini and Shiv, with Kiran-ji and Jassi, of the crowds walking in through the gallery, of the empty gilt frames and my parents' postcard. Vidya arrives to say hello and congratulate me, and I even get to meet the king and queen finally. "Be good to our son," the king tells me gently.

"He'd better be good to you, too," says the queen.

We walk around and meet guests and many of the local artists whose works are up in the first room. Sheiza clasps my hand, and I am so, so glad her puppets are here. I lose track of all the conversations, but each one is special. New people, new artists, gathered here together to make tonight possible. I video call Mamma and Baba, then Whitney and Lilyn, to walk them through the exhibit, and they—Mamma and Baba especially—seem so proud. Mamma even cries a little at the postcard introducing the art.

In the gallery hall, where people are mingling and drinking wine and eating hors d'oeuvres, Shiv takes my hand. He pulls out his phone and a pair of earbuds, and smiling a secret smile, he hands me one.

When I place it in my ear, music bursts out, Bollywood music that makes me laugh. "What's this?" I ask him, high on the evening and the romance and the magic of this semester abroad here in Jaipur.

"I thought it was time we finally had that dance."

So I close my eyes, circle my arms around his neck, tuck my head into his solid chest, and we dance, slowly in the gallery that is ours—his palace and my curation. When the music ends, Shiv and I separate, and his eyes, dark and golden and filled with love, sparkle. "I'm so glad you dropped your journal on that train," he whispers.

"I'm so glad you picked it up." I hold him close to me.

"They're going to ask you to make a speech," he says. "I see Kiran-ji plotting to bring you up." He squeezes my hand. "Are you ready?"

I survey the gallery, see how perfectly everything I hoped for has come together. "I am," I confirm.

Within moments, Kiran-ji and Jassi are ushering me to the front. I'm pretty sure I black out during most of Kiran-ji's introduction, but I catch Shiv and Mohini clapping, cheering me on. I take a deep breath. And then I hold my head up as Kiran-ji points in my direction.

"And now, presenting Archi Dhawan!"

Epilogue

What Next?

Dear Whitney and Lilyn,

I guess I can officially say my Capstone project was a success. Really, this whole semester was a success. Well, all except for my ridiculous plans for a "boy-free semester." Someone should have told me that was never going to happen! Especially not after I met Shiv on literally day one. I can't believe my time here is almost coming to an end. There are a couple more weeks before I get back, but I wanted to get everything written down for our in-person debrief. We'll have to do it over chai—I'm bringing Shiv's good cardamom back with me.

The exhibit was amazing. It ran for three weeks, and every day, we had more and more people show up. The Times of Jaipur article got a ton of buzz, and I got interviewed for another local paper about how I managed to get the KAVI piece. It was so cool to get to say "I can neither confirm nor deny" when they asked me questions about her.

Mohini and I spent the rest of the month before exams exploring more of Jaipur and Rajasthan. I went back to see Sharmila Aunty again, and she came to visit Jaipur with the kids to see the exhibit, too. It was wild. #ReadytoReturnHome was trending online for over a week.

Shiv and I hung out a lot more, too. I got to see where he lives, finally, in the residential part of the palace. He's going to be applying to universities this year. He's taking a gap year till then, visiting his family and working on expanding social programs in Jaipur. And he said he's always wanted to see D.C. I told him it's nothing compared to Jaipur, but he said he's sure he can find something special to visit there, maybe this summer. :-)

To bring back for my Capstone project, I have photos of the exhibit, but I also got to take one of the empty frames with me. It's heavy and metal, so the Rathore Gallery is mailing it to school for me. It'll be nice to have a piece of everything at home. Kiran-ji said I have a standing offer for an assistant job if I ever want to come back. I think I will return to Jaipur someday, at least to visit, but there are a lot of other places I want to see, too. And more art I want to show the world.

I'm excited to see you guys again for graduation. I'm going to miss VBIS, obviously, but I miss Odyssey, too. And Mamma and Baba. Mohini and I are going to keep in touch, and I'm going to try to send letters and postcards to my coworker Jassi, too. It's been a pretty wild ride, this semester. Ups and downs like I wouldn't have believed, coming into it. But is it weird that I'm grateful for it all, even the downs? I wouldn't change a thing.

I'm sure you're both wondering: What's next for me? Honestly, I'm wondering, too. There's so much I want to do. I can't stop thinking about what the future holds. I have a million things on my list, a million ideas for exhibits and art demonstrations. After I got a KAVI painting on my first try, I remember thinking, How am I going to top this? Except since then, I can't stop coming up with more ideas. It's like my water broke, or something. Wait. The dam broke? What's the saying? LOL. Anyway, as soon as I get home, I'm taking a very long nap. Beyond that, Shiv and I are still going to date. I like him, and he likes me, and things are going good. Why mess that up?

The future is uncertain, but that's okay. And whatever happens, at least I can say I fell in love with a prince.

Love,
Archi

Dear Shiv,

I hope you get this before your flight to D.C. I'm writing from the rose garden behind the Smithsonian Castle thinking of you. Tulip season passed while we were in Jaipur, but I don't think I missed a thing. I can't wait for you to visit. My parents are excited to host a prince—they're going to overwhelm you. I have an itinerary written out, but as we know, sometimes it's okay to deviate from the plan. When you're here, we can do a sunset garden date on a different continent. The flowers are blooming for you.

Yours,
Archi

Author's Note

When I first received the opportunity to write this book, it really did feel like a sign from the universe. I remember looking at the pitch and seeing that the main character's name was slated to be Archana and her story would take place in Jaipur, Rajasthan. Archana is a family name, and my mother grew up in Jaipur. I knew I had to say yes.

This book has been a fascinating, collaborative experience: a whole team worked on the plot and vision, and I'm lucky to have been part of this project and helped bring these ideas to life. Though this book takes place in the very real city of Jaipur, with very real historical sites and details, I have taken several creative liberties.

Much of this story takes place at Jaipur's City Palace and, within it, the Rathore Gallery at the Maharaja Sawai Man Singh II Museum. The museum is real, and it is at the City Palace, but it consists primarily of a textiles section and an armory. There is also a space where artisans showcase their creations and tourists may make purchases, which is officially called a gallery, but it is not the kind readers may be accustomed to. In *Love Craves Cardamom*, I invented the Rathore Gallery, a separate structure that functions as a formal museum displaying historical artifacts, paintings, and sculptures. In the real palace gallery, local artists display their art and are available to speak with visitors about their work. Archi's decision to invite local artists for her Capstone project is an homage to that space.

Most of the Rajasthani art mentioned in the book is real, but since the Rathore Gallery is invented, the works were not stolen from this particular museum. The artifacts mentioned in the open letter to UK museums include both real and fictional Rajasthani art. For example, at the time of writing, the British Museum holds the Setmalar Ragini, a page from a bound silk folio, made of watercolor and gold on paper, from nineteenth-century Jaipur. It also has multiple Rajasthani paintings in the style of Nihâl Chand, the eighteenth-century chief painter of the court of Kishangarh. The non-Indian stolen artifacts mentioned are all real, such as the Nigerian sculptures and the Easter Island moai. While the British Museum has refused to permanently repatriate looted artifacts, other museums across Europe have taken steps to return stolen art. In 2021, France returned twenty-five artifacts to Benin. As of this writing, the British Museum's official website includes a page on "contested objects."

The Gharana Art Studio is fictional, created to recognize

gender nonconforming artists and pay respect to the Hijra community. Hijras are one of several third-gender groups in South Asia and can include people who identify as non-binary, intersex, or transgender. All-Hijra communities and lineages are known as gharanas. I chose the names Laxmi and Madhu for the Hijra artists in this book after Laxmi Narayan Tripathi, a Hijra-and-transgender-rights activist, and Madhu Bai Kinnar, India's first openly transgender mayor. The Hijra community, which has its roots in ancient Indian society and is mentioned in Hindu holy texts, has long faced discrimination and violence, which continues today. I hoped to honor a marginalized and lesser-known (in the West) Desi community by including them in this book, which touches on so many other themes of culture and archival history.

As for other modifications, the Jaipur City Palace does have a garden, but it is not open to the public. I took liberties in describing the garden and making it more personal to the characters. VBIS is invented as well, inspired by the many colleges lining Jawahar Lal Nehru Marg. I additionally took liberties with the transit options, so some of the sites in the story appear closer to each other than they are in real life. As for the prince, Jaipur does still have a royal family, descendants of Maharaja Sawai Man Singh. However, the royal family in this story is entirely fictional, as are the palace rules about privacy for the prince and princess.

Writing *Love Craves Cardamom* has been an exercise in balancing authenticity and history with the fiction of a love story. I am not a historian, and this blending may have created some factual inaccuracies, though I hope that any errors, besides the intentional ones mentioned in this note, are slight. It was important to me to showcase the beauty and culture of Jaipur and touch on the political history of monarchy and colonialism in the backdrop while also creating a fictional, alternate universe for Archi and Shiv. I hope I have honored my family home while also maintaining a focus on the joy and fun of a rom-com. Thank you for giving Archi a new destination: wherever it is you're reading.

Acknowledgments

A novel is always a team effort, and this one is especially so. There are so many people to thank, in no particular order.

I am so grateful to Laurel Symonds and the kt literary team for everything you do to make writers' dreams come true. I love working on projects with you!

Thank you to the Electric Postcard Entertainment team for giving me the chance to bring Archi to life: Dhonielle Clayton, Haneen Oriqat, Connolly Bottum, Kristen Pettit, Eve Peña, and Suzie Townsend.

Love Craves Cardamom is infinitely better thanks to editor Bria Ragin. Your insights and guidance made even the rough edges of this book sparkle. To the cofounders of Joy Revolution, Nicola and David Yoon: What a dream to have your eyes on something I've written!

More thank-yous to the rest of the team at RHCB—

Wendy Loggia, Beverly Horowitz, and Barbara Marcus, for ushering *Love Craves Cardamom* into the world, and to Tracy Heydweiller and Colleen Fellingham for your work in turning a Word document into a real book. To the design team, Michelle Cunningham, Liz Dresner, and Michelle Crowe, and to the cover illustrator, Bex Glendining. This book is so beautiful because of you.

I am honored to be a part of the Love in Translation series, alongside the incredible Ravynn K. Stringfield and Stefany Valentine. Thank you for writing Whitney's and Lilyn's stories.

I could not have written this book, or any book, for that matter, without the support of so many people I love and admire. Thank you to my sister, Arushi. I hope I can be more like you when I grow up. To Mamma and Baba, for taking me to the library so much when I was a kid and buying me books for every birthday and for letting me sit at the Costco book section when you grocery shopped. To my grandparents, for making a home in the city Archi loves.

To Emily Zeng, I am so lucky to have you in my life. Thank you for my author photos and so much else. Thank you also to my dear friends who make me better, and because of that, make my writing better: Meg Shriber, Margaret Cirves, Emerson Toomey, Evelyn Rubinchik, Jasmine Park, Aimee Clark, Ryan Meyer, and everyone else who has been in my corner during my writing endeavors, especially my Berkeley, law school, D.C., New York, and Boston communities.

I am particularly thankful to my college English

professors. Thank you so, so much to Melanie Abrams and Vikram Chandra for changing how I write for the better. I hope to hold on to everything you taught me and to keep learning.

Thank you to Lane Clarke and Taj McCoy for your friendship, advice, and our brunches, and to the Andrea Brown Literary Agency team, especially Caryn Wiseman and Jemiscoe Chambers-Black, for your mentorship and support. I hope to always keep learning from you.

Many thanks to the writing community, all the agents and editors and authors I've learned from and admire so deeply. There are far too many of you to name. I am grateful even if we shook hands at a book signing.

I wrote this manuscript and write these words now as Israel and the United States wage genocide against Palestinians. These words themselves are not activism, but they are an acknowledgment I cannot leave out. In a book critiquing colonialism, demanding that history and culture and people be honored, and that students and artists use their voices to be disruptive, neither these characters nor I could go on without joining the call for liberation everywhere, from Palestine to Kashmir to Congo, from Sudan to Hawai'i and beyond. All these struggles for liberation are interconnected; in the words of Black activist Fannie Lou Hamer, "Nobody's free until everybody's free."

Thank you, finally, to Desi readers, to diaspora kids. Everything I write is for you.

About the Author

Aashna Avachat is an author of young adult books from California. She is a graduate of the University of California, Berkeley, and Harvard Law School. When she's not writing, she's probably reading on a sunny patch of grass, going on long walks to grocery stores, or hanging out with one of her many foster kittens. *Love Craves Cardamom* is her debut novel.

aashnaavachat.com

TURN THE PAGE FOR A SNEAK PEEK AT . . .

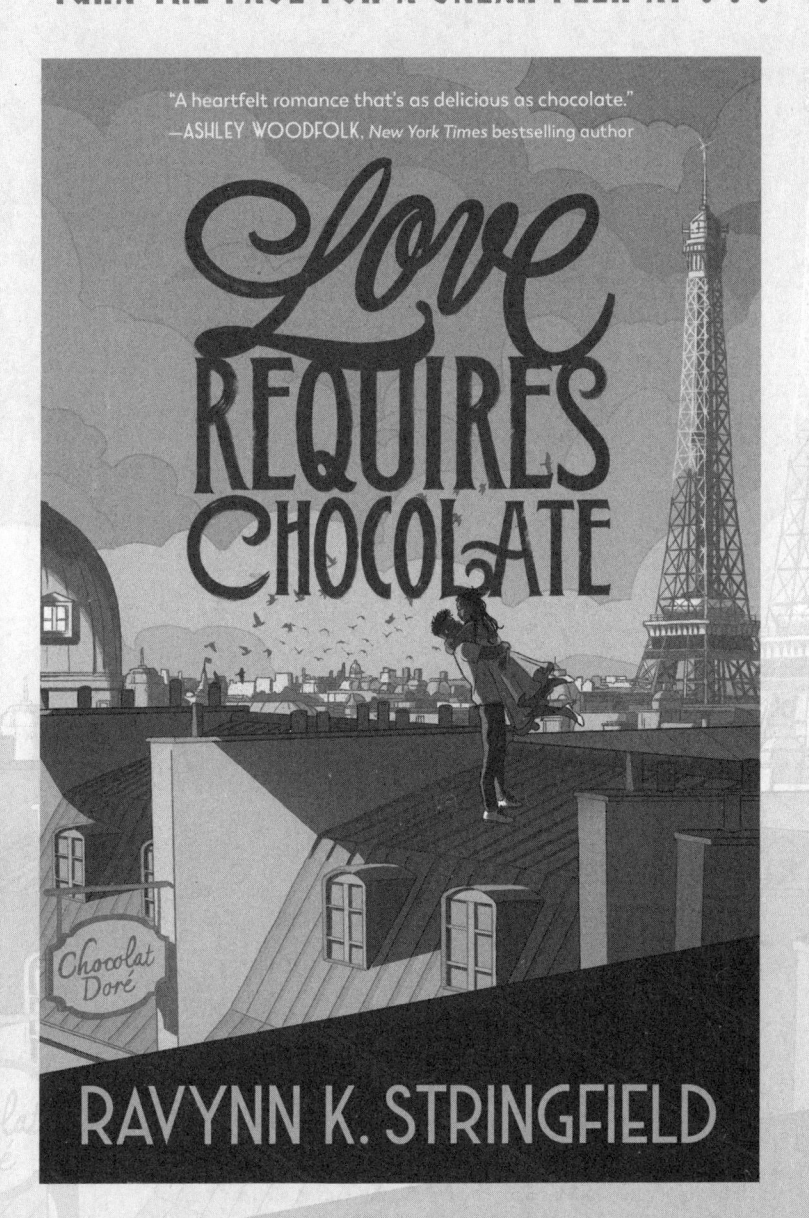

"A heartfelt romance that's as delicious as chocolate."
—ASHLEY WOODFOLK, *New York Times* bestselling author

Love REQUIRES CHOCOLATE

Chocolat Doré

RAVYNN K. STRINGFIELD

SCENE ONE

SOME PEOPLE DON'T APPRECIATE
THE VALUE OF A GOOD LIST!

"Mademoiselle!"

An out-of-breath man's face crowds my phone screen as I slowly turn, capturing the bustling street outside Gare du Nord. The sound of the city is at a reasonable volume, so I can hear myself think. Though, admittedly, all the French landing on my ears is super jarring. I feel like a fish dropped into a huge new tank. Every voice jolts me, because even though I know the language, I can't make my brain translate words fast enough to keep up yet.

The man's face wobbles on the screen as my hand trembles with excitement. *I'm here!*

"Uh, hi!" I say, lowering my phone, then lifting my cat's-eye sunglasses. "Or bonjour! You're kind of in my shot." I point to my phone with what I hope is a charming smile. The man's cheeks are red from the heat, and his expression tells me he is uninterested in my shot.

"Are you Whitney Curry?" His thick accent nearly swallows my name.

"Yes! That's me! The one and only!" I say, my stage smile turning into a real one. I finally notice that he's holding a letter-sized piece of cardstock that has LYCÉE INTERNATIONAL DES ARTS À PARIS (LIA)—**WHITNEY CURRY** printed across it. My name is bolded, and I'm impressed by the fancy school insignia embossed at the top. I wonder if he'll let me have the sign for my memory book.

"I am Monsieur Guillaume Polignac, your ambassador from Lycée International des Arts, Paris, here to escort you to the dormitories." He mops his brow with a handkerchief, and I immediately stick my hand out.

"Enchantée—" I start, but Monsieur Guillaume Polignac cuts me off.

"This way." I try not to bristle at the fact that he ignored my attempt at French. My nose wrinkles at the rudeness anyway, but since he *is* my ride to my new home, I try to keep pace as I follow him up the sidewalk. When we stop at a tiny blue car, he struggles to lift my monogrammed trunk with the letters "W.C." in spiraling white type on the front, and my brown leather valise, mumbling and probably cursing to himself in French.

"What do you have in here—a whole person?"

"Oh, just the essentials," I tell him brightly. "Costumes, accessories, special lights. You know . . . everything a girl needs to thrive. There's no such thing as being overprepared!"

Monsieur Guillaume Polignac raises his eyebrows at me before giving the trunk one last shove to pack it inside. "Such strange luggage."

"It's vintage. Very rare." I climb into the passenger seat and buckle myself in, making sure to pull my braids out from under the seat belt. My heart is thudding against my rib cage, and I do my best to remain still. I want to do my "I'm excited" dance, but a quick glance at my stone-faced driver curbs the impulse.

Monsieur Polignac does not ask any questions, nor does music come on when he starts the car, which is just as well, as it would only interrupt my daydreaming. Before we've even started moving, my mind is buzzing. I am envisioning myself renting a car and driving out to Château des Milandes, the old estate where Josephine Baker spent much of her life with her children, on the weekends I have off from my rigorous Parisian art school schedule. I need to stand where she stood. I need to breathe the same air she did. I need to soak it all up so that one day I might be as iconic as she was.

I'm trying to manifest greatness, but my phone is vibrating in my pocket incessantly, making a grating noise against the car door. Texts flood in from my mom, asking a thousand questions about the flight and reminding me to turn on my location sharing. Another deep inhale and exhale before I dig my phone out and turn it on do not disturb.

Not right now, Mom. I'm drinking in Paris. I try not to think about my mom's anxiety about me traveling alone for the first time and all the fights I had with her that led to this moment. I feel a little guilty that I do consider texting Nana instead, wanting to share this momentous occasion with at least one of them, but I ultimately decide that updating them both will have to wait. I sit back in the seat and think, *I'm soaking up my new life far, far away from Mom's fussing.*

Monsieur Polignac inches through traffic down a picturesque street. You know, like the ones on postcards, with beautiful gardens enclosed by iron lace and cream-colored buildings that could double as elaborate cakes. We pass gorgeous glass storefronts spilling over with perfumes and scarves and purses. Beautiful people window-shop or clutch fresh flowers and baguettes. I even think I catch a glimpse of a chocolate shop. Bicyclists navigate the paths. It all feels like something out of a guidebook of Paris rather than the real thing. Excitement runs like lightning through my body, but I feel a small pit forming in my stomach. There's so much to see. How will one semester be enough time?

"First visit to Paris?" Monsieur Polignac asks.

"Oh, oui," I reply, slowly peeling myself away from the window. "I've wanted to come here my whole life. It's my nana's favorite city. She used to live here." I rattle off Nana's entire artistic career as a relatively well-known performer, singing and dancing throughout Europe and often in New York City in her twenties. But it's not enough to just be the granddaughter of the incomparable Diana Curie. I've got to make a name for myself.

The *legendary* Whitney Curry.

Monsieur Polignac's bushy eyebrows move up and down, and I know I've probably lost him at some point in my speech as we wind down another narrow street. But then his eyes have an unexpected mischievous sparkle, and he makes a turn.

"Well, it's out of the way, but everyone should see it

as soon as they arrive . . . ," Monsieur Polignac mutters to himself. After several minutes in thick traffic, the buildings begin to fall away, and I can see the river, the Seine, with boats drifting down it, toting tourists taking photos. This is the river of songs and poems, the one that couples in romance movies walk along together. My heart is so full after these first few minutes in this city, and I'm suddenly sure I know what those lovers in all the classic Parisian-set stories feel.

On the street, people walk, bike, drive, and ride scooters around this busy area, making use of the many bridges to cross to the Left Bank. I have an urgent need to hear the chatter of the boulevards, to be out wandering the streets. I'm here to study, but I'm ready to be among them, getting to know the city as well as I know my audition materials. I consider leaving the window up so as to appear a little bit saner, but one only arrives in Paris for the first time once—and it's imperative to do it right. I roll down the window and let the wind blow across my face as I take pictures with the Polaroid I stuck in my purse. The pit in my stomach starts to shrink, and I imagine it spiraling away like a ribbon in the wind. It's replaced with a molten excitement that electrifies every vein in my body.

We arrive at a bridge with huge winged horses stationed on pedestals on either side, looking infinitely statelier than any of the numerous statues I've seen thus far. All of Paris looks elaborate, elegant, but these lions are positively ornate, and my eyes greedily drink them in.

"C'est le Pont Alexandre III," Monsieur Polignac informs me as we join the line to make a turn to cross the bridge. I lean farther out the window, trying to snap a photo of the sculptures before they are no longer in view. Monsieur Polignac clears his throat. "You will want film for this. . . ." He points ahead and a little to the right.

My mouth drops open.

There, right in front of me, is the Eiffel Tower. Its base is partially obscured by trees and buildings, but the iron structure is unmistakable. It's *tall,* towering above the landscape, sunlight glinting off it. Years of dreaming of this moment, and here I am, zipping across the Seine in a car on the most beautiful bridge in the world, looking at one of the most iconic monuments ever. And with the window down, all I hear is snatches of French—and maybe bits of other languages I can't discern. Folks around the world want to be where I am right now. Before I know it, my throat is tight, and my eyes are itchy as they fill with tears.

I know Monsieur Polignac is looking at me with concern, but I can't hold it in. Tears are streaming down my face, and I hiccup like a baby. I'm overwhelmed in the best way.

"Ça va aller, mademoiselle?" he asks, peeking at me from the corner of his eye.

"Oui, ça va," I reply. "I just want to remember this moment."

And even though the picture I'm about to capture will never tell the full story about how I feel in this moment, I lift my camera to my face to capture it anyway.

"The school is just ahead, near la Sorbonne. We are in le Quartier Latin. You will be but a short walk from the

Seine," Monsieur Polignac says after a while. We've passed the Eiffel Tower, where I got a few more pictures and cleaned my face with a handkerchief, courtesy of my guide, who continues weaving us through the city. I get the sense that he's not taking the most efficient route, instead allowing me to see a few more sights, including the edge of the Luxembourg Gardens. We arrive in the fifth arrondissement, and I see lots of school campuses and cafés. Young people who I assume are students sit in front of the cafés, smoking and laughing with their friends, textbooks likely shoved into bags under the tables and forgotten.

There's so much to see, and the prospect is thrilling, but I can already feel anxiety swelling in my chest as I think about navigating these streets on my own. When I first started driving, Mom always joked that I'd get lost going to school. She wasn't wrong. . . .

But that's a Tomorrow Whitney problem. Today Whitney is still experiencing her first Parisian car ride through intense Parisian traffic. The views are definitely worth focusing on.

I pluck my paper map from my bag and trace my short—but tastefully nude-colored—manicure over the different neighborhoods, which coil around each other like a snail shell. I colored in each one and annotated places I wanted to see. "Well, I can check 'experience the Eiffel Tower for the first time' off my list!" And after placing the annotated map on my knees, putting my journal on top of that, and steadying my hand, I do.

"Is that how you will be seeing Paris?" Monsieur Polignac chuckles. "By list?"

"Lists have never failed me. There's nothing wrong

with writing things down and checking them off. Gives me a happy feeling." I wave my list gently in his direction.

"What do you have on there?"

I clear my throat and poke out my chest. I've been researching all summer. Whitney Curry's Epic Parisian Bucket List has been vetted and obsessed over. Ironclad. Thrice approved, by three generations—Nana, Mom, and moi.

I start to read:

"First was see the Eiffel Tower. Then, have a luxurious picnic under it, with cheese and . . ." I cough to cover up the word *wine*.

He laughs.

"Second, visit all the museums, especially the Louvre, of course."

"Bien sûr," he replies.

"Third, spend an entire month investigating all the churches. Notre-Dame, Sacré-Cœur, Sainte-Chapelle, et cetera . . ."

"Et cetera . . ." His eyebrow lifts. "Don't forget that our beloved Notre-Dame is still under construction from the fire. It is not yet open to the public again."

"Oh, right. I will just have to pay my respects from afar. I have every major church marked." I point at the elaborate map, a supplement to the list currently spread out on my lap. "I have to see the Moulin Rouge and learn to make macarons and éclairs. But I'm still investigating the best pastry workshop to attend. Then I'll need to stroll down the Champs-Élysées and stop at all of these shops." I tap my route. "I need to experiment with perfume and make my own and get out to Versailles, and I *have* to visit a chocolatier . . ." My mouth can barely keep up with my list, causing me to nearly stumble over that last item. One of my greatest loves in life—after vintage dresses and midtwentieth-century theater—is *chocolate.* I almost don't want to taste it here; it'll probably ruin chocolate for me for the rest of my life.

"You've got a lot of things you want to do," he says, giving me a look that's somewhere between bemusement and amusement. Either way, I can tell he's done hearing about my list even though I'm not halfway through.

I am nothing if not prepared to have the best semester of my life, starting with checking off everything on my Parisian bucket list. Most of it is for research purposes (that just happen to be lifelong dreams), which will inform the writing and execution of a fantastic one-woman senior thesis show, something my nana would be proud of.

He glances over at me before turning left down a dead-end street. The shrubbery falls away for a moment, and I can see a soccer field filled with boys about my age chasing a black-and-white ball. One boy sneakily cuts across the group and kicks the ball in the opposite direction, causing the rest to yell in protest. The boy's focused face is disrupted by the barest grin, which causes me to smile.

Monsieur Polignac notices me watching and finishes his thought: "You will discover more if you wander. This is the type of city where magic can be found in the most unlikely places. People miss it when they run around the city with their guidebooks and websites."

I nod and smile. Whatever.

He's not a believer in the power of lists.

And he's missing out.

I could never leave my study-abroad experience up to chance. Magic is made, not discovered.

He points. "Et voilà!"

At the end of the cobblestone road is a massive building the color of cream, with bright shutters, iron balconies, and rose-colored window boxes spilling over with flowers. A gingerbread house. That's the first thing that pops into my head. Something out of a fairy tale.

"Welcome to the Lycée International des Arts!"

I look up. The warm light from the window washes over us.

"Welcome home, Whitney Curry," I whisper to myself. I take a steadying breath and open the car door.

NEXT STOP IN THE
LOVE IN TRANSLATION SERIES:

TOKYO, JAPAN

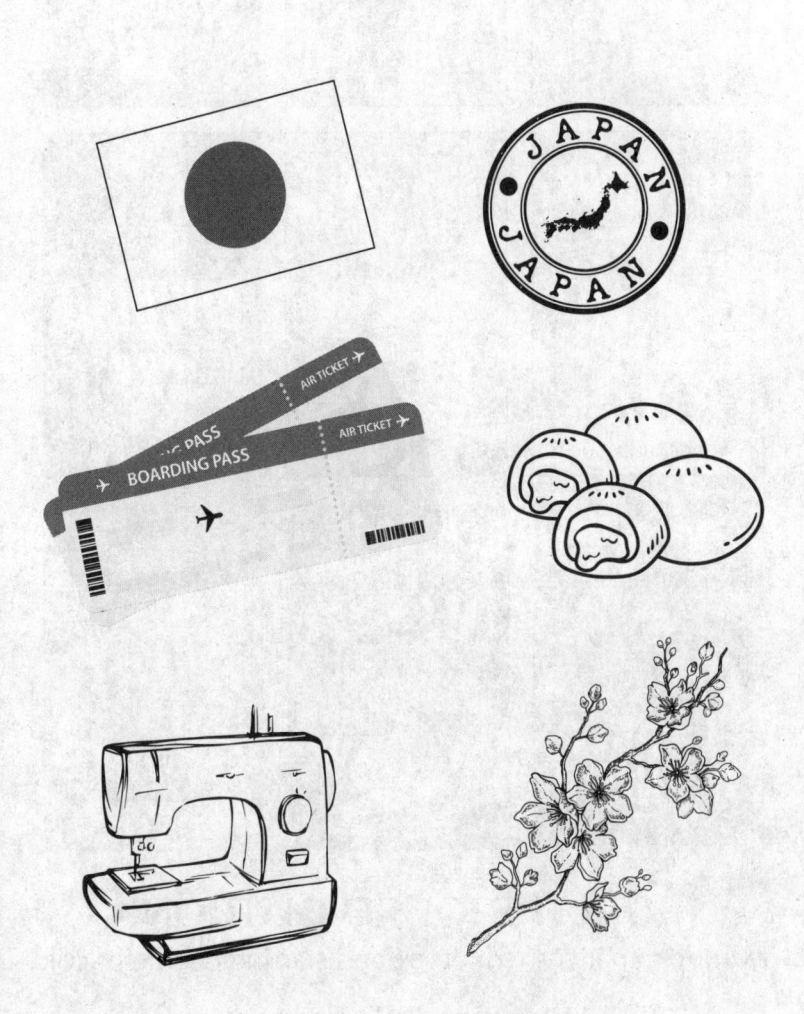

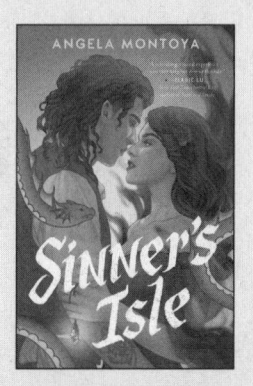